A Dreamer
Book II

Channeled by, Jess Hartley

Vera Hawk Press—Grass Valley, CA
Paperback ISBN: 979-8-9892209-3-9
Hardcover ISBN: 979-8-9892209-4-6
eBook ISBN: 9798989220953
Library of Congress Control Number: 2024908465
Title: *A Dreamer: Book II*
Author: Jess Hartley
Digital distribution | 2024
Paperback | 2024

This is a work of fiction. The characters, names, incidents, places, and dialogue are products of the author's imagination, and are not to be construed as real.

There are historical references and facts shared from two Native American Tribes, the Nisenan and Cherokee (Tsalagi), as well as Ayurvedic wisdom, however, all characters of this book are fictional.

Dedication

This book is dedicated to all the beings of Earth. All Fauna and Flora.

With the hope to inspire a more liveable, healthy, loving world, of tolerance and compassion and recognition of the sacred gift that is life. To create a healthy beautiful ecosystem that is respected for countless generations to come.

May all beings feel belonging.

May all beings feel loved.

May all beings know peace.

Chapter 1
Guardian

I was back in the water, dark as ever, only lit with the distant stars and their twinkling reflections, like always. Tonight it felt like I was gliding through a glass of cool water. I could feel my body drinking it in, overwhelmingly refreshing. I closed my eyes and called out from my heart song. My higher pitched, youthful version of ancient song then harmonized with a mature, lower pitch. Feeling the harmony resonate through my body, through my bones, it made my heart melt back into the feeling of Oneness. Like Mother's arms, like laughter, like a hug. I sang a different tone, harmonizing into a song that was more uplifted. Witnessing how my conscious shift in energy affected our entangled energy.

It felt like I was soaring effortlessly on the strings of our melody, as if our heart song was real and tangible in the water. The feeling was incomparable. I twirled my body in it, wrapping myself in the strands of our music. The ribbons spiraled around me, tickling me, and I giggled, then burst out in loud laughter. Then I sang at an even louder pitch than I had ever felt confidant enough to do before, belting it out with every bit of my being. She let me sing alone, sharing my heart with the world around me.

"Whyla!" I called out. "Whyla… I love your name, Whyla. Why did you not correct me when I called you Whyttee?"

"You were not incorrect to call me Whyttee. But yes, my name known to most is Whyla. But names are just labels to separate the One, and so you see, it's almost more appropriate to call me Whyttee, a sacred word meaning One."

Her booming yet soothing voice rang through me. Sometimes I wondered if she was only speaking inside me, or if her voice could be heard by others. I didn't feel her words through the water, like her heart song, but rather just in my head and heart.

"Liluye, would you like me to call you Lila? Is that name more true for you? See a name is just a name, but there are infinite names for the One."

I felt this message, deep in myself, deep in the parts of myself that had still been doubting this idea of Oneness, the part that was still identifying with a 'me' and 'I.' Lila, Liluye, were basically the same, but were still identifiers of single perspectives that "I" *i*dentified with. "I" was still a "me."

"There is no you and me, there is only us." She sang through me strongly.

Her words rang through every cell, and in and around every space between the cells, and suddenly burst outward into fragments of light through the water. 'I' was suddenly the water. Consciousness moved and 'I' was surrounding and becoming warped into form. Into Whale, into Whyla, into Whyttee, 'I' became. This body moved with ease and danced through the fibers of One with grace. Then we sang out from our heart, a harmony of divine conjuring, with all life breath, in the ever spiraling void of all, feeling and sharing sacred Oneness…

"Lila, Lila!!! Come on baby, I need you to wake up now. Lila!!" I heard Mom in a panic, and felt our rocking, and a gentle tapping on my face. My face. *My* face. *I* was back. It was strange and there was little feeling in my body. Looking around felt somehow a little foreign, even though this had been my room for as long as I could actually remember, the only room 'I' really knew.

"Are you alright? Lila? Are you ok, honey?" Mom sounded in a panic again, I felt her heart beating fast and her tears running down her cheeks. I felt her pain in her heart, mixed with relief. I was feeling her, from inside her, inside me. I could always feel her emotions before, but this felt different, heightened and intense.

"Mom, it's ok, calm down. I'm fine." I was speaking, but it felt more like I was watching a movie of us, observing myself from outside myself.

"Oh, Lila. I was so worried. It's nearly 8:00! I've been trying to wake you for over 45 minutes. Are you sure you're ok?" She was crying now, tears of relief and overwhelm. She was also sad. Sad that I was just like Dad, with an incredible ability, that was possibly also a curse.

"I'm alright, Mom. It's ok." I closed my eyes, but held her hand as she held me, and we rocked more together for a moment.

"Lila, I want you to go see a Doctor. I want you to go see the Doctor that your Father used to see."

I thought for a moment, and didn't know what a Doctor of our world could do for me, how I would explain, or how they would respond. A cramp in my stomach suddenly pinched me forward. It didn't feel like a good sign.

"I need you to see this Doctor, for my own peace of mind. Please." She was wiping her tears now, and almost seemed angry, or at least poised in a guarded stubborn energy. I knew that it was hard on her, witnessing Dad's downward spiral, witnessing my journey now. I understood her fear.

"I mean, I guess I can. I just don't know how they can help me, and what they would do. I don't want to go on any weird medications or anything, like Dad did."

"I know, sweetie, I don't want that either. I just want you to talk to him and see what he suggests. I know there were mind tricks and exercises he taught your dad to come back out of the dream more easily." I could tell she really needed me to do this.

"I'll make the appointment for you today. He books out a little bit, so it will likely be a week or two or more before he could even see you."

"Alright, I guess I can do that. But really, I'm fine, Mom. It's ok. I just had another amazing, beautiful, awe-inspiring dream. I was…"

"I don't want to hear what you were doing, Lila. Are you kidding? 45 Minutes! That was 45 minutes of hell for me, wondering if you would ever wake up. I know that the dreams can be amazing. I've heard. You have no idea how scary it is for me to have no idea…" She started crying, sobbing, her hands burying her face in her tangled mess of hair. I reached out to her and held her in my arms, and rocked her now.

"Mom, I am so sorry for your burden with this. I feel how it is so difficult for you. You must trust though. Trust, as I am trusting as well. This is an important mission. I think I may be some sort of chosen one, set to this mission after Dad failed to complete it." My head lowered down, realizing that Dad's death was possibly linked to this dream and the mission. I knew it all along, but didn't admit it to myself until right now.

"What mission?" she asked, semi agitated, not seeming to believe me.

"Well, there's a great mission, within this Dream, that I always return to in different ways. I'm learning many powerful things there. Mostly from the spirit animal guides. I have been blogging about the lessons. I did a new one last night. But there's a lot that I can't explain. I'm sorry to say. I don't want to have to explain this to a Doctor either." I kind of rolled my eyes.

"Well, it's not up to you. I'm your mother and it's my duty to look after you. I cannot sit back and witness for you what happened to your father. I won't."

"Fine." I knew that the only way to satisfy her right now, was to just go along with her needs.

I was late to school, but surprised Mom let me go still. She brought me and walked me in to see Mrs. Pombokom, explained my tardiness and then they gave me a slip to give to Mrs. Averie. I said bye to Mom and we hugged and said I love you. Then, as I was leaving, and assuming Mom would be too, I noticed her go back into Mrs. Pombokom's office. What was she going to tell her? She was my boss now, and was my principal. My stomach got the jitters. I couldn't go back in. I was so late to school already and Mrs. Averie hated when I was tardy. So I walked to class, imagining their conversation. I felt somehow betrayed. I also felt like an outcast.

"Lila, lovely to see you, and nice of you to join us," Mrs. Averie said in a genuinely sweet tone. She was so pleasant, it made me smile with relief.

"Have you your homework then? The write up of the first 3 steps of the Hero's Quest, as gathered from your book of choice?" She said, a bit more passive aggressively.

"uhhh…"

"Please stay a few moments after class to speak to me."

Damn. How did I forget to do that homework? I completely spaced on it. I did my science and math homework, but didn't even pick up my reading book once. I was so preoccupied with reading Dad's dream journal, and caring for and spending time with Mom. I really liked Mrs. Averie and didn't like to disappoint her. I felt her disappointment strongly though, and sunk down in my chair. I hadn't even allowed myself to acknowledge all the other eyes and ears on me.

"Alright, class, sorry for that disruption. Let's get back to discussing the 'Belly of the Whale' moment."

The belly of the *Whale*? How? What? I scrambled my eyes over the handout we'd been reviewing piece by piece, and had somehow not read the word Whale yet. I got chills and felt my new familiar ache for Whyttee, Whyla. I closed my eyes in daydream of her.

"Pst, hey, you should probably pay attention," I heard Lina's voice whisper from my right.

I guess there was no way for me to be in my own little world today, I was on a stage.

"So what's going on, sweetie?" Mrs. Averie asked me, after class. I only had 10 minutes to get to my next class and I kind of had to go to the bathroom, so I needed to keep it brief.

"Oh, I'm sorry, Mrs. Averie. I've been very distracted lately. My mom was just diagnosed with breast cancer..."

"Oh my dear sweet girl! I am so sorry to hear that. It must be very challenging for you right now. I'm sorry I put you in the spotlight like that. Here I was assuming you were just sleeping in and being a bit of a lazy teenager maybe. I am so sorry I assumed those things. Can you get the homework done tonight?"

Wow, that was easier than I thought.

"Thank you, Mrs. Averie. Yes, I will get it done tonight. I am sorry for not having myself together. I will try to be more on top of things."

Then she pulled me in for a hug, which was surprising and warmly welcomed. I didn't realize how much I did actually need a hug.

"Thank you, Mrs. Averie. Thanks for being so understanding. I hope you have a good rest of your day." I smiled and walked toward the door.

"You too, sweetie. You too," she replied as I opened it. We smiled at each other.

The rest of my school day was admittedly a blur. I was lost in all kinds of thoughts and dreams and feelings, A Lot of feelings. It truly was as if I had developed a heightened sense of feeling, overnight. Middle school was a crazy place to be when you could feel other's feelings. It was exhausting. So I found myself tuning it out and going inward more. I even decided to go for a walk by myself at lunchtime, walking around the baseball field a few times. I saw Acarya as I was coming back and I smiled at him. He smiled back, then joined me, walking along side me. He didn't say a word, he just wrapped his arm around me, and I could feel his Love. It was sincere, genuine, and deep. It felt like being in the water, in the Dream, like being with Her. It was all the kinds of Love; friend, mother, father, protector, lover, all rolled into One. I felt tears forming in my eyes and I stopped and turned to him, looking him in the eyes. Then I just walked forward, arms outstretched, fitting like a puzzle piece, neatly into the swallow of his arms, a perfect fit. He hugged me, lightly at first, and then grew to squeeze me tighter, until there was no space left between us. We were One. It was more like home than I had ever felt home to be, here in this World. I felt one tear slide down my right cheek. He saw it fall and reached down to wipe it, and then held my face in his hands and looked deep into my eyes, right into my soul, and said, "Everything is alright. It's exactly as it should be." He really knew exactly what to say, always. I dug in for another hug, and this time I squeezed him tight, my head dug into his left ribcage and nearly his armpit. I felt like a child suddenly, clinging to their parent, and I pulled away. We looked at each other and smiled again.

Then he started singing, in the British Indian fashion he couldn't avoid having, a Bob Marley song, "Every little thing, is gonna be alright... Rise up this mornin', smile with the risin' Sun, three little birds, each by my doorstep, singing sweet songs, a melody pure and true, saying, this is my message to yooouuu. Singin' don't worry, about a thing, cause every little thing is gonna be alright..."

I smiled and even giggled a little, and wiped my eyes. Then he did something I wasn't expecting. He reached out and interlaced his fingers with mine. A rush of tingling went through my whole body, starting at my palm, where our hands felt like one hand.

When we got to my classroom, he pulled my hand up to his mouth and sweetly kissed it, looking down into the soul of my eyes once more. I felt a melting through my whole being. I loved him, so much, it was overwhelming. Someday, I'd get the courage to tell him that. Meanwhile, I just smiled and slightly blushed.

"Are we going to Mr. Peen's this afternoon?" he asked.

"Oh yeah, I guess so. I kinda forgot. Maybe we can do a shorter session today."

"Sounds good. I have some homework to do tonight," he replied.

"Yeah, me too."

"Alright, I'll meet you at the spot after school." He tucked his hands up high on his backpack straps, like he did, and winked as he walked away backwards as the door shut.

The next 3 classes were done in a flash. Admittedly, I was completely checked out. Although, once again, I answered a question correctly in Math without a clue of what the teacher was talking about. I felt both guilty and proud, and laughed with gratitude at the Universe looking out for me, or at my brain for having some awareness of the present still. Then I went straight back to my daydreams of Whyla and the Dream.

"Hey, are you ready to walk the trail of doom?"

"What?" I asked with pretend shock.

"Just kidding, it's just a normal trail, like any other.... Don't worry, I'm here to protect you," Acarya said, wrapping his arm around me again, and then he flashed his side smile. Melting my insides again, like a candle on a hot day.

He was talking about Kokiba trail, which really did always put me on edge, and was my least favorite spot in this 'perfect' little town. I felt myself hardening again, at the thought of all the horror stories.

"Don't worry! I *will* protect you…always," he said, pulling me closer.

What did that mean? Was he thinking about being with me forever? I mean we're 13! I'm not even 13 for another week. But then again, I knew he was right, and it felt absolutely true, and even maybe meant to be. He *would* be my protector forever. Somehow, I think we both knew. The thought made me melt again, this time even more gooey. Geez, what was I becoming? I straightened up my posture and regained strength in my knees.

As we got to Kokiba, I felt myself apprehensive and a little bit scared again. I clutched to Acarya and looked around. He slightly puffed up, with some sort of manly instinct, and I truly felt protected by him. But I was on alert, there did seem to be a threat nearby.

We walked along, and there seemed to be nothing, so I let up my guard a bit. We were talking about some kind of project he was doing in wood shop class. I was trying to pay attention, but I still felt that there was a threatening presence nearby. I felt myself quickening our pace and glancing around.

"Is everything ok?" he asked.

"Yeah! Sorry. I am feeling some kind of something. That's all." I kept looking around. I knew I was looking paranoid now. But it was closer, I could feel it.

Then I saw him.

A man, standing in the woods, just staring at us, seemingly in the middle of nowhere. Not on a cross trail, just in the middle of the woods, he was just standing in the brush, watching us. I felt every piece of me go on alert, every hair stand up, butterflies flutter with fear in my stomach, and I may have even jumped into the air a little.

"What is it?" Acarya asked, as he turned to look in the direction I was staring.

"Come on, let's go," Acarya said and grabbed me tight, quickening our pace. He was scared too. Then I felt the energy of this person, standing by himself in the woods. It was laden with negativity and anger, a lot of pain, and guilt. I felt it, and it brought tears to my eyes, and made me feel almost nauseous. I felt myself go a bit limp and Acarya held me up by my ribs, grabbing me tighter. We walked past without an issue and he didn't seem to move, except his head, which seemed to watch me pass until he couldn't see us anymore. I breathed a big breath in as soon as I felt far enough away from his energy.

"Are you alright?" Acarya asked, pulling me to look him in the eyes.

"I'm fine. Are you? That was quite an energy on that guy." I found myself saying, very comfortably, knowing that Acarya knew exactly what I meant.

"You *are* my protector!" I said confidently.

"I got you, girl," he said, with utmost sincerity. "But yeah, dude was a total creeper." He turned to be sure the guy wasn't following us, and then we both quickened our pace.

I didn't like how affected I was by that guy's weird energy. It was unnerving.

But we walked the rest of the way to Mr. Peen's, hand in hand, feeling strength in our hold with each other, in our Oneness. I truly felt loved and protected by him.

When we got to Mr. Peen's, we realized he wasn't there. His truck was gone and the door was locked. So we decided to leave a note at the door. Which read,

"Dear. Mr. Peen,

We weren't sure if you were expecting us today, but we came anyway. We will come by tomorrow after school again. We hope you're doing good.

Sincerely,

Lila and Acarya"

Just in case he didn't wish us to come tomorrow, we also left our phone numbers.

I felt a bit of uneasiness for Mr. Peen's absence, still slightly on edge from the stranger in the woods. I took a deep breath in and exhaled away the fear. I somehow felt that he was alright, but he just didn't know if we'd be here today. So we walked back towards our houses, holding hands again, as it was feeling more comfortable than not.

"So, have you had any cool dreams lately?"

"Well, yeah, actually. I've been meaning to tell you about it all. My mom finally dug out my father's dream journal, and it's pretty crazy."

"Yeah? How so?"

"Well…I don't know exactly what is going on, but it seems we are in the same Dream World. I know that this is going to sound strange, but we are just different characters, embodiments in this other realm, different than we are here in this world. He described the same Whale figure, and the Forest. Then…I saw him. I mean dreamed about him in the Dream World, his character, Mikasi. He didn't look like himself at all and he was younger than I remember him being. He was in many ways nothing like the man I knew as a father, but in ways he was, and I knew and felt that it was him…It wasn't a good dream. In fact, it was a hard dream to take in. He was conniving, afraid, and I think he did something really wrong there. I think he may be responsible for the way the Dream World is now; dark, desperate and sad. I have to pick up the pieces that he left broken and unfinished. I don't know exactly what the mission is entirely yet, but it seems urgent and extremely important. I wake feeling more and more disconnected from this realm, but go deeper and deeper every night, into the Dream."

"I wish I could go there with you! How crazy! How can you be sharing the same dream experience?" He was amazed, but not understanding that it was possibly a real place.

"I'm not totally convinced that it's not all real. That perhaps we are able to simply shift consciousness into another dimension or something. I am telling you, this place is as real as what you and I are experiencing right now, here in present time on Earth. It's a different timeline there though. Time is not the same there, and I can be there for literally days, in the Forest, and it is only an hour or two of sleep here. Then I can be in the water with Whyla the great Whale, and it can feel like mere moments, but Mom will have been trying to wake me for nearly an hour. Yeah, that's why I was late this morning. I guess I couldn't wake up for a while, she was pretty upset. My Dad used to be like that. I feel I am digging deeper each time I go, and more and more that I am supposed to be there… and a longing to be there."

"Whoa, your mom was trying to wake you for an hour this morning??"

"Well, like forty-five minutes or something, but I am totally fine…"

"Lila! That's sketch! I'd be totally freaked out if I was your mom too. Poor Tihana! And your dad used to do this too? Lila, you know what road that led him down. I don't want that to happen to you." He was starting to sound panicked, like Mom.

"I'm fine, it's all ok…Every little thing, is gonna be alright." I started to sing in my best Bob Marley impression I could muster.

"I'm serious, Lila. This really kind of freaks me out. I'm worried about you."

"Well, don't be. I'm fine. It's fine, really!"

I felt myself wanting to squeeze his hand tighter, and wanting to let it go at the same time. So we continued just holding hands, but barely touching our palms together. I felt like I needed to change the subject.

"So have you been meditating at all? I always forget to. Last night I fell asleep breathing with these prayer beads though." I pulled the strand from tucked inside my shirt. I could slightly smell their woodsy intoxicating scent, and it made me close my eyes for a moment.

He stopped and faced me straight on, looking at me seriously.

"Lila, I am honestly worried about you. I know this sounds weird, but I got a cramp in my stomach the second you said that your mom couldn't wake you this morning. It feels wrong. It's scary. I want you to maybe come over and talk to my mom about it. I know you and your mom are supposed to see her later this week for an Ayurveda session, but I think you need to see her today, before the dreams get anymore intense. I don't know if she can help, but I just feel a strong urge to have you speak to her. Can you come over for a little bit?"

He was genuinely concerned and it was the least I could do, to please him and ease some of his worry. I was actually excited to talk to Mrs.Varma though. I had meant to ask her about the sacred shape I saw last week, the circle of spheres that intersect. I did feel she might have some insight, so we re-directed our course towards the Varma residence. Acarya pulled me closer, under his wrapped arm, like a bird or my guardian angel.

Chapter 2
Believe

Hello, children! What a pleasant surprise! I thought you were going to Mr. Peen's today."

"Yeah, we did too, but he wasn't home. We left a note for him though," he said and then kissed his mother on the cheek.

"Alright, well that was good to leave a note. I hope he is well. Would you two like some Ojas balls and Chai?"

"Oh, yes, please!!" I replied quickly. The thought of it made me realize how hungry I was. I hadn't really eaten much all day, completely distracted by my thoughts and everyone else's energy.

"Lovely, I'll be right back. Your father is in his study, if you'd like to say hello."

I had only seen Acarya's father maybe twice. He was like an elusive endangered animal that you rarely ever got to witness in its natural environment. I found myself curious to see him, and my eyes a bit widened.

"Oh cool, I'll go say hello," Acarya said.

He gestured for me to come with him, and led me upstairs, just passed his own room, so just passed the 'line' I had ever walked over in their huge old Victorian home. I honestly didn't know how many rooms there were, but I started to count and realized it was a five bedroom house! Wow. Ours was only three, and only one story, and everything a fraction of the size. If you were to equate it to back in the time when they were built, the Varma home was for someone who was already rich, struck it rich with gold, or was maybe a mine manager or even owner. Our home belonged to a miner working down in the dark mine shafts. It was funny to witness the extremism of class and separatism still present today. A lot of their home was built with Redwood, which is no longer really found around here anymore. It made me sad to suddenly imagine and visualize the rapping of these wild lands back then, what this forest would have looked like two hundred years ago. Then I shook off the daydream and focused back to the charming, sweet, hospitable family that lived in these walls of wood, and worked hard to be here, and I felt their love and appreciation embedded here.

"Hi Dad."

Mr. Varma had his back to us, sitting on what looked like a giant ball, at his desk that faced the window. He turned around and took off his glasses.

"Ahh, son! Welcome home. I thought we weren't expecting you for a while. Lila dear, it's lovely to see you. It has been a while. It's nice to be able to work from home now on Mondays." He said in his thick British Indian accent, and he smiled his jolly smile that he did. A smile that took over his whole face, including the squinting of his eyes. He had a rounded face and large round eyes, but he was not a very big man. He was maybe a little bit rounder in the belly, but he was sort of petite. He was pretty much adorable. I always wanted him to be my Doctor, but he was too specialized. I wondered for a second where Acarya got his height. He was at least six inches taller than his father and mother, who were nearly the same height.

"Well, I imagine you two have some homework or things to attend to."

We smiled sweetly at each other and then Mr. Varma brought his hands to his chest in prayer and said "Namaste" to us both. We repeated it back and I considered that our moment to let him go back to work, so I motioned to leave.

"Lila, I am so sorry to hear about your mother's health. I am praying for her and sending her healing energy."

I turned back around to say thank you, and as I did, I noticed a small framed image on his desk, that I didn't see the moment before. It was the circle image from my dream, with the interwoven flower-like shapes.

"Thank you, Mr. Varma. I appreciate your kind words, and the healing energy for my mom…Umm, sorry to change the subject, but I just noticed that circle image there. Can you tell me more about it?"

"Oh, the Flower of Life Mandala?"

"The Flower of Life Mandala…" I repeated in wonder, pondering out loud.

"It is a very sacred mandala. It portrays the cycles of life, with sacred geometric patterns. It is said to be the way the Universe creates, where all form stems from, and it all begins with one circle, depicting that we are all originated from the One. I find it helps me to feel my place in all things. It is both calming and uplifting to me."

He smiled. I smiled back. Completely in awe.

The Flower of Life Mandala. Wow. My body had chills. I had heard the word Mandala, but didn't really know what it meant exactly. Instead of asking further questions though, I decided to look it up more when I got home. I tried to mask over my extreme excitement and curiosity.

"That's so beautiful. Thank you for sharing." I put my hands back up in prayer position again, it was becoming more natural for me. This time, I used it in a way that said 'thank you' and 'good-bye', which didn't seem to be the meaning, but felt like an appropriate thing to do. He bowed in prayer to me back, confirming my gesture was acceptable.

Then Acarya looked at me and we smiled and he said, "Alright, Dad. We'll let you get back to work now."

We walked back down to the kitchen, and I pondered more about the mandala.

"What are you thinking about? You suddenly look really deep in thought," Acarya inquired.

"Oh yeah, it's just interesting. That symbol was a major part of one of my dreams last week. I was a little lost in the whole idea of it, I guess."

"Wow! You had a dream about the Flower of Life Mandala??! Dang! Your dreams *are* sweet!"

"What is sweet?" Mrs. Varma chimed in as we reached the kitchen.

"Mom, Lila has been dreaming about the Flower of Life Mandala, and didn't even know what it was. How cool is that?" He almost boasted.

"Well, I just had one dream about it. But yeah, it was pretty cool." They had no idea how cool though, and I could never possibly describe it to them.

"What? Wow, Lila. That is very powerful, and auspicious. The Universe is speaking very clearly to you, pay attention. Are you writing your dreams down?" She asked very seriously.

"Yes, actually, I am. Yeah, they feel like very powerful dreams."

"Wow, just wow. That is truly remarkable, Lila."

I felt her sincerity, and it only heightened my feeling of anxiousness about my mission, solidified it as important and sacred. I knew this already, but somehow this symbol seemed to be able to communicate across the worlds, it seemed to be a key in understanding and communicating. I still had chills, but was now feeling my nervous system revved up, ready to go back into the dream world already. Somedays felt really long.

"Here, eat this grounding and nourishing snack, and support your Vata which is probably a bit high right now. It is through the forces of Vata that we connect to the realm of Spirit." She handed me a beautiful small turquoise ceramic plate with 3 rounded balls of yummy dates, nuts, seeds, and spices mixed together. They smelled like Cinnamon and Ginger and seemed to both enliven my mind and warm my heart, simply with the scent. The creamy Chai was steaming in a golden mug. I felt so much love around me, from Acarya, from Mrs. Varma, from the room, from the food. It was exactly the vibe I needed, and I took in a deep breath of gratitude, and closed my eyes for a moment.

"Thank you, Mrs. Varma. This is so wonderful and delicious."

"Oh my dear girl, I am so glad."

I felt the most 'at home' that I had truly felt in my heart, in years. At least for here in the waking life. Being with the Varma's felt so much like swimming with Whyla.

"Lila, I was thinking yesterday, after we met, that if you ever wanted to apprentice with me, to learn about Ayurveda and Herbalism and cooking nutritious foods, I would absolutely be honored." She said with a warm smile and an invitation in her sparkling eyes.

"Oh my goodness, really?? I would love that so much!" I was beaming with the idea of learning all of these incredible things, from such an incredible woman, that I admired so much.

"Wonderful! Well, after your snack, if you're interested, you can help me finish encapsulating the herbal mixture I made for your Mum."

"Oh yes please!! I would love that." How exciting! I couldn't wait to see how it all went. I found myself starting to shove the Ojas snack balls into my mouth.

"No, no, take your time. I'm in no hurry. Enjoy and relax as you eat, it helps with digestion." She smiled and gently touched my arm. My arm seemed to melt under her hand, which spread through my whole body. She had a magical touch. Acarya had very amazing parents, both deeply spiritual healers, who were also well educated and professional. I absolutely admired and respected them.

When we were done with our snack, Acarya and I walked back to his mother's office, where she was sitting at her desk, transformed into an apothecary work station. There were jars of powdered herbs, scoops and bowls, and a little contraption that seemed to be for filling the capsules. She was wearing gloves and a surgical mask, which she pulled down when we arrived.

"Alright, so you can just watch me do one, and then I will let you fill up a set. My sweet little capping machine only holds 24 capsules at a time, and we are going to make ninety-six. I have already blended up the herbal blend here, including Guggulu, which we spoke about yesterday. Here would you like to smell it?"

She handed me the jar of the dark gray, almost black, powder and I took a big inhale to smell it. It was so much like the powder in the little carved box, from the Dream, but it wasn't exactly it.

"What was the one that was very similar to this?"

"Shilajit." She answered.

My body got chills as she said it. That was it. "Could I possibly smell that one?"

"Sure, it's right over on that shelf." I walked over to the wall of jars, all containing healing medicinal plant medicines, and I could feel their power. I could feel their strength. I could feel their Love.

"Wow," I said.

"Yes, aren't they powerful? I can feel them too." She smiled at me. "You know, it can be very powerful to meditate with the herbs. You just place a little in your hands and sit with them for a while, closing your eyes and smelling them into your senses, then ask that they share with you their secrets. It is amazing what can be revealed. We are all part of the living circle, and these plants are highly intuitive and engaging, they want to connect with you. You see that is their dharma, to offer healing, love, and connection, to animals and humans. They are elated when they are acknowledged. It heightens the potency of their medicine. Go ahead, pick one and go into the other room and meditate with it. You too, Acarya. See if they reveal any wisdoms to you. See if you can open your heart and mind to receiving the message." She instructed us. "Just put a little on your hand with a scooper." She handed each of us a little metal scoop. I looked up and down the wall of literally hundreds of jars, and couldn't pick just one. They were all singing out to me. I felt the room suddenly holding so much more energy than I was initially aware of. I stepped back in overwhelm. Then I saw it, the small jar that read 'Shilajit'. I had to know more.

There was only a small amount in the jar and I imagined it was rare or more expensive than some others, so I only took the tiniest little bit. Holding it in my hand brought back a flashback image of witnessing it in my Dream, in the little spiral carved box. It smelled like burned sweet wood. Or, truthfully, it reminded me of a farm with sheep or goats, the scent of their manure. It was strangely intoxicating though, I found myself wanting to keep smelling it. Acarya picked one too, an off white powder that had a lightness to it and fluffed into a little cloud of particles when he opened the jar.

"What did you choose?" I asked.

"Ashwagandha," he said, having fun with the pronunciation.

"Oh, that's interesting that you were drawn to that one, Acarya. I was going to make you a blend with that herb soon. I actually put a small amount here in your mother's formula too, Lila. Alright, well you can do the next batch of capsules, after your meditation session."

We all smiled and then Acarya led the way back out of the room, to the living room, where the meditation pillows were.

"So we just close our eyes and meditate like usual, but ask the herbs to reveal their secrets to us?" I asked, recapping what Mrs. Varma had just instructed.

"I guess," said Acarya, smiling. "See you on the other side." He winked, then closed his eyes and adjusted his posture.

I looked down at the dark black partial powder, partial small shale rock, of this dense resin. It reminded me of shiny Obsidian, nearly glass shards. I closed my eyes and felt it in my hand, felt it trying to connect with my hand. I asked with my inner voice, "Dear precious Shilajit, will you please reveal what I long to know about you? What is your purpose on my mission? What do I need to know?"

I felt it responding, or my hand suddenly responding to it, more in tune, a communication forming. Then in my mind, I was on a cliff of a mountain side, towering massive mountains all around. Powerfully raw with energy, I could feel the mountain was alive, breathing, witnessing. I looked down and there was a small crack in the rock, and then a feeling that I must release something, like a cough or a sneeze. I felt this energy gathering from my feet, moving its way up my body. Then I exhaled forcefully, and felt a black tar-like substance moving up out of the crack. It was a relief, and I felt cleansed but also exhilarated, much like the relief of a good sneeze. Then I noticed a person walking up the path toward me, they were carrying a small pottery jar and a metal scraping tool. They gathered the sticky substance. Then stood and turned to me, making a gesture in prayer. My heart was happy. Then I was suddenly in the view of the ceramic jar, moving down the mountain now. All I could see was sky and a bit of the woman's face. She was old, but I intuited she was actually much, much older than she even seemed, somehow able to traverse this steep terrain. I felt the gratitude and joy in her heart and it made me smile. Soon I was in a small hut, being made into a tea, and then offered to a man holding his hands out for me. I reached out for him too, feeling a mutual longing. Then he drank me, and I slid down into his body with comfort and ease. I was in his stomach now, I think, and the walls were all pink and smooth. Until I turned around and saw a dark black spot, that was rough and wreaked of pain. I moved towards it, curious and aching to make it pink again. So I took what felt like my hand and started wiping it away, little bits falling off. I touched my hands firmly against the wall and felt the energy here was scared, angry, and sad. I smiled and was able to override the feelings with a feeling of peace, contentment, soothing and nurturing Love, like the energy of a big hug. The black spot slowly began to fade and I could see the soft smooth pink layer below beginning to resurface. I felt my heart opening, the layers over my chest flaking off, and I looked down to see that a bright white light was radiating from my center. I allowed my light to shine brighter, into all the dark corners of the space and then my heart grew so bright and I felt myself letting go of my awareness of my self, and everything went white. I was simply an awareness of a feeling, a deep feeling of peace.

"Wow, that was cool," I heard a whispered voice say.

I slowly opened my eyes and saw Acarya grinning kind of a silly grin.

"Wow, is right. I just went on a pretty incredible journey. What did you experience?" I said, needing to gather myself a bit more before speaking.

"Seriously, I'm not quite sure if it was really working or not. I may have just had a delusional daydream." He laughed. "I was suddenly wearing a cape and felt like I had superhuman strength and powers. Then I felt so loving, like super warm fuzzy feels. It was like I was a character from Sesame Street." He said proudly.

I smiled at him, a little surprised, and then burst out laughing. "I'm sorry, but that is so cute. Not what I was expecting to hear. I just totally pictured you as a puppet character though. That's Adorable." I laughed again.

"Alright, alright, so what did you experience?"

I told him the whole vision in detail, and he slouched in overwhelm with big eyes. "Woooowwww. Now *that* is crazy. Dang girl, you should go tell Mum."

Mrs. Varma thought it was beautiful and then told me that I had 'a natural gift.' It was extremely amazing to hear, especially from her, and I felt a little taller. I also felt more reassured about my mission and the Dream. Perhaps I was a chosen one for a reason. Then Mrs. Varma said something that changed me, and my mission, in a second… "Perhaps *you* will be the one to heal your mother."

…I felt the words moving through every cell of my body, like it was lightening, lighting hidden torches within me. I felt flushed all over. Then I got chills over my entire body. She could see my reaction, it was apparently as visible to others as it felt in my being. She got up, walked over to me and put her hands on my shoulders, looking me in the eyes, and said, "Lila, I have heard a little bit about your dreams, and from what I witness of you and your enthusiasm for the healing arts, I believe you are going to be a very powerful Healer indeed." Then she leaned in and kissed my forehead. It felt like an initiation.

"Talk about warm fuzzy feelings!!" Acarya said, witnessing us in our moment. I felt so much love and gratitude, I could've burst.

Acarya decided to walk me home. He didn't want to let me walk by myself after we saw that creepy guy on the trail. So, like a gentleman, he escorted me home, the third of a mile to my house, bringing his skateboard for a quick ride back.

"Your Mom is so wonderful, Acarya."

"Yep, she is! So is yours!" He smiled.

"Yes, I know, but I mean, wow! Your Mom is seriously so wise and caring and sweet, and she knows SO much stuff."

"Yup. …So is and does your Mum."

"Yes, you're right. I am not trying to say that my Mom isn't these things, I am just having a moment of serious gratitude for yours. I want to be her apprentice and learn everything I can from her."

"Awesome! You should!"

"You're right though…I think I do sometimes idealize your mother, because, well, she isn't tired, sick and sad all the time…I love my Mom, but sometimes I feel more sorry for her than I feel proud of her, or wanting to be like her. She sacrifices so much for me too, it makes me feel so guilty saying that. Plus, this whole thing has really shifted her attitude and approach to work, so maybe things will be better soon," I said with hope.

"Lila," he said, stopping me and turning me towards him, "everything is going to be alright. Your mother has been through a Lot more than mine and she is still the most sweet, caring, kind, and gentle woman I have maybe ever known. I admire your Mum, in high high High regards. She just needs some love and nurturing right now."

Gosh, he was wise for thirteen. I felt his words ring true. She was separate from the One, not feeling loved and supported by Great Spirit. I needed to remind her of the Truth.

I hugged Acarya around his middle tightly, and he wrapped his arms around me too. I looked up at him and smiled, he was looking at me with more Love in his eyes and heart than I had ever felt from him. I wanted to kiss him. Something stopped me though and instead I leaned back in for one more hug. I felt the excited butterflies, then I felt myself blushing red. I turned to leave rather quickly, and then turned back to look at him. He was still standing there looking at me, waiting to make sure I would get inside the door I guess. I smiled again, and he smiled back.

"See you tomorrow, Acarya."

"Mom, I'm home!" I called out, as I opened the door. I was still feeling all the feels.

"Lila! I wasn't expecting you until a bit later."

I ran to her and wrapped my arms around her so tight. I thought of all the things I loved about her and squeezed her tighter, consciously sending love vibrations into her body, into her chest.

"I love you so much, Mom. I appreciate you so much. You are amazing." It felt good to say, and absolute Truth in every bit of my being. I knew that it was good for her to hear too. She hugged me tightly back and then pulled away and brushed my hair from my face, grabbed my cheeks with her hands and kissed me on the forehead. I felt truly blessed.

"I have your herbs from Mrs. Varma. I got to help capsule a few. She has this cool little machine that takes the cap tops off and then you spread in the herbs, and then push them down in there with this poker tool, then when they're all filled you just push the upper level back on and all the tops are popped on. It was so fun. Plus, I meditated with Shilajit and had this crazy journey starting as a mountain and then ending up in someone's stomach and..."

"Whoa, Lila, slow down. I don't know most of what you're talking about. I'm excited that you're excited though. It's just a lot to process at once. Let's talk about these herbs...do they have instructions? I hope they weren't too costly for her to make. It's very hard for me to accept all of this from Mrs. Varma. I'm not even entirely sure I believe it will help."

I felt my heart sink into my toes. What did she mean she didn't *believe* it would help? I couldn't believe what I was hearing her say. It was devastating on many levels.

"Mom, I think believing is sort of part of the healing path. It's necessary. Do you believe you can heal?"

"Lila, I believe in science. I am a nurse. I believe in medicine and surgery and other such procedures, and then rest and rehabilitation." The devastation sunk its claws in deeper, right into my gut.

"Well, I *believe* that I am a healer. So what do you think about that?" I said boldly, standing proud, but inside I was shaking like a bush in the wind.

"Lila, I am proud of you for having such a big heart and wanting to help me, and for wanting to help the world. It makes me truly inspired and I find it very endearing. I don't know if it's a good idea for you to be spending too much time with Mrs. Varma though."

There went my heart, right out my feet and buried six feet

under. I felt the frog back in my throat. I couldn't even believe what she was saying. Did she know me at all? Did I know her at all? I couldn't even think. Everything went numb. Then I felt a small rage growing inside me, building with a heat that had been hiding, like lava deep in a volcano.

"Mom, I absolutely can't do that. I believe in this." It was all I could get out, and with a stifled tone. I walked away to my bedroom.

I believed in healing. I believed that I was a healer and that I needed the proper training, and that time was absolutely of the essence. Mom couldn't get in the way of that. But my heart was broken. I didn't know if I could heal her, if she didn't believe in it. I didn't know if the herbs would work as well as they could. It was all so disappointing.

After doing my homework for a while, we made a nice meal of Lentils with Carrots, Celery, and Spinach, spiced with fresh Thyme and Oregano. It was delicious, warm and nourishing, really hit the spot, and even helped me get a bit out of my funk. I was still bummed out though. Bummed with a mixture of a rebellious inspiration, a fire was definitely lit. I felt dared to prove this stuff to her. It was just hard to not have her support and approval.

"Lila, I wanted to apologize for how I was earlier. I am inspired by you, by your natural inclination to want to study alternative healing. It truly is a foreign place to me, and so...it kind of scares me. I was raised to believe this sort of thing was similar to witchcraft, so I have some reservations about it."

"Well, Mom, just because you don't know about it, doesn't mean it is wrong."

"I know that. You're right. I am willing to try to open my mind to it."

"Good. Thank you. I believe all you really need to do is open your *heart* to it. ...The plants are here to experience Life and be a part of the great cycle too. Their great dharma is to provide healing and balance. Isn't that beautiful? If you open your heart to understanding them and accepting that they are alive, with a purpose, too, and embrace their gift to you, you will receive their power magnified. Faith is not something we have to try to find or understand with our minds, it is something we have to simply allow with our hearts, moving the blocks and barriers we create. Those blocks are formed when we don't understand how the Universe is unfolding, when we try to control things we can't or shouldn't, and when our hearts feel loss. I think we need to focus on filling back up your heart, and creating Trust that 'everything happens for a reason'."

"Well, ummm… are you about to turn thirteen or fifty? How are you so wise beyond your years?" She reached out and held my hand, smiling softly, and looked deep into my eyes with love and appreciation. Then she picked up my hand and kissed it.

"I love you," was all she said.

I decided not to read Dad's journal again before bed. I didn't want it to influence my dreams, and I wanted to just continue strong on my mission. I was feeling extra motivated and inspired. However, my mind was having a hard time turning off. I couldn't stop thinking about the conditioning we have toward fear, how Mom was raised to believe that healing was witchcraft, and that witches were obviously bad. Did she believe that they should've been burned at the stake? Some seriously messed up stuff. Witches were likely just healers! How very sad this realization made me. Instead of going down a small rabbit hole of sorrowful thoughts, I decided to do some deep breathing, using the prayer beads, and just pray.

"Hey…You…Universe…God…however I am supposed to address you… I just wanted to say that I am sorry that humans are so ruled by fear and ignorance. If there was anyway you could possibly just help us to shift this self-defeating, planet killing, perspective…that would be amazing. If we could all experience dreams like you've shown me, I think that might help. Or even better, One collective realization at the same moment." Right as I said this, I realized the possibility and depth of my mission. Was it true? If I completed it successfully, would it really influence us here? The thought made my body tingle, I felt that feeling of inspired fire within. So I focused on breath, the soft rhythmic flow of taking in molecules of the One, and letting go of the One, being ultimately connected to everything around and within me in a sacred ebb and flow, and I finally drifted off to sleep…

…I was back in the second forest, the one with the taller trees and slightly less shrubby ground. I had my satchel and walking stick, but I didn't have the glowing white rope. I looked around and didn't see any movement, or sense any sound. It was so strange to be in a forest with no bird or bug sounds, no creaking of branches. I felt afraid for a second, to be so alone. Then I inhaled, closed my eyes, and felt myself connecting to the Oneness, to the silent stillness that was connecting everything. I opened my eyes and looked down, to see my light tan arms chiseled with muscles and wrapped with fine strips of leather of various shades, from presumably various animals. I felt their protection and connection. My suit was a darker brown leather, and the metal spikes somehow glittered with a light. I wondered where the light was coming from and searched for it. Then I realized the stars were barely visible peaking through the tips of the trees, which were growing so close together at their canopy, maximizing their intake of light. A little managed to escape their grasp though, and I was reflecting it. Somehow this gave me a boost of energy and motivation to get back to my mission. I started walking gently, making hardly any sound, feeling the ground below me and the sky above me, the trees all around me. I definitely felt like I was being watched, but I also felt like I was completely protected. Then I remembered, I was part of the forest, I could feel its feelings and think its thoughts. Then all I felt was Oneness, a certain peace mixed with excitement and gratitude. The forest was happy I was there. I glided through, using my staff at moments to guide my fluid movements. I was never good at Parkour, but Acarya had occasionally tried it in town and wasn't half bad. I was a Parkour Queen here, and I owned it, pridefully and with joy in my strength and agility. It ultimately seemed to come from a place of feeling the rock or ground below me, being a part of its energy as much as this body I seemed to inhabit. I could feel where we met, it was more like I was the space between us. It was surreal and seriously fun. I felt my heart bursting with joy. Then I saw my heart starting to glow bright, through my leather. I slowed down, in shock of seeing light go through leather. It must have been extremely bright. As I slowed, and questioned my light, it faded back down and I couldn't see it anymore through the layer of dense hide. So I focused again on traversing the forest ahead, connecting with Love to the energies all around, making my way to the Tree of Life.

I heard a crack of a branch nearby and felt another entity. I looked to my right where I heard the noise. There was a person standing there, it appeared to be a man. They were dark and ominous and I couldn't make out any details of their appearance, but their energy was disturbing. Then they literally disappeared before my eyes, reappearing on the left side of me, a few feet closer. Every hair stood straight up on my skin. I felt afraid, anxious, unsure. Then it turned to slightly left of my 'pathway' and blazed away at lightening speed, leaving a trail of dust. What the?? I felt scared and even shaky. It was creepy and weird. Then I realized it had left a trail. Perhaps even wanting me to follow it. My mind said run the other direction, but my heart was strangely curious to follow after. I felt myself stuck in indecision for a moment, my heart beating quickly. It was everything in me to fight my mind and the fear of following this strange energy, but something in my gut told me to trust it. So I started to follow the trail of upturned dirt, about forty-five degrees to the left of where my initial instinct told me to go. I felt weary of the decision at first, and my legs seemed to be slowed with inhibition, but I couldn't help but wonder, and I couldn't help but trust that I was supposed to follow. The forest was on my side, I was One with it. Then I was also One with this foreign energy. So I felt my pace quicken and a new curiosity version of excitement, as I tried to catch up to it. Feeling the space between my feet and the ground, feeling all the roots of the trees, their interconnectedness, I was again part of this beautiful web. Then I was no longer running, but rather moving through with conscious awareness of the spaces around, as if witnessing it all on a three dimensional screen, navigating it like a computer. I surged ahead at lightening speed and then came to a place where the trail suddenly ceased. Without a trace, there was just a stopping place, in a new spot in the forest, still in the middle of it with nothing but trees as far as one could see. I looked around for the figure. Nothing. I felt that sense of fear rising again, but took in a deep breath and cleared it away. I wanted to simply sit, and close my eyes, feeling a strong need to touch the ground at this place with as much of me as I could. So I laid down, opening my eyes, and looked up at the dense forest canopy above. It was beautiful and I felt hugged by the Earth here, nourished by the heavy, moist energy. Then I heard the Hawk cry, and it awakened something inside. I opened my eyes and saw that I was being sort of swallowed by the forest floor, a layer of moss and soft roots creeping over me. I struggled and freed myself and got up. It didn't feel bad to become part of the forest, it was deeply peaceful and comforting, like being with Whyla. Yet I knew I had a mission and I needed to stay focused. I redirected my course to where my initial instinct and inner compass always led me back to and I charged forward at full speed, this time using the awareness method of moving through space at the speed in which my mind could comprehend my surroundings, basically flying through. Nothing could distract me or lead me off course now…

Chapter 3
Coyote

"Lila, honey, I have to go to my appointment soon, you NEED to wake up now. You're already going to be late to school, again," I heard Mom saying and the familiar rocking and shaking. "Lila, it's already 8:15. Wake up!"

I was groggy and it was hard to pry open my eyes.

"I'm awake," I managed to say, "It's ok, Mom. I'm here."

"Lila! Oh thank God." She held me close and rocked me for a second. Then she got up almost angrily and said, "Now, please hurry and get dressed. You'll have to eat in the car before I drop you off at school." Then left the room in a little fury.

I was SO tired and I felt like I could just sleep for the rest of the day. I knew I needed to go to school, but did I? Or did I need to return back to the Dream and continue on my mission? It felt like a no brainer to me, but then again, *this* was the 'real world' that I was brought into, for a reason as well. I needed to pull myself together and be conscious. I had a mission here too.

Being conscious and being *present* were two different things though. I could tell it was going to be a challenge to pay attention today.

Sure enough, the day was an absolute blur. Again. My peer's hormones were raging extra hard today and I had to block out their energy, enforcing my shield that was becoming stronger. I was counting down the seconds to the last bell. Time seemed completely different and irrelevant though. Moments seemed fleeting, but to stretch on forever. I was lost in daydream, and every time I blinked I saw the Flower of Life mandala, so I spent much of the day with my eyes closed. Picturing everyone's glowing orbs and spheres of light, the true essence of everyone, all intertwined, helped me cope with their pettiness and insecurities which led to blatant cruelties.

Until, I saw an orb that was flickering, struggling to spin and spiral with energy. I suddenly came-to with awareness of the 'real world', the physical world around me, and realized I was looking at Dustin Smith. Dustin was a boy that was sort of always picked on, by other kids mostly, but also teachers. He wasn't the brightest, school seemed to be very difficult for him. He was never very clean, kind of always had this smell that was musty and offensive. He didn't seem to like anyone and was always sort of angry or irritable. He went down into the forest at lunch to be by himself, away from everyone. He was someone everyone sort of ignored, pretended they didn't see, or worse, someone they took their own stuff out on, because he just seemed to take it. I always felt sorry for him. His Dad and my Dad had somehow known each other a long time ago. I remember seeing my Dad stumble out of his Father's truck one night, when I was maybe five. I think they were friends. Mom didn't like them hanging out though. He was always cussing more after he'd been with him. I always imagined that his Dad was the reason Dustin was the way he was. He looked less angry and more…empty today, though. It seemed like he was even paler than normal too, and he had slightly dark circles under his eyes, which were puffy. I resolved to try to speak to him after class, but I couldn't stop staring and wondering what was going on in his head. He was clearly not paying attention to the teacher as much as I wasn't. I thought about how vastly different his energy sphere was from the rest. Could these spheres of energy be correlating to what Mrs. Varma described of Ojas? Was poor Dustin's Ojas so low that his essential energy field was failing? I thought about feeding him an Ojas ball, and visualized him clean and smiling, his sphere spiraling with joyful energy. It made me smile to imagine it. Alright! New mission found!! I was suddenly more awake, inspired, but also overwhelmed with sadness and shame. He was bullied his entire life and I was only just now seeing that I should try to help him. Why hadn't I helped him before? I mean I was never the one saying anything mean to him, but I certainly didn't stop them, and I often didn't look at him as he passed. I definitely never wanted to be paired with him in any kind of activity or group assignment. I was part of the problem. I ignored his flickering light. Obviously, his home life was rough and he was never well cared for. I actually started to tear up, then I gathered myself together and started to pay attention to the teacher.

After class, I watched as Dustin quickly grabbed his things and was the first one out the door. I had to rush to gather my stuff, to chase after and catch up.

"Hey, Dustin! Wait up!" I called.

He turned to look at me and made a scowl, and then turned around and walked faster. We still had one more class, but it looked like he was going down into the woods, like he was about to ditch last period. I called out again and this time he didn't even turn around. I ran to catch up.

"What do you want?" He said in a grumpy tone.

"Where are you going?" I asked.

"None of your business, and why the hell do you want to know?" He said as he scrambled through his back pack. He pulled out a pack of cigarettes.

"Oh, um, I just wanted to see if you were alright. You seemed sort of down. Well, extra down."

"Why the hell do you care?" He flicked his lighter and lit up a cigarette in far too familiar of a way for a 13 year old.

"Oh, well, I, uhh. I just noticed is all."

"Well, thanks for noticing." He exhaled smoke directly at me, purposefully offensive, trying to get me to leave.

"You should probably not smoke, it's really bad for your

health," I said, coughing and waving the smoke out of my face.

"Yeah, you should probably get to class, before you get us both in trouble," he said again exhaling smoke in my direction, in an even more obvious gesture.

"Fine, I just wanted to say, 'it's not always going to be like this for you. You are powerful. You are loved'." I didn't know why I said those things, but it felt really good to say. I turned and walked back up the forested hill with my head held high and my heart, beating extremely fast, wide open with Love. I was proud of myself for reaching out to him. I turned to see what he was doing. He wasn't looking at me, he was looking off in the distance, pondering my words perhaps. Then he put out the cancer stick, leaving it on the ground which absolutely irritated and concerned me, but he did seem to be pondering, cause he suddenly smiled. I felt my heart burst open a little more.

As I got back up to the school yard though, there was a yard duty lady standing there, looking very disappointed. "Smoking cigarettes? Principal's office. Now!"

I walked into Mrs. Pombokom's office and didn't feel ashamed, but was more excited to tell her of my good deed. She was looking at me though with a lot of concern and also a bit of disappointment.

"I can explain…"

"Lila, I am going to have to call your mother. This is not something we take lightly. You're only twelve!"

"I'm thirteen in a week and a half…not important…Mrs. Pombokom, I wanted to just find out if Dustin Smith was ok. He looked like he was going to pass out or cry or have a fit of rage or something. I guess I had an awakening to the fact that he is so sad. I wanted to tell him that it's all going to be alright, that he is powerful and loved."

"Oh Lila, you really are a special one, aren't you? Well, that is commendable. You still left the acceptable areas of the school grounds though."

"I was curious where he was going. I know. I'm sorry. It felt important to tell him these things today and I honestly thought he was leaving to go home, ditching last period or something." I didn't feel that I could describe what I was now able to see and feel and where my urgency was coming from, she might not understand.

"Well, I guess Dustin is really the only one in trouble here then."

"Oh, but truly, what kind of punishment. Don't call his parents. I have a feeling that won't be in his benefit at all. Truthfully, I think his parents are the reason he is smoking and the way he is. Wouldn't calling them make things worse?"

"Well, Lila, you are a wise old soul. I will take this into consideration. Now hurry up to class, you've already missed the first 10 minutes," she said with a side smile. As I was almost to the door, she said, "Lila. You are powerful and loved too." She smiled a little bigger. I smiled bigger back. Dustin was waiting to go in next, he looked at me with that same scowl (likely because I probably was responsible for him getting caught), but then he nearly smiled (perhaps appreciative of my words). I felt my heart singing it's song...no one could hear it but me, but I was beaming with my heart song.

I met up with Acarya after school, to go together to Mr. Peen's house again. We were a little more on alert going down Kokiba trail, but we didn't see anything or anyone this time. I told Acarya about my day and experience with Dustin. He was blown away that I could see the energy spheres. I told him that I couldn't always see them, but if I sort of stared through everything, they would be there. It was very meditative. He seemed like I was telling him a story about ghosts, curious and excited but also apprehensive and a bit scared.

"So, his energy sphere was all messed up and slow? That's super sad, dude."

"Right?! I know! Doesn't it make sense though?"

"Yeah, it does, I guess. That's so incredibly sad. I'm going to say something nice to him tomorrow," he said pridefully, but also realizing the same sad truth I had earlier, that it was way past time for this realization and resolution.

"Well, if we can try to just realize how much our actions or inactions are affecting life around us, and act in ways that only benefit others, we will not only be a part of the good cause, but we will lead really good lives," I said, as if I was some wise elder.

"Amen, sista! I'm inspired!" Acarya said emphatically.

The truth was, he was always nice to everyone and already made gestures of good deeds wherever he went. He was bullied a little when they first moved here, for his accent, the smell of his food he would bring to school for lunch, for his culture, and sometimes even for his skin color. Made me realize how insecure and bizarre our species was. Scared of anything that was different, yet not recognizing that we're not different. At all.

When we got to Mr. Peen's, his truck was there and he was sitting out on his front porch again, smoking from a Sherlock Holme's style pipe. He smiled as we walked up.

"Well, I owe you both an apology for not being here when I said I would on Thursday and yesterday. Thanks for being so dedicated. I really appreciate your help and I don't want to put you two out."

"It's fine, no worries, Mr. Peen," Acarya said.

"Well, I don't feel good about it and I want you to know I'm sorry. Some things came up for a friend and I needed to be there for them."

"It's really not a problem, Mr. Peen. We enjoy the walk." I smiled.

"Alright, well, thanks. I guess you can just pick up where you left off. I think you're ready to start really cleaning things off now that it's all upstairs. I have really appreciated having space in my living room again."

"I bet, that was a lot of stuff cluttering your space," I said.

"Yeah, well, I'll be getting rid of it soon enough," he said in an almost defeated but also angry kind of tone.

"Mr. Peen, is there anyway these things can be preserved in a local museum again?" I asked naively with concern.

"Not unless all of a sudden people start caring," he said.

"Well, we care! And we didn't know until you told us the history. People just need to know the truth and then they would care," I said.

"You really think that if people knew the real story of the native people here, and the truth of the gold rush here, that they would embrace that part of their history? People don't want to acknowledge mistakes and horrible things they, or their ancestors, did."

"Well, I think we are removed enough now, generationally, it's been a hundred and seventy years. It's time to know the truth and heal this horrendous past of these beautiful lands," I said with inspiration and passion. "It's time for us to say sorry, on behalf of those ancestors, and ask for forgiveness of this cruelty. I also believe that it's time to learn of the ancient ways of balance and sustainability with this land. We need the native secrets and the energy of Connection, that has been lost."

I could nearly see a tear forming in Mr. Peen's eyes. He was grateful for our words, and our genuine interest and sympathy for his culture. I don't think we nudged his Hope meter much though.

"Well, children, I really appreciate you saying these kind words. My heart feels some peace from them, so thank you. But I'm afraid it's a little too late for learning our ways. Our ways are lost. Lost with the minds and souls of the broken few who remain. We are already returning to Source, and with us our way of living and knowing."

"Don't you know the ways? Can't you teach us?" Acarya chimed in.

"I know some, but the ways of my people have been ridiculed and chastised for so many generations now, that many of the ways have already been lost, simply not passed down to the next generation. But there are certainly some things that I know, and I could teach you both, if you were really interested," he said, standing a little taller.

"Oh my goodness, that would be so amazing! Yes, please!! Anything you can teach us, would be so beneficial. Perhaps we can do a half hour to an hour of lesson, and then help you finish this project of cleaning the artifacts?" I proposed.

"Well, you know, that could actually work. Wow, kids, are you sure you're really into learning the old ways?"

"Yes!!," we both said in unison with enthusiasm.

"Well, alright, then," he said smiling with a bit of surprise and pride. "Let's begin tomorrow. I need to gather my thoughts and ponder where to begin with you."

"That's great. I think Tuesday and Wednesday would be great regular days for us, does that work for you?" I asked.

"That'll be just fine, we'll say 4:00-6:00 on Tuesday and Wednesday, and I'll offer you guys some of the wisdom bestowed upon my people." He almost seemed to be tearing up again. "Well, alright then. You guys can go ahead and head up to start cleaning those things. Here are some horse hair brushes, they're for dusting off anything that can't be wiped with a wet cloth, like the skirts and hide robes."

"Thank you, Mr. Peen," Acarya said as he took the brushes and smiled at both of us, then gestured to me to walk up the stairs first, like a gentleman.

I was lit up inside at the thought of learning the ancient ways from Mr. Peen, *and* from Mrs. Varma. It felt so right. It felt like I was about to begin school for the first time, my real school. I couldn't fathom all that I might learn.

I must have been looking pretty lost in daydream, because Acarya suddenly said, "Hello! Anyone in there? Where are you right now?”

“Ah I was just thinking about all that I am going to start learning, from Mr. Peen, and from your mom. I’m so excited! It feels so right and so needed, for my mission.” I heard myself say it out loud and it brought chills to my arms.

“Your mission?” Acarya asked, suddenly breaking my bubble of a daydream.

“I mean, it just feels relevant for my path in life.” I felt myself getting anxious to talk about my mission, and Acarya getting too curious. I wasn’t even totally sure what my mission entailed yet and I didn’t want him to feel my anxiousness, he might fuel it.

“Yeah, I’m excited too,” Acarya agreed, and put it to rest.

Spending time with the artifacts, even though they were so old and most were falling apart and seemed lifeless, I could feel the energy of the people. It was a heavy energy, filled with sorrow. I tried to feel beyond the grief, to a time when the people were happy and living in harmony with each other and the surrounding lands. I could only imagine it, the feelings were just depressed. It took everything in me to not absorb their pain, but this only encouraged my heart to want to help them even more.

When I got home, Mom was there, and I was so excited to tell her, that I completely forgot that she had been to some appointments today. I blabbed on about my day and told her about my interaction with Dustin Smith, temporarily leaving out the bit about seeing his energy sphere, telling her that I just picked up on his heaviness. She told me I had a big heart, but sort of disapproved of my gesture, ‘wandering out of the acceptable areas and getting in trouble didn’t help anyone.’ But I knew that I had helped him, in some maybe small but important ways. Then I told her about our deal with Mr. Peen, how very excited I was to learn of his people’s old ways. She was encouraging of this.

She came in for a big hug and said, “I really am so proud of you, Lila. You are such a bright light in this world. It gives me great hope for the future."

I felt her words ringing through me, delivering strength and power that made me feel taller again, while soothing and relaxing me with love. I felt amazing for a few minutes. Until, Mom told me about her day. It had gone well with her primary Doctor, Dr. Cassidy, and apparently most of her blood work showed she was actually pretty healthy. Then she saw the Oncologist, Dr. Brennan, who recommended that she have a full body MRI, scheduled for Thursday. This Doctor was sort of dry and black and white, Mom said, and he didn't paint a good picture for her. She left his office feeling scared and insecure about her future, which she hadn't been made to feel yet. The Oncologist told her that likely she would need to have a *double* mastectomy (even though there was only one tumor on one side), chemo therapy, radiation, and then be on a medication for the rest of her life to prevent any reoccurrence. It was heavy and Mom was feeling it.

"Well, you know the MRI will maybe make things more clear, and you don't have to work with this Dr. Can't you get a second opinion?" I asked.

"Yes, I was thinking I might do that, after we hear more from the MRI. I would prefer to be with someone who is a little more hopeful and a bit more inclined to minimize my treatments, not maximize them. But then again, I'm not an Oncologist and I trust what is to be," Mom responded. She seemed deflated though, the wind out of her sails.

"Well, we can't dwell on what we don't know yet still. I guess until Thursday we should just be doing everything in our power to send your body healing love and picture it healthy," I heard myself saying, soothing even me with the words. Mom inhaled a big deep breath and smiled.

"Thank you, sweetie, for always being my rock." She took my face with her hands and looked me in the eyes, and kissed my forehead.

I laid in bed for a while that night, thinking about everything. It had been a very full day and I was exhausted, but also turned on with too many conflicting thoughts and feelings. I tried deep breathing, holding the sandalwood beads that were becoming a very familiar soother, like the pale yellow blanket, 'nigh nigh', I had when I was younger. Somehow I was just too wound up tonight though. So I decided to read more of Dad's journal…

"…I was back in the woods, this time I knew exactly how to get there. I closed my eyes and *imagined* myself running through the woods with lightening speed, and witnessed my movement with my mind. I traversed the dark forest without stepping a single foot forward. Suddenly, I saw it, just up ahead, and I surged forward even faster. There it was, the Gate. Although, it had taken me years to realize it was a gate, since it was invisible. I sensed the energy line now though, and knew that it was a race for your life on the other side of that line, if you didn't know the Three Truths. I knew that the moment I stepped foot over that line, the game would become more intense. So I stood there, pondering my next moves, and wondering if I would actually reach the Tree of Life tonight. I felt hesitation and fear at all that lay beyond this threshold and I felt a subtle tremor inside. Why did it have to be me? I always felt that I had a major purpose in life, but I also never thought that I was some kind of chosen one, some kind of hero. It felt like a lot of pressure, and what if I failed? Would I fail everyone? Everything? That's insane. I somehow knew that I was only dreaming, so how could it be real? I took in a big breath, feeling strength in my body and might in my mind, I stepped over the invisible barrier line, entering into the heart of the woods. I felt the wave of energy, like a scan of electricity through my body, mind, and soul. There was a loud sound of booming base, mixed with choral singing, mixed with children's laughter, with Whyla's song, with my mother's voice calling my name, all wrapped up in wind. I felt my heart burst open and the beam of light shoot out, lighting a path ahead. It was breathtaking and immense to experience this breakthrough. Truly unlike anything I could ever describe, but I guess the closest thing would be to imagine the combination of a warm hug from someone who cares deeply for you and an incredible orgasm with a great love. Now add an epiphany moment, mixed with a little butterfly from a rollercoaster, mixed with the feeling of accomplishment when you did something you didn't think you could. Oh, and then add the explosive love fest from a basket of fluffy kittens, and maybe toss in a first kiss. Then, and only maybe slightly, can you begin to understand the feeling. It was needless to say, intoxicating. I'm hoping that this is a regular thing here.

My heart was shinning a light that I thought was illuminating the darkness to show me through, but I realized that it was actually highlighting a pathway that only lit up when I was facing it. So if I veered with my chest in the wrong direction, the pathway would disappear. As soon as I corrected my facing, there was the pathway, illuminated with a glow like that of a flashlight in the dark of a moonless night. So of course, I followed it. Glancing around occasionally, to see if there was anything coming or watching. I felt a presence, an ominous one, something dark looming near. It felt like fear mixed with a deep anger. I felt the hairs on my neck stand up. There was nothing there though, anytime I looked. I kept following the light path, and my pace grew a little faster, with the small growing fear that I was being stalked. I hated that feeling, that there was something, that I couldn't see, watching my every move, playing me the fool, the victim. I was not a victim. So at last instead of running, I turned around and yelled "Show yourself!" in my deepest booming voice.

It was then that I saw him, the demon that haunted my dreams since I was a small boy, the snarling raggedy Coyote with piercing yellow eyes. He creeped towards me, fearlessly, burning through my eyes and right into my soul with his disturbing glare. Suddenly there were others all around him and they were all advancing towards me, creeping with exaggerated shoulder blade movement, heads low, to perfectly calculate and intimidate the stalking of their prey…me. My heart started racing, and my immediate response was to turn around and run, but instead I walked towards them. I was shaking with fear and it took everything I could muster to continue moving towards their gnarling teeth, dripping with saliva, ready to devour me, but I kept walking. When we were all about six to eight feet away, well within striking distance for them, I stopped. Something told me to kneel on the ground, become passive, and let them smell me like dogs meeting for the first time. I curled up in a ball on the ground and then rolled over to expose my scared belly, hands up over my face submissively, and closed my eyes. I felt the energy creeping closer, and then the warm air of breath, and a loud sniff. Then they were all investigating me with their noses, hovering above me, closed in around. I knew if I didn't remain calm, they would devour me in a heartbeat. I exhaled a relaxing breath. Their energy shifted and I knew it was safe to open my eyes. As I did, the one with the creepy yellow eyes, licked a great lick up the length of my face. I felt the acceptance and love. I let out a loud laugh and they all flinched, a few even ran away. I knew I needed to be mindful of their skittish energy, but I was honored to be accepted by the pack. Right as I went to stand up though…I woke up. I felt a mixture of feelings, one was that of relief. I had been afraid of this creature, that haunted my dreams, for so long. Now the feelings had changed, I had figured out a way to no longer be chased by him. It felt amazing. I also had a deep aching longing, an emptiness I couldn't describe other than the cliche of depression. It felt truly like my joy was missing. I couldn't even smile. That feeling of pure bliss from walking through the invisible energy line was gone, what was left was an empty vessel."

I pondered Dad's writing for a while. It had so many trigger words in it. I often blocked out how Dad was at the end, how he died. It was too painful to remember. But witnessing his inner journey through this dream journal was a trip. I could understand where he was coming from, but I also couldn't. We were so different. We perceived things so differently. He was more susceptible to feeling. I guess I had an inner strength that was more like Mom, and Grandma, with less of a need for pleasure, more of a need to do what's right. I wanted to look up Coyote Medicine, it had to be something meaningful.

Coyote
~Trickster~

Coyote...you devil! You tricked me once more! Must I sit and ponder, what you did it for?

Many Native cultures call Coyote the "Medicine Dog." Whatever the medicine, good or bad, you can be sure that it will make you laugh, maybe even painfully. You can be sure that Coyote will teach you a lesson about yourself. Coyote has many magical powers, but they don't always work in his favor. His own trickery fools him. No one is more astonished than Coyote at the outcome of his own tricks. He falls into his own trap. And yet he somehow manages to survive. He may be banged and bruised, but he soon goes on his way to even greater error, forgetting to learn from his mistakes. He may have lost the battle, but he is never beaten.

Coyote is sacred. In the folly of his acts, we see our own foolishness. As Coyote moves from one disaster to the next, he refines the art of self-sabotage to sheer perfection.

Contained within trickster medicine is the humor of the ages. The cosmic joke is not just on ourselves but on everyone else, if they are following Coyote or have strong Coyote medicine.

Snooze time is over if you have pulled this card or possess this totem. Watch out! Your glass house may crash to the ground at any moment. All your self-mirrors may shatter. The divine trickster is dogging you, and you may trip. But get ready for more laughs, lots more.

Are you playing jokes on yourself? Is someone tricking you? Are you trying to fool an adversary? Go beneath the surface of your experiences. Ask yourself what are you really doing and why?

You may not be conscious of your own pathway of foolishness. You may have conned yourself, your family, your friends, or even the public at large that you know what you are doing. But listen, Coyote. You have created a befuddling, bewildering, confounding trick. See through the genius of your acts of self-sabotage. Find it amusing and laugh, trickster, laugh. If you can't laugh at yourself and your crazy antics, you have lost the game. Coyote always comes calling when things get too serious. The medicine is in laughter and joking so that new viewpoints may be assumed.

Wow! Spot on, again. Dad *was* a jokester. He was the life of the house, always making us laugh with the absurd things he would randomly do or say. He was always lightening up our heavier times with silliness and play, especially with Mom. He was also subject to his own folly, his own traps of self-sabotage.

All the repressed feelings of anger, sadness, and anxiety creeped in again. Then I remembered the time that Dad and Mom were in a little quarrel and he turned around and stuck a carrot stick, that he grabbed slyly off the counter, into his nose. Mom burst out in a laugh and they lightened up about how they were talking about the issue. He really was the Coyote.

I laid there for a while before I fell asleep, with a little tear in my right eye. A tear that represented so much; the joy of remembering the happy times with Dad, the anger and sadness I held, but mostly the immense pain of simply missing him. Eventually, I did finally fall asleep…

…I was back in the water. I instantly felt my body melt with ease and sink a little more into the nurturing abyss, my eyes closing with mild ecstasy. It was the perfect temperature again, and I could barely feel its silky smoothness against my skin. I glided and twirled, feeling my heart opening again like a lotus blossom. I called out with my heart song, feeling myself vibrating a lower, heavier pitch. My song was more sorrowful tonight. She answered, but not with her song and twirling about me, like she usually did. This time, just as the first time I dreamed of her, she came up from under me and lifted me to rest against her dorsal fin, riding through the water on her. She was so big and so powerful. My legs barely wrapped around half of her belly, and here in the Dream, my legs were fully grown. I felt her strength. She was not just physically, but emotionally supportive of me. She felt me as much as I felt her. I felt our Oneness again. I closed my eyes, picturing our spheres of energy intertwining. She felt often times like my mother, a similar persona and role. I loved her, with every cell of me. We glided through the still, silk waters. I admired the heavens all shinning brightly above, billions of stars everywhere, lighting the darkness with their twinkling beauty.

"Whyla? If I fail this mission, will I die?" I heard myself ask, the anxious question coming easily to the surface from an unknown depth.

"Liluye, if you fail this mission, we *all* die," she sang softly, not really matching the weight of the words. I felt a flood of emotions spiral through me.

"How? How am *I* the one with the fate of the World in my hands?"

"Worlds, Worlds plural, Liluye…everything is counting on you."

"Why? Why me?"

"Well, you, and the one who failed before you, are the last

remaining ones who have come to my call. I cannot reach through to anyone else. Their consciousness is closed off, they have forgotten their Connection. The darkness has reached too deeply in their hearts. You have not forgotten the Truth."

"I am scared. I fear that I might fail."

"So are you not even going to try, then? Like your Father before you."

I felt the words hit me like a ton of bricks, bashing against my head and heart.

"Did he try and fail, or did he just not even try?"

"He betrayed the Forest, betrayed me, and everyone. Then, like a coward, he ran and never returned."

It was what I had thought, what I had pieced together. I still didn't know what he did, but I was pretty certain he had stolen the precious seed.

"Liluye, you are not like the one before you. You are stronger. You are wiser. You are not betrayed by your own needs and desires, the darkness has not reached your heart."

"What if I fail?"

"You can only succeed, if you see yourself doing so, and you wish it with all of your heart. Knowing the great connection of Spirit, you can use the Good that is coiled at the True Heart. You are still connected to the innocence of childhood, so you're blessed with resilience and naivity, which will support you on this journey. You are also blessed with the Oneness still residing in your Heart. Trust it and follow it. The mind gets in the way of this Light, as we age and think we know more than the Truth, or think we are owed something in return. The Ego is the ultimate defense system of the darkness. You must stay led by the Light. Trust your Light to guide you. Know this is the Light of Life, given to you by the One, forever connecting you to the great powers of Great Spirit. Allow your journey to be led by your heart."

I felt her song spiraling around and within me. It was so

nourishing and replenishing, filling in any cracks or holes that were questioning my wholeness. I felt reassured of my strength, reminded of my preciousness and my abilities. I knew I couldn't wait any longer, as much as I just wanted to stay here, hugging this sweet mother and hearing her nurturing advice. I had a mission, and time was of the essence…

"Lila, are you there? Wake up, honey! Wake up!!" I felt the familiar shaking and fear from her.

"I'm awake. I'm awake." I was groggy and frustrated. I really needed and wanted to get on with my mission. I knew that time was limited and the more time I spent here in my waking life, the less I was getting accomplished in the Dream. I felt sad that I had to still participate in the affairs of this dark planet, angry that I couldn't just go back to sleep. Then I remembered that I would be learning from Mr. Peen today after school, learning of ways that I believe are part of the remembering, and needed on this great mission. So I wiped my tear and sat up and hugged Mom. I knew I had scared her again. Last night wasn't even a long dream, from my perception of it. Then again, every time I dreamed I was with Whyla, the hours seemed to go by in a flash.

"Well, I tried to wake you earlier today, because we've been so late. So you're actually on time for once," Mom said proudly, and got up to leave. "So get dressed and come down for breakfast."

I was almost annoyed at Mom for this. I could've dreamt more and gotten farther on my mission. I had a full hour before school started. Then again, a nice mellow breakfast with Mom sounded lovely. I decided to take a shower even, since I had enough time and was too lazy the night before.

Chapter 4
Origins and Prophesy

I was so refreshed after a shower, walking into the kitchen with a beaming smile, I took a big inhale of the creamy steel cut oatmeal Mom was making. So warming and comforting, it actually kind of smelled like cookies.

"Is that Cinnamon? Mmmmm."

"Yes, and also Cardamom. Isn't it yummy? I have never really used Cardamom before, but Mrs. Varma recommended it. It smells a little like heaven in here." She smiled brightly.

I had to agree. It made me just want to close my eyes and take in deep breaths. Ha! A meditational breakfast! Awesome.

Mom had a nice idea of saying what we were grateful for, to start out our day feeling gratitude in our hearts.

She started by saying, "I am grateful for you, Lila, for being your Mom. I am so so sooo grateful for who you are and your amazing big heart. You make me so proud and so blessed." She took my hand and looked me in the eyes, smiling a beaming smile. I felt her love and warmth showering at me, like she was the mighty Sun.

"I am so grateful for you too, Mom, for who you are and all that you do for me. I am also grateful to you for who I am. I am proud of who I am too, and I wouldn't be me without your influence. I am *so* grateful for you too." I smiled beaming back at her, still holding hands. She was my Whyla. Always there to nurture, nourish, and keep me safe, and teach and guide my heart song.

I felt amazing heading to school. It was strange how having that time with Mom, feeling my gratitude, and filling my belly with warm delicious food affected my mood, energy, and whole perspective. I felt like a different person, refreshed and revitalized. Since I was walking up to school earlier than usual, I saw Acarya sitting out front, where he often was, reading a book, skateboard hooked into his backpack. He was often reading required material for school, but sometimes he was reading something of his choice. If you asked, he'd say, "What? I like reading. Gets my mind creative and juiced up for school." Somehow he was able to be dorky and cool at the same time. I loved when he wore his reading glasses too. He was so cute in them. He quickly took them off when he saw me walking up though.

"Hey, Lila. Fancy seeing you here, so early."

I laughed and said, "Yeah, my mom woke me up early today," with a semi-annoyed tone, but also ashamedly, knowing I was perpetually late.

"Well, it's a nice surprise," he said ridiculing, but playfully.

We walked together toward our classes. It was weird to not have a class with him this year, we had been in the same class from first through fifth grade, then had at least 1 class together in both 6th and 7th. This year, he was in higher level classes. He was just really smart and exceptionally hard working. We luckily had lunch together, but he was sometimes doing things with various clubs he was a part of. I always found it interesting how much he actually did in a day. He was so relaxed about it though, he just rode the tides of life like he did his skateboard, generally smooth and cool.

As we reached my home room class, he touched the small of my back, as he sometimes did, and the tingling sensation formed there.

"Well, you enjoy this class immensely," he said exuberantly, with obvious exaggeration, except he was sincere. He loved school and learning. He meant it genuinely.

I smiled and said, "Yeah, you enjoy too, Acarya. I'll see you at lunch."

"Oh, I have my student council meeting at lunch today. I will meet you after school by the light pole, like usual though." He smiled his flirty smile and adjusted his hands to the top his backpack straps, like he always did. Gosh, he was cute.

"Hey, Acarya," a few girls said as they passed by. He was more popular than I was maybe aware of. I didn't like not being in any classes with him. Was he flirtatious with them? Who were those girls? I hadn't even seen them before. They were probably from the smart classes too. Oh man, he was probably the cutest nerd in school. They probably loved him. I suddenly felt a rush of emotions and feelings, and my face even flushed pink, I could feel it. Alina was right inside when I walked in, and she could tell I was thinking and feeling a lot of mixed things.

"Are you alright? Hey, you're here on time for once. Good job! What's up though, you look like you just saw a ghost."

"Nothing, nothing, I'm fine. I just am thinking about a million things at once, a million things that don't matter and aren't what I should be thinking about."

"Like?" These were exactly the moments that Lina thrived on.

"Just realizing that Acarya is maybe more popular than I thought he was. Some girls just tried to flirt with him right in front of me."

"Well, yeah! He's a cutie. Plus, yeah, he knows everyone! But don't worry, he's totally in love with you." The second she said it, my heart lit on fire and my cheeks went red again. "You can totally tell. But yeah, he *is* pretty flirty." Wait, what? He is? I didn't like the idea of it, and I felt a strange feeling of jealousy for the girls that got to spend the whole day, flirting away with him. Wow, I was really falling head over heels. My head was definitely upside down.

Then I thought about what Whyla said last night. I was still connected to the innocence of childhood. This was key for my journey. I knew that if I pursued romantic love with Acarya, I would be losing some of that. I felt myself blocking that path with him. Yet, our innocent love was also possibly something that was key to my perspective and abilities. I felt empowered by it, by our love, by him loving me. I felt held by our innocence, like the magical places captured inside a snow globe. That place was my well of happiness these days. So I gathered the negative thoughts of jealousy, fear and anger and I exhaled them out, trusting the love that we had for each other was real and worth taking our time being sweet, innocent and young, like puppies.

Most of the day was sort of typical, along with my new 'norm' of being hyper aware of other's energies. Occasionally, I could intentionally block them, but most of the time it was unavoidable. I couldn't see the spheres today though, even when I tried to, which I found extremely disappointing. All this feeling, and blocking of feeling, was exhausting by the end of the day. As I walked into my second to last class, I was pretty much dragging, and I plopped down in my seat. Just before the bell rang, I heard the door slam shut and shoes clunk in angrily and loudly. It was Dustin Smith, and as he sat down in front of me, I was able to see his spheres of energy, spiraling erratically with more speed than normal. He was furious. I came back to seeing his physical form, and noticed he was shaking, with rage, a bright red mark across his left eye and cheek.

"Are you ok?" I asked quietly.

No response. He slouched down in his chair, pulling his hat over his eyes. Eyes that were scowling with intensity. He looked like he could burn a hole through something with his laser vision.

I retreated back.

"Looks like someone got their ass handed to them," Simon Harbunkle said snidely, making two or three other idiots laugh. "Well, if you didn't smell so bad, and if you actually washed your clothes, and..."

"Shut up!!!" Dustin suddenly jumped up and shouted loudly. He looked like he was going to explode.

"Hey, what is going on here," Mr. Baker asked. "Dustin, please, sit back down. Simon, if I hear another word from you, it's the principal's office for you."

I was feeling so low suddenly, recognizing that my *one* act of kindness and reaching out to him hadn't done much. I felt guilty again that this poor kid was so neglected of love and light in his life. I felt so bad for him. Then I felt his anger, his pain. He was about to explode, like a volcano, I could feel it welling up inside. I could suddenly imagine all the terrible things he heard and witnessed, all the cruelty spewed his way. I felt compelled to stand up and speak, and before I could tell myself not too, I did.

"Listen up everyone. Life is precious and fragile. Words and actions that are mean, are harmful, in a really serious way. You think that your cruel words won't hurt that bad, but really, you mean to hurt with them. That makes you someone who likes to torture, which makes you sick, and evil. I am ashamed and guilty for not standing up until now, for those that you insist on belittling. For what? So you can feel bigger, more powerful, cool? So you can feel better about yourself and your insecurities? What if you had a hard family life and didn't have the same ability to wash your clothes or be cared for in your basic needs? What if the fact that your *parents* were having a hard time was constantly being shoved in your face by harsh comments from your so-called 'peers'? You guys lack empathy completely, and that scares me. It makes me ashamed to be sitting beside you, seen as one of you. I am sorry, Dustin, for all the times I didn't stand up and say these things." I sat down, my whole body shaking. There was silence, and then a few girls on the left side of the class started clapping and then more joined in, including Mr. Baker. I didn't want an ovation, I wanted change. I looked up at Dustin, and saw him thinking about my words and digesting the whole experience, still looking like he wanted to just run away.

Then I saw a little hint of a smile from him, and I took in a deep breath and full exhale, and my shaking calmed.

"Alright, well, thank you for that, Lila. I hope you can all take her wise words in and really learn from your brave peer here. Now, let's take this altruistic way of understanding and discuss Democracy..."

When I saw Acarya after school, I was overwhelmed with feelings and just ran to him. Somehow knowing that other girls were lusting after his attention, made me want his attention even more. I ran up and gave him a big hug. He hugged me right back and then he grabbed my hand. Instantly assuring me.

We walked interlacing our fingers like lovers, swinging our arms like children, perfectly content to be whatever we were in between.

We headed down the Kokiba trail and he was filling me in on his day, I was filling him in on mine. He was proud of me for standing up for Dustin, which made me feel more proud too. There was still guilt there though, for this being the first time, when I had watched Dustin Smith get bullied for at least five years. I was still worried about his energy. Then while thinking about energy, I sensed one from behind us, and whipped my head around quickly.

Standing, not eight feet behind us, was a beautiful Doe, ears erect in our direction. There were a lot of White Tailed Deer in our area, but you didn't often see them right in town. She was majestic and seemed curious about us. She even seemed to be following us.

"Awe, it's my Totem animal," Acarya whispered, putting out his hand to her, as if she might come right up to him. His Totem animal? I didn't think he was into Animal Medicine, and I had no idea that he knew one of his Totems. I wondered what Deer represented.

Then Acarya reached slowly into his backpack and grabbed an

apple he hadn't eaten from his lunch. He slowly offered it out to her.

She sniffed the air, catching the scent of the juicy sweet apple, and she advanced forward. She was hesitant when she got close, and motioned to bolt away, not fully trusting that we would just be feeding her something without a catch. Acarya reached the apple out farther and then placed it on the ground. She stepped closer still, and began to nibble on the light green apple. She realized we were trustworthy and allowed herself to be consumed by the apple, stepping slightly closer. She was watching us though and she could easily escape if we tried to capture her. Of course we only wanted to witness her, which she gratefully came to understand and even let out a little bit of tension in her belly, releasing it a little lower to the ground, signaling that she was relaxed. It felt amazing to be this close to her, and to have this mutual trust outside of the barrier of species. Her energy was sweet and innocent in many ways, but also loaded with fear, and distrust. She was just about done with the apple when a loud crack of a branch happened just to our left and her right, scaring her off into a double legged prance, into the forest. I looked to see what had cracked the branch and couldn't see anything, but felt another eerie energy was watching us.

"Come on," I said, grabbing his hand again.

"Wow, that was soooo cool! I can't wait to tell Mum about that. God, I love Deer. What a beautiful, graceful creature."

He was lost in the daydream of her. A little twinkle in his eye, and for a second I pictured him like an Anime character, and giggled.

"I can't wait to look up what Deer Medicine means. I didn't know you thought Deer was in your Totem. I think you're right."

"Yeah, I have had a lot of pretty cool experiences with Deer. They eat Mum's Roses sometimes, which has always made her very angry, but I was always mesmerized by them, and I would just watch them eat the Roses and see how close I could get before they would leave. Mum was angry I didn't scare them away from her flowers, but I was so excited when they would let me get close. They almost always let me get right next to them. They're really pretty sweet and gentle."

"Just like you," I said smiling at him. I was going to have to read about Deer later.

When we got to Mr. Peen's, he was in his rocking chair out front, smiling at us as we walked up his stairs.

"Homoja bemi! That means, "Welcome!" Well, are you two ready for more school?" He grinned, a smile I don't recall seeing before.

"Go ahead and sit down, you're in your classroom." He laughed, taking a puff of his pipe, and rocking in his chair.

We took our backpacks off and sat with our backs against the railing of the steps, Acarya on the step above me. I felt like a little girl in school again, excited to learn what was next, bright and wide-eyed. I had a pencil and notepad and was ready for pearls of wisdom.

"The teachings of my people have always been told in the form of story, passed down through generations, whispered in starlight and firelight. Mukum, which means, 'they said long ago,' is how all stories would begin. These stories play from each other and connect to each other in great circles and spheres of knowledge. It is not as simple as starting at 'in the beginning' ...cause, everything is circular and connected, you see? So..." He puffed his pipe and gathered how he would begin to tell us this ancient knowledge and way of being. He was slow to speak, slow to choose the right words, very deliberate with his speech. It took him three to four times longer to say something, than it would for most. I was soaking up every syllable and finding time slow down.

"It has been told to us from elders upon elders that when we speak our language, other beings understand: the water, the trees, the animals. We must use our language, as that is our direct connection to Mother Earth. So it will be incomplete to even teach you these things without using the Nisenan language, but I will do my best to teach you of some of the ways and stories. Many of our stories have been lost, many teachings incomplete now. Too many generations of children taken into foster care or sent to missions, too many attempts to 'civilize' us, has done its job. The job of stripping our people of the full span of knowledge and ways being passed down. Only a small remnant remains. I, myself, only began to learn the Way when I was already an old man. I was raised in foster care and didn't have the ability to really learn the ways until I was an adult. I turned my back on it for a long time though. Then it found me, hiding and unsure, and I finally came home." He paused to take a puff of his pipe. It smelled vaguely like vanilla, but made my nose tickle.

"My people inhabited these lands for thousands of years, before the white man came. There are many sacred places around here that were very special to my people, many large healing stones, and many powerful spiritual places of worship. The rivers all speak the voices of our ancestors and those yet to come, and we honored the rivers as sacred spirits. We lived off the land and in balance with each other, as small tribes and villages, trading goods and tools with each other. The white man claimed that we were uncivilized, barbaric, but our ways were just simple, honest, and everything evolved around community and family. We honored the Earth as our Mother, and lived in harmony to the best of our ability. We never took too much, and when the harvests were smaller, we took less. We honored the land and all that it gave us. I wish that I was able to have been raised with the old ways of living, our ways were already long gone before I was even born. During the Gold Rush, our people were systematically erased, most killed for bounties placed by the US government. Others forced into foster care, typically through the Catholic Church. Our land and food was all but taken, and we were no longer able to continue living in our ways. Somehow though, there has been some information saved and passed down, or was written down by anthropologists who actually cared to take account. Blessed be these people who helped some of this knowledge to not be completely lost forever. Praise be to my elders and ancestors that endured such hardships and challenging times, and through all the suffering and torment, managed to preserve small bits of wisdoms and connection to Great Spirit, through the old ways. Even though they were threatened continuously for even using the language. Our ways may not ever have a place in society again."

"That's not true! I think we need to return back to these simple ways," I cried out passionately, feeling Liluye deep within me.

"Well I appreciate your enthusiasm, but I'm not sure. It's sweet and endearing that you two are so interested and caring though. Thank you for that. You know my people are responsible for the landscape of this area having so many trees? There were mostly just grasses, which were actually quite nourishing and a large staple of the diet too. Mostly, however, my people ate Acorns and Pine Nuts from the groves of Oak and Pine that they planted and lovingly tended. It takes years for an Oak to produce acorns, so they were very conscious about their care for these great creatures. Sometimes, they were simply tending to trees for the next generations to come," he said and puffed his pipe again.

It was a beautiful thought to imagine this land without buildings and streets, just grove after grove of revered giant Trees, lovingly offered to future generations. What an incredible gift to their children and grandchildren.

"Do you know of your people's ideas of creation? That always fascinates me?" Acarya asked.

"Well, there are many different stories told. One belief is that the Creator made Earth as an island on a great body of water. The land was held up from sinking by four great spirits holding the ropes tied to the four corners of land. If they loosened the ropes, the land sank a little, thus creating floods. If they raised land a little, then a dry period would occur, and if they shook the ropes we would have earthquakes. I always liked another story I read once, that states that the Creator was born first and then he made Coyote out of clay. The Creator next made the Earth, the mountains, the springs and rivers, the animals, and everything that was on the Earth. Coyote talked about what ought to be done after it had all been made. There are many tales of Coyote being the deceiver who tried to disrupt the once-perfect existence the Creator had made on Earth. Coyote reminds us of our trickster, trouble making ways, which is ingrained in the Human consciousness, and is always trying to undermine our ability to be more like Great Spirit. I feel a humble relationship with Coyote…I see how I and everyone I know have a little bit of Coyote in us."

"That's fascinating," Acarya said in response.

I thought about my father and got lost in thought for a moment.

"The Shaman of the village was someone who was believed to have control over the spirits by dreams and through mystic experiences. They represented the supernatural and were a dominant figure in rituals and ceremonies performed at the round house, or sacred ceremony house. Our last Shaman is now very aged and in her last years. She is already mostly on the other side now, connecting to Great Spirit."

I wondered if he was referring to, Mrs. Pombokom's mother in law. I didn't feel like divulging my connection with her right then though. I also got lost in thought about Shamanism and if that was what I was connecting to in my dreams.

"Since you kids have expressed so much interest in learning of the ancient ways of the Native peoples. I thought you might want to also take a look at this book, "Voices of Our Ancestors," by Dhyani Ywahoo. It's of Cherokee teachings, well actually they call themselves the Tsalagi, Cherokee is the English name that white man gave them. This book came to me at a time in my life when I was seeking a lot of answers. It basically shifted my entire life, and is what brought me back home, to the Way. There's a considerable amount of information that has been kept alive from their lineage, and it is truly mind-blowing information, particularly their philosophies and creation stories. You can borrow it, if you'd like."

I reached out and grabbed the book, feeling a tremendous energy as my hand touched it. It sent a wave of chills through my body. I couldn't wait to learn more, in fact I had never felt so eager to read a book before.

"Well, I think that's enough for today, kids. I'm feeling a bit tired now. We can pick up again next week. So I will say again Mokum, 'long ago they said,' this is how my people would also end their stories."

"Oh, really? That's all?" Acarya asked sort of impolitely, a little out of character for him. He was obviously entranced in the wisdom too.

"Yeah, I don't want to overload you with too much information at one time," Mr. Peen said and smiled. I could tell he was touched. "Although, hearing these words brings a great peace to my heart and a little hope for the future. You both being interested in learning these ways, is truly warming to my soul. You know, it was illegal to practice the native ways until 1979, with the American Indian Religious Freedom Act. Even then, it's been means for scrutiny and persecution, so there is always a little bit of fear and caution that comes with telling these Truths and speaking of the Way. But I appreciate your innocent wonder for it. It truly does bring joy to my heart, and I know my ancestors are happy for it too."

"Well, thank you for sharing these wisdoms and truths of your people. I can't wait to learn more and read this book too," I said with enthusiasm and gratitude. "I wonder if you could maybe write a book someday about the Nisenan people."

"Well, to be honest, it's something I have been thinking about and even working on for a long time now. I just didn't know if anyone would ever care to read it. Although now, I have some renewed motivation and hope." He smiled even bigger, a faint hint of a sparkle in his eye, and he got up and went down to his workshop. He turned once, still smiling behind his pipe, and I imagine he was feeling pride and gratitude for our session and words. We got up to go continue the wiping away of years of neglect.

We got upstairs and I just had to open the book a little. It was too tempting, calling me with its ancient wisdom. I flipped to a random page and started to read out loud.

"Fire is illuminating. It lights where there is darkness. There are considered to be 'three sacred fires,' the Elder Fires Above, which are *will*, *love*, and *active intelligence*. Through these basic teachings, we infuse each moment with the fundamental principles of *intention*, *compassion*, and *doing good*. This is the foundation of the knowledge bestowed upon the people. Everything is related to cycles of relationships, the relationships are the manifestation of the sacred fires. *To be in good relations with yourself, your family, friends, neighbors, world, and universe, is the primary purpose of life*. We find meaning in this purpose through the fundamental principles of intention (will), compassion (love), and doing good (active intelligence)."

"What the what? Are you hearing this?"

"Oh so much, yes!" Acarya said, shaking his head slightly with an almost scowl and pouty lips, while clapping his hands, like a Southern Baptist affirming to his Pastor that he was feelin' the gospel. He cracked me up. I smiled and then continued reading.

"Life and death, manifestation and formlessness, are all within the circle, which spirals out through all dimensions, even time and history dance along the spiral. Patterns of the past echo in the present and resound through the future. Our time-keeping system reflects the spiral as interlocking wheels of energy and consciousness always in motion together."

"Wow, this is some seriously loaded information," Acarya said. I nodded in agreement, and had to keep reading, it was too intriguing.

"Hey, Lila, hold up, I want to record this," Acarya said, always the tech guy.

"Alright, then, you good? Where was I? ...alright, so... 'throughout history there have been certain teachers that express the same essence in their teaching, the same wisdom, and come at appropriate times to remind the people of harmony. It is a cyclical reincarnation of pure mind and it is still going. As the Pale One, the Peacemaker, and Quetzalcoatl walked upon this land, so shall there be another teacher of great compassion to rekindle the wisdom fire of right relations for all people."

"There are many similarities between our worldview and those of Buddhism, Christianity, Judaism. All people and all religions trace their roots to the one Great Tree of Peace. We must all look deeply into the patterns woven by our thought and action and develop mindfulness and generosity for the future generations. May compassion arise within our hearts that we may see all beings as our relatives in this dream of life. The opportunity of life is very precious and it passes very quickly. If all beings lived in right relation, all beings would realize freedom from suffering. May the Great Fire of Wisdom burn in our hearts and shine in all we do, as enlightened action benefitting all our relations."

I had tears in my eyes. It was so simple, so beautiful and so pure. I felt the words in my heart, and through my whole being. It broke my heart in a million pieces though to think of these wisdoms being lost, these teachings being seen as inferior to the mentality of money-grubbing fools that have governed our country since the time of forcibly removing these wise beings from the land. It was our World's greatest tragedy. I felt the pain and suffering that has endured unnecessarily. I thought about Mom's health and all that her life has to be to provide basic needs for us, just because our society has been molded by people who think that these teachings are 'savage,' that it is better to work yourself to death for the sake of earning some money and accumulating things. This knowledge was Everything! Everything that heals, harmonizes and makes right. We could live free of suffering by these teachings and ways.

"I can't believe this isn't basic knowledge taught in every elementary school. It's crazy to me, that we are still basically taught that the Native ways are "barbaric" or "savage". I can't imagine what this World would be like if the white settlers and miners had listened to these ancient and pure ways instead of destroying them." I said, with a tear now rolling down my left cheek.

Acarya nodded in agreement and looked at me with a sweet expression while wiping my tear away. I turned to another page and kept reading.

"From the mysterious void came forth a sound, and the sound was light, and the light was will, intention to be, born of the emptiness: "Creator Being," fundamental tone of the universal song, underlying all manifestation."

"That sounds a lot like what Mum describes of the sound 'Aum', how interesting, I'll have to tell her about this," Acarya said. The thought was true and so fascinating. I continued reading.

"Compassionate wisdom arose as will perceived the unmanifest potential of mind streaming forth. Will and compassion together gave birth to the fire of building intelligence, and thus was formed the sacred triangle from which all matter is derived, the Three in One. It is a Mystery, we say." I smiled and tried to comprehend what we were reading here.

"The first "thought beings," *tla* beings, carriers of mind's pure light, existed like cells in one body, of one mind and purpose: to explore the mysteries of mind. Coalescing along 12 vortices of activity, elemental lines of energy or force, mind took form, the One became the many. Star Woman fell to Earth, from the star system known as the Pleiades, where the first spark of individuated mind arose, opening the way for star beings to manifest in pure light mind on Earth. The Three Elder Fires precipitated the planets and the animals, while the people were the dream children of the angels, their dreaming arising with the primordial sound."

"The twelve original tribes each exemplified a particular vortex of activity, a particular creative energy, all moving cohesively together. Tribe One was about quality of will. They were the Crystal caretakers, maintaining clear thought and rituals to keep form in order. They were the timekeepers, the drummers. Tribe Two were the healers, caretakers, and high teachers. Their chief was the Peace Chief, who never shed blood. Tribe Three were those with understanding of sacred geometry and astronomy, watchers of the skies, giving instruction on proper building. The Fourth Tribe were masons, builders of the form shaped by the Three. They were administrators, responsible for good clan and community relations. They were also the craftspeople, creating objects of beauty for prayer, contemplation, and utility. Tribe Five were scientists, mastering and teaching the wisdom of particulars. They observed patterns and possible futures. The Sixth Tribe were great caretakers of the temples and holy gardens, where the sacred food was grown for the communities. They were the keepers of ritual. Tribe Seven were sacred warriors, warring on ignorance. They were the shakers, transformers, life force makers. They were the guardians of correct action. Tribe Eight were ambassadors with other realms, having access to consciousness. They possessed planetary understanding and could even affect weather systems, distributing energy for the benefit of all beings. Tribe Nine communicated with stars, creating inventions for clear communication. They expressed a more ethereal manifestation of the conscious building seen in the third line of force. They were world shapers, magnetizers. Of the tenth, eleventh and twelfth lines of force we do not speak, for their function is beyond words and cannot be understood. These star people came to Earth in Elohi Mona, five islands in the Atlantic Ocean, later known as Atlantis. Before the star people came, there were great waters upon the land, and male and female still existed in One body. There was emotional nature but not yet the mind to actualize and complete the intention of Earth being a place of learning, a place of dreaming what is good. So the purpose of individuation of mind and the descent from the stars was to quicken life upon the Earth. The star energy came to spark the fire of mind…that all might return again to the Mystery."

What??? Mind blown.

I was stunned with this load of information, and this beautiful but seriously trippy creation story. I was only really familiar with the Christian creation story from the Bible, before today. This was fascinating. I also understood the conflict of interest this all would have had, and still obviously has, with the Christians. This was almost implying that people came from outer space, like aliens. Wait…?

"So what they're saying is, these people have the knowledge that we are essentially aliens?" Acarya asked, on the same wavelength exactly.

"Right?! That's what I got too."

We looked at each other with wide eyes and mouths slight open, and then laughed, in excitement and nervousness. It made a lot of sense in ways, but was such a trip to imagine, such a foreign thought.

"The Pale Face One, or the Peacemaker, were they possibly Jesus?" I asked out loud, for some reason it had struck me. "Oh, there's a number here beside it, hold on," I said as I flipped to the Notes page in the back of the book. "As examples of this pattern of cyclical reincarnation of specific wisdom energies, consider the birth of the Pale One in 873 B.C.; Wotan, one who was miraculously conceived and then born in the normal way, and was of a highly realized consciousness, was born around 100 B.C.; the Peacemaker in 1573; and of a possible contemporary incarnation of the same wisdom in 1983 (Shearer discusses the "echo system" in detail in *Beneath the Moon and Under the Sun*)."

"Ok, this is some mind blowing stuff here. Obviously, I believe in reincarnation. That's a basic understanding in my family and our lineage. But I never thought about the connection with various enlightened beings," Acarya said.

"So Wotan sounds to me like *he* was Jesus. Miraculously conceived?" I assessed.

"Yeah, that's pretty fascinating," Acarya agreed. "How exciting that there may be another one out there now too. They would be what, like 35 now?" He pondered. I nodded in agreement and wondered who might it be. It gave me a strange but welcomed sense of peace knowing that there may be another enlightened being here on Earth right now.

I went back to the page I was reading before and continued to read, totally consumed by my fascination.

"The Peacemaker lived around 1570, and there is prophecy of another individual born in the year 1983. It is thought that they will bring the wisdom of the East back to the West, uniting and bringing harmony, while ushering in the First Heaven."

"First Heaven?" I asked, bewildered, then kept reading.

"The Tsalagi ceremonial calendar is based upon the Mayan calendar, in which measurements of time relate to the movements of Venus, Mars, the Pleiades star system, and Sirius. This calendar came originally from the lands that sank below the Sea (Atlantis). The mathematical formulas derived from mystic understanding of zero, and the relationships of stars were seen as a road for all peoples to realize wisdom's clear light. The mathematics were brought to Earth from the Pleiades with the wave of star beings who are ancestors to every Tsalagi." We looked at each other again with wide eyes. I kept reading.

"In this sacred calendar, a "world" consists of 22 periods of 52 years each. In each world there are nine hells, the times of obstruction of the wisdom fire, and thirteen heavens, the times in which enlightened thought and action flourish for the benefit of all beings. Each complete cycle, or world, equals 1,144 years, which is 25 worlds- 28,600 years-comprise an era. We are currently living in the Fifth World, and entering the Sixth World, the beginning of a new era. First Heaven brings new opportunity to understand Earth as a living being and develop systems of transforming waste rather than increasing pollutants. There is an image associated of a Bear dancing on fear and ignorance. It is a time of recycling old ideas, healing the poisons of improper invention, bringing forth that which benefits life. Clear intention and good will brings about inventions that bare fruit for generations to come, done by those who are of right relations and consider themselves ancestors of generations not yet born. Inventions born of the creative flow of mother-father energy, quickened by faith's inspiration, are gifts to serve rather than enslave.

Each human is composed of elements from Mother and Father. Even the perfection of "that which cannot be explained" exists within. That wondrous perfection arises as joyful appreciation for all beings and creative intelligence to benefit all, when mother-father are realized in your heart. When you have mother's understanding and father's skill of doing what's needed, the riddle of your life will unfold, for the benefit of all.

From the Earth, energy arises, feeding you through your navel. Heaven's insight spirals down through the top of your head. Heaven and Earth meet within the heart, setting free the choice and voice to do. Oneself, a sphere containing all possibility,

Earthward flow being intention, Heavenward flow being the energy to accomplish. From East to West the winds of inspiration blow, carrying joy, making apparent one's gift to be shared. From West to East the wind-that-blows-away-that-which-is-no-longer-needed shakes its lightening wand. The vision is realized through the cross. Quartering the circle defines the Vastly Vast, giving shape to form, up and down, East and West. The cross, and the swastika, are ancient symbols of energy's manifestation. The same principles of world formation apply to human life. Receive life force from Heaven and Earth, spiral out compassion from your heart. See that all are relatives in this great dream."

My mind and heart were blown wide open, and if we were in the Dream world, my heart would be glowing for sure. I felt chills all over. Every word felt like magic, like whispers from God into my soul.

"This sounds so much like what Mum talks about. I'm sort of trippin' on this. These cultures didn't have contact way back then, but they share some seriously similar truths," Acarya said. "We're already over half way through the First Heaven though, technically, if it started in 1987," he said, pondering some math, looking at a circular chart in the book. The last marked time was 1987.

"There has definitely been a shift happening, since the introduction of the internet, I guess, which has been in this last time period. I wonder if we're on the brink of a serious shift in human consciousness. How rad would that be?" He said with a huge grin.

"I believe it is happening already," I said, and felt a flood of energy rush through me, and then the butterflies return to my stomach.

"Well, it seems to me, according to these ancient teachings and the ones of my ancestors from India, our purpose is simply to live in right relation, within one's self, with others around, and with the Planet," Acarya said. "Seems that is the shift in human consciousness that is happening, and needs to continue to happen. That all people may live from this place." He was wise beyond his years, and although I was thinking the same things, I always appreciated that he was on the same wavelength.

We smiled and then I closed the book, realizing we had spent a lot more time reading it than we had planned. We needed to probably get some work done. Our minds were lost in it all though, and our conversations were some of the deepest and most profound discussions of our lives. Time escaped us though and soon it was time for us both to head home.

We thanked Mr. Peen again, now wonder-struck from all the incredible information we had just read. I really wanted to borrow the book, but I actually let Acarya take it home to show his Mom, who I knew would be super into it too.

The words in that book, the eloquent words of Dhyani Ywahoo, sounded so much like Whyla. It made me ache for her, but also appreciate her on an even deeper level…and made me wonder if the Truths weren't the same, the words coming from the same Source. The thought gave me a deep warmth.

Chapter 5
Sacrifice

When I got home, Mom had made a lovely dinner of Mushroom Rice Pilaf with Broccoli. It was actually delicious. I filled her in a little bit on our time with Mr. Peen, but due to Mom's Christian background and slightly fragile nature at the moment, I neglected some details. Hopefully, soon, she would be in a place of openness to these truly remarkable thoughts and ways, and origin stories. The psyche can only handle so much sometimes though, and a life threatening illness can sort of take over. She had given her self a lovely day of self care and rest, just doing little things around the house. She had written in her journal a lot too. I encouraged her to go take her soothing bath and call it an early night. It was another big day tomorrow.

I went to my room, needing to get a little homework done first, but then I remembered about our experience earlier with the sweet Doe, and Acarya's feelings for Deer, and had to look up Deer Medicine.

Deer
~Gentleness~

Deer...so gentle and loving you are. The flower of kindness, an embrace from afar.

One day Fawn heard Great Spirit calling to her from the top of Sacred Mountain. Fawn immediately started up the trail. She didn't know that a horrible demon guarded the entrance to Great Spirit's lodge. The demon was trying to keep all the beings of creation from connecting with Great Spirit. He wanted all of Great Spirit's creatures to feel that Great Spirit didn't want to be disturbed. This would make the demon feel powerful, and capable of causing them to fear him.

Fawn was not at all frightened when she came upon the demon. This was curious, as the demon was the archetype of all the ugly monsters that have ever been. The demon breathed fire and smoke and made disgusting sounds to frighten Fawn. Any normal creature would have fled or died on the spot from fright.

Fawn, however, said gently to the demon, "Please let me pass. I'm on the way to see Great Spirit."

Fawn's eyes were filled with love and compassion for this oversized bully of a demon. The demon was astounded by Fawn's lack of fear. No matter how he tried, he could not frighten Fawn, because her love had penetrated his hardened, ugly heart.

Much to the demon's dismay, his rock-hard heart began to melt, and his body shrank to the size of a walnut. Fawn's persistent love and gentleness had caused the meltdown of the demon. Due to this gentleness and caring that Fawn embodied, the pathway is now clear for all of Great Spirit's children to reach Sacred Mountain without having to feel the demons of fear blocking their way.

Deer teaches us to use the power of gentleness to touch the hearts and minds of wounded beings who are trying to keep us from Sacred Mountain. Like the dappling of Fawn's coat, both the light and the dark may be loved to create gentleness and safety for those who are seeking peace.

If Deer has gently nudged its way into your cards today, you are being asked to find the gentleness of spirit that heals all wounds. Stop pushing so hard to get others to change, and love them as they are. Apply gentleness to your present situation and become like the summer breeze: warm and caring. This is your tool for solving the present dilemma you are facing. If you use it, you will connect with Sacred Mountain, your centering place of serenity, and Great Spirit will guide you.

How fitting. Acarya *was* a Deer. Oh, how I cherished him. What an amazing creature, the Deer.

I decided not to read Dad's journal and instead go right to sleep, I was yearning to go in to the Dream for myself, hoping to connect with Whyla, but eager to move forward on the journey...

...I was back at the edge of the Gateway within the Elder Forest, my staff, white rope, and satchel all with me. I raised my head up, inhaling courage and strength, and walked forward over the invisible barrier line. As I stepped through, I felt the overwhelming awareness of Oneness rush through me. I heard all the heart songs singing, and felt the ultimate Connection of every living being around me, feeling my heart beat the drumbeat of the Earth. As I stepped to the other side, I was surprisingly able to witness a grid or matrix of energy, similar to the interweaving of spheres I saw before. This time it involved the trees, plants, and the ground, the Earth itself providing the heart of the matrix. I blinked in astonishment of what I was witnessing. Then I closed my eyes and breathed with the subtle ebb and flow of the Earth's breath, feeling completely centered and intimately connected to everything around and within. The Forest breathed with me, accepting me as a conduit of consciousness, allowing me to enter.

I walked a little ways, making effort to reach out and say hello to anything I could touch. I could feel the feelings of the Forest, and the Forest was scared, sad, confused, and was longing for something. There was a deep wound somewhere that needed to be found and healed. I began searching, using my new double vision of seeing the form and its energy field, I looked for the weakness. I was following a compass in my heart. I knew that I was intimately connected to this web and it was leading me to where I was needed. So I trusted my path and continued forward, sharing my heart's light in the darkness that had spread here. It was both draining and energizing. The fire inside me was growing stronger, while my physical form seemed to be slowly disappearing. I was suddenly not a form at all, but merely consciousness, and I wasn't *me* anymore, I was Everything. I was the Earth herself. I felt suddenly a deep aching pain in my heart. It was nearly unbearable and I felt an intense need to cry. The feeling of crying and a song of longing filled me, and it began to rain. The sky poured out tears of sorrow, compassion, and healing love. The healing was palpable. I felt myself drinking it in, filling all the empty spaces of myself with the nourishment of her tears. It felt like a hug or a blanket wrapping around and within me. The spaces were filling and the feeling was dissipating, but there was still a deep wound somewhere. Instead of looking around more, with vision, it came to me that I could simply tune inward and *feel* for the place. It led me on a twisted journey of warp speed to the massive Tree at the center of this maze, and then I saw them, the dancers, the Protectors. The agonizing expressions of torment on their faces made me weep even deeper and more intensely. I felt the tears coming from ancient places of suffering, ancestral and primal. I felt a deep crack filling with the healing power of Love. So I wept with them, holding them, rocking with them in their lamenting torture. I didn't know why we all wept, but it was cathartic, and profoundly releasing. We cried until there were no more tears and the pain had slightly subsided, then we took in a deep breath and exhaled out some residual pain. It was liberating. There was however a heaviness left, a weight that hadn't fully released. There was still work to be done, but this was a wonderful healing session, the first of many. Being aware of everything at once now, I breathed deep heavy breaths.

I was the Earth, I could feel everything and witness everything all at once. Then I knew the way to heal this planet, I had to heal myself...

"Lila, it's time to wake up," I heard Momma say, her hands gently pushing on me. She was being more quiet and calm than normal, so I knew it was one of her first attempts to wake me. I felt the tears still flooding my eyes. I felt a slight pain still residing in my heart. Opening my eyes, I reached up to wrap my arms tight around Mom's neck. She held me and rocked me, and I felt the pain subsiding.

"I love you, Mom."

"Lila, dear, I love you more than all the planets in all the universes." She was beaming with love, I felt it radiating through her. She had a look of peace on her face. Something had shifted in her, she was how I remembered her from when I was a very small child. It brought tears to my eyes to feel her here again. I don't know where she was or how she suddenly returned, but I was so grateful to have her back, fully present.

"Well, today is the big day, and I am feeling very optimistic. I had a beautiful dream last night that I was walking through a glorious meadow, butterflies and flowers everywhere, birds singing. I was dancing and prancing around. Then I laid down in the soft grass, looking up at cloud formations, and suddenly I felt like I was being hugged, by the Earth. Then I heard the voice of God, whisper in my ear, 'I love you, my child. You are well.' It was so serene and peaceful and real, and I can feel the feeling still inside me," she said with sparkling eyes of wonder.

I hugged her again, this time with my head on her breast, and I felt the little place where she still held her pain. She had healing to do. We both did. But today was for celebrating a little peace of heart, a space of grounding in this crazy journey. It was no small feat to feel calm and grateful in the middle of what we were going through.

When I got to school, the first person I saw was Acarya, and without hesitation, I walked right up to him and hugged him tight.

"Aww, good morning! How's my girl, this morning?"

His words echoed through me and ignited that flame again. 'His girl?' It melted me. Then I looked up at him, smiled, and said, "It's going to be a really good day!"

"Yes, it is!! Mum was wondering if you ladies were coming over this afternoon."

"Oh yeah, I nearly forgot. I'll send a message to Mom at lunch and check in to see. I'd love to come over and learn more from your mother, regardless of whether my mom is up for it or not."

"Awesome, she'll be stoked. So…I can't stop thinking about all the stuff Mr. Peen shared with us yesterday. Some seriously deep stuff. Pretty awesome, but also really sad. I truly am heartbroken at the idea of these things, and their whole way of living just being forgotten, neglected by arrogant people who thought their ways were superior. And bounties for their lives? Our government literally funded a genocide and we're not taught that in school at all. We have so much healing and re-education to do."

"I hear you 100%. My thoughts and feelings, exactly. I think I need to write a blog post," I responded. Feeling helpless and small.

"Yeah, that would be awesome. You should do that. I wish we could help Mr. Peen even more, and all the indigenous people of this country. I really can't stop thinking about it, like it might be my mission in life or something. It's weird, but there's this fire lit inside me now, to render justice and restoration of a new way of living, based on old ways of living. I mean Ayurveda is pretty much awesome, and it's over 5,000 years old. These old wisdoms need to return to mainstream awareness and be the norm."

His words lit my fire even brighter too. He was speaking the words of my heart and mind. It felt so right and so needed. There was a deep healing that needed to take place in our country, and the world at large. Perhaps, this was where we were supposed to make a difference.

"I know, I feel so strongly about it all too. That was a life-changing conversation with Mr. Peen yesterday, for sure," I said.

"I wish there was a way to make the teachings more public."

"I know, exactly!" He agreed. We pondered this, walking the short last distance to our classes.

Until we saw Dustin Smith walking by, with his hair cut, fresh and clean. He wasn't wearing a hat, and his head wasn't cowering low. He was looking where he was going. This may seem like no big deal, but this was huge! I had never seen Dustin with his head up, in the five years I had been in class with him. I felt a flutter of joy. His energy actually felt kind of good. His clothes seemed to be cleaner than normal too. He seemed like a completely different person, more confident, less angry.

Acarya noticed too and being the guy he was, he stuck his knuckles out for a fist bump and said, "lookin' sharp, brotha." Dustin half grinned back and returned the knuckles. I knew it was going to be a good day!

Later, after school, Acarya met me at our normal spot, and I skipped over to him. It was a cooler day and the wind was blowing a bit, feeling more and more like Autumn, the season of change. It was my favorite season. Mom was going to actually meet us both and give us a ride over to the Varma's. We had coordinated through texts at lunch.

She pulled up about five minutes later, and seemed a little less radiant than when I had seen her last, but she was still smiling. I kissed her on the cheek as I jumped into the front seat, Acarya behind me.

"So? How did it go?" I asked immediately.

"Well, I haven't actually gotten any results yet. I have my follow up tomorrow morning."

"What? I thought we would know things today," I said, disappointed.

"Well, I guess I wasn't really thinking about the fact that the Radiologist would need to evaluate it and then the Oncologist would need to schedule a different appointment to discuss the results and the pathway. I'm sorry I misled you. We'll know more tomorrow," she said.

When we got to Acarya's house, Mrs. Varma greeted us as she always did, with a big smile and a warm welcome. She always offered tea and some kind of delicious food. Their house smelled of wonderful spices coming from the kitchen where a large pot was simmering.

"Mmmm, smells great, Mum," Acarya said, as he kissed his mother's cheek.

"How was school, dear?" She said, sweetly smiling at him.

"Great!!" Acarya said emphatically, as he ran upstairs to deliver his backpack to his room real quick.

"How are you, doing Tihana? How were your appointments this week?" she asked Mom.

"I'm doing pretty well. My appointments were fine. I'm not sure I really love my Oncologist. He's a bit more extremist with his approach than I like, and feel might be necessary. I find out results, of the MRI I had today, tomorrow morning. The unfortunate part of what I found out today, which I hadn't mentioned to you yet, Lila, is that I can't actually choose to get a second opinion. I'm in-network with our local hospital with my insurance, since my work is affiliated. We're such a small town, there's really only the one Oncologist here, so I have to sort of go along with what he thinks I should do." She sounded a little defeated, almost nervous.

"Oh Tihana, you know you can always make your own decisions, regardless of what the Doctor suggests. It's your body, it's your choice. You can decide to have a lumpectomy instead of a full mastectomy. You can decide to do radiation, but not chemo. You can decide to *not* take the pill you have to take for the rest of time. You can decide to do it all, if you wish and feels right. You can also decide to do none of the above.

You can use herbal remedies, cleansing and rejuvenating practices, deep psychological purging and healing, therapies and practices to balance the senses and your energy field. All healing treatments that have been done since the beginning of written history. You can choose to love and nourish yourself with these things, at the same time as pursuing the western medical approach with your Oncologist. This is what I suggest. It is truly up to you though. My prayer is for you to feel strong and empowered, and this is coming from a Doctor's wife. You hold yourself confidently and see yourself shining in health and wellness. Sometimes we must be our own best cheerleader, first and foremost," Mrs. Varma said with utmost sincerity and sympathy for the difficult decisions, but with a passion of being almost a warrior of healing.

She was preparing us Chai and Ojas balls while she spoke, placing them on a light turquoise plate with two Koi fish swimming in a circle, chasing each other's tails, around them a row of lotus flower petals. It was a lovely little plate. Six Ojas balls were evenly space around it, that she sprinkled with Cardamom and Cinnamon. It was art.

Acarya was back by now too, so Mrs. Varma made him his own plate of three balls. Then she kissed him on the forehead, before ushering us back to her 'office,' healing space.

Walking in, I could feel the healing energy held and infused there. The smell in the air was so good, I found myself closing my eyes and inhaling deep. My eyes even slightly rolled back from overwhelm at the goodness.

"What is that smell?" I asked, breathing in deeply.

"Isn't that divine? It's actually a blend of a few different essential oils that are all healing and soothing to the heart, including Rose and Sandalwood, my favorites, and also Clary Sage. I added a small bit of Cinnamon today for warming from the chill in the air, and the presence of Vata season coming on. I think it overpowers a bit, but I am partial to the subtle smells of Rose and Sandalwood, myself."

"Vata *season?*" I asked.

"Yes, the doshas that I mentioned last time are influential to climates and environments, and the seasons. We recognize that the Vata season is the dry, cool season of Autumn and early Winter. This is also reflected in an increase in anxiousness and ungrounded feelings (of the upcoming cold of winter) and an increased desire for that which provides warmth and comfort. That's why Cinnamon is so soothing in Fall, it is warming and grounding. It's the time of year to be eating less raw fruits and veggies and more cooked or baked things, warming and easier to digest. Vata season can bring on irregularities, mimicking the wind, and we need to nourish our digestion carefully to prevent forming ama. Ama is improperly digested food matter that accumulates in the body when our digestion isn't optimum, remember? So we want to nourish our digestion with more spices, and warming ones now, verses the cooling ones of Summer. I'll talk more about the other seasons another day, as we have a lot to discuss today and I want us to focus on this current season. Vata is the main source of your imbalance, although it has manifested as a Pitta-Kapha disorder. We discussed this last time, but just to reiterate our reasoning and approach, and the overall big picture here. So when there is loss, irregularity, hidden lost emotions in the body, pain and or trauma, Vata is present. Pitta and Kapha come to the rescue, so to speak, to bring in a warm hug. They literally seek to warm the body and protect and comfort the body, to balance the opposite qualities that Vata has brought in. The symptoms are just alarms to the mind that there is healing work to be done there. So we must really be mindful of all three doshas, presently, and they are going to dance a bit together in the process of untying this little knot. I thought more about it, and I really think it would actually be beneficial to do a type of cleanse, and I definitely want you to do bodywork too. You need to purify and release. We also need to really nourish you with the deeply nurturing Ayurvedic massage, known as Abhyanga. I know that money is tight right now, but I am willing to let you pay me as you can for these services and to offer them to you by donation, so whatever is available to you, it can be a very small amount. I am offering it all as my gift, because I care for you both, and if I can help, I want to and I will. How does all of this sound so far?"

"Wow, I am really very grateful for this offering. Are you sure though? I don't want to put you out, you don't have to do all this for me," Mom said in hesitation.

"Nonsense. I already told you I am honored and wouldn't have it any other way," she again said, with that Mrs. Varma way of being both kind and stern at the same time.

"So where was I then?...Ah yes, Kichadi! Kichadi is going to be our main meal for the next little while. It is both a cleansing food and a nourishing food, very easy to digest and providing all the simple components of nutrition necessary. Did you manage to get the mung bean dal?"

"Yes, we did. We haven't cooked any of them yet though. We made lentils instead," I piped in.

"Lovely. Alright, so I would love to talk you through the process of making it. There are many ways, but I find it easiest to prepare the rice and legumes separately from the veggies, then to mix them together at the end. Many recipes call for a large pot to cook everything together. Either way, it is very simple. I like to begin with dry toasting some spices, usually Cumin, Coriander, Fennel, Mustard and Ajwan, which is Celery seed, or sometimes Thyme. I usually use a small iron skillet to toast all of the seeds. You can just toast them in your pot too. But I like to do it this way so that the end result is a nice powder of spices, whole spices left as they are can be harder to chew fully. So as soon as the seeds start popping, and it starts to smell delicious, put them into a grinder or mortar with pestle and grind them up. That will be the base for the flavor of the dish. You can use fresh Ginger and Turmeric root, or add dried Turmeric too. Turmeric is one I would put in just about everything, it is both nourishing and purifying to the body and boosts immune strength. So use Turmeric whenever possible.

We want to choose a variety of vegetables that are balancing to all three doshas and that are in season. The more we can eat seasonally to our environment, the better. Our digestion has evolved with the plants and we receive what we need if we eat with the rhythms of Nature. It is a blessed miracle and an evolved brilliant design. Everything is connected, in a great symbiosis. We are all here together.

So I'd love to see if you can follow my recipe and try it out for yourself first, and if you need support, we can do a cooking demo. I think you two will make a lovely Kichadi though. And remember that it's about the journey sometimes, not the destination." She winked at me.

"So how was everything else we discussed and suggested for you this week?" she continued.

"Well, I think it went pretty good actually. We went to the health food store right after we left here on Sunday and got most of the things on the list, and we have been eating very well all week. Wouldn't you agree, Lila?" Mom asked and motioned to me to speak.

"Yeah, it was really fun to go to the co-op. I loved people watching there, such interesting individuals," I said, half giggling.

"Yeah, and I was pretty avid about journaling as well. It was hard at first, but it's actually getting much easier. I'm not sure I'm ready to share it yet, though," Mom said shyly.

"Sure, that's understandable. I'm just thrilled you are journaling and that you are taking time to see what is in your mind and heart. What needs to come out with pen on paper. That's wonderful, Tihana," she encouraged.

"Thanks. Yeah, it feels good," Mom said nonchalantly, she really didn't like to speak about herself or to be doted upon. Humility was a strength, and a flaw, of hers.

"I feel like I am trying harder to love myself and speak kindly in my inner thoughts to myself. I also am allowing myself to rest more, which I haven't really ever done. It also feels good. I feel guilty a little bit though. I really need to get back to work this next week, and I am not sure how I can afford to not work as much as I have been doing. I am using sick time right now, but that's limited. I really don't think that I can afford what you want to do with me, as far as the cleansing and body work go. I know you say it is by donation, but I don't want to utilize your time without properly compensating you for it," Mom said reluctantly but stubbornly and with a hint of guilt.

"Mrs. Hickey, Tihana, listen to me now. It is my gift to you. If you feel like paying me a small tip, that is perfectly fine, but I have been blessed with financial stability and I do not need your money. I hope you can just accept this gift and continue to allow this healing. I can't sit back, knowing how to help you heal, with the ability to do so, and *not* help you. I also do believe that you will take it more seriously and hold yourself more accountable if you do invest in yourself and this. I have seen and been taught of a sacred bond of interaction, that says there should always be some sort of exchange," she said with an elegant and caring authority, and a gentleness, knowing she was personally blessed to not know of my mother's pain and sufferings.

"Well, I am truly honored then. Thank you," Momma said. Making me so proud.

I smiled at them both, so grateful for them, so inspired to be beside them.

"Alright, so how are the herbs going for you? No strange side-effects or feelings? Any insights on your body's reaction to them?" Mrs. Varma asked.

"I am not really sure. I guess my first instinct was that the one formula had a weird burnt smell, but also strangely intriguing. I haven't really noticed any affects yet, I guess. While, the herbs with meals, for digestion, seem to be working well though. I have had more appetite lately, so that is definitely nice," Mom said, as she evaluated her last few days in her mind.

"Well, it's also too early to see for much with the other herbs, they take a little longer to affect things. But I am glad you are taking them regularly and not feeling any heat or cold or negative change in digestion or energy."

"Nope, I feel actually pretty good."

"Wonderful, well keep doing all that you're doing. Plus, I'd like to add another thing for you to try. That is, some visualization meditation."

"Oh wonderful, I actually was doing some today, before and during my MRI. I had no idea what I was doing though." She smiled and lightened.

"How wonderful. What did you visualize?" Mrs. Varma inquired.

"Well, I visualized God wrapping me with a hug and angels all around me," Mom said.

"Lovely. How absolutely beautiful. Alright, you can use this same image if you like, or another such vision, and simply repeat this practice daily, for a few minutes. While you do this, visualize the essence of the illness evaporating from your body, and your body perfectly well. The more you can visualize your cells all healthy and happy, the more they will respond with such." She smiled.

"I think that will be a really good thing to do, and that sounds great," Mom said, softening. I could tell she felt seen and held, trusting in Mrs. Varma, for holding space for and encouraging mom's way of spirituality.

"I also want to introduce an affirmation to you. It is one that is specific for breast cancer, but you wouldn't know it if I didn't mention it. What I want you to do is repeat the affirmation 3 times, while you are visualizing and feeling your angel guides and your connection to God. The affirmation is this… 'I take in and give out nourishment in perfect balance. I care for and nourish myself with love and with joy. I lovingly forgive and release all of the past. I choose to fill my world with joy. I love and approve of myself. We are all safe and free.' I wrote it down here for you, so you can just read from the paper and repeat it a few times. These words are from the great author Louise Hay, from her book, "You Can Heal Your Life." Her affirmations are based on physical manifestations and their correlations to emotional and psychological states. It's brilliant work and it aligns ever so nicely with Ayurvedic philosophy. So here's your affirmation," and she handed Mom a small piece of paper with the wise words written out.

Mom read it over silently, nodding her head slowly 'yes,' and thanked Mrs. Varma.

"So beyond those things, I think we can just continue to do all that you've been doing, and just relax and nurture yourself, while lovingly releasing all that needs releasing. It's a blessed journey of ups and downs."

"Ha. Yes, it is. Alright, this sounds good. Thank you, again, Anjana. I truly appreciate your time and your wisdom."

"Well, truly it is my pleasure." She put her hands in prayer position at her heart and slightly tilted her head, as an adoring mother would to her child, and said 'Namaste.' We both repeated the gesture, and she put a hand on each of our cheeks and smiled at us. It was a gesture that spoke a hundred words in a split second of a touch and look. She was truly honored to help Mom, it was genuine Love and kindness.

Acarya was doing his homework at the kitchen table when we walked out. It hadn't been very long, a much quicker session than before. She might have sensed that Mom was getting tired, as I had sensed also. I wanted to stay and visit and pick Mrs. Varma's brain some more, but I thought I should probably just head home to help Mom with an early dinner. So we said our goodbyes and thank you's some more, and Acarya walked us out, like he always did. This time he reached out for a hug, which he really never did in front of either of our moms. It was usually me that was just pouring myself onto him, but not this time. I embraced the hug excitedly and felt the butterflies return. He smelled good, and he felt even better. I breathed him in, and then separated, and went toward my home. I always felt renewed, walking away from the Varma residence.

"Well, what do you think? You think you can give it a try?" I asked as we walked to the car.

"Lila, I actually do believe in angels and perhaps Mrs. Varma is one. I know that I have my reservations about this, but what she says always resonates with me. So, yes I can be on board. It is really challenging to not pay her what I know her time and knowledge is worth though."

"It's ok, I think that's part of the shift we all need to make. Money is evil. There is so much pain and suffering that comes from the pursuit of money, which I know we have to do in order to live. But doesn't that seem sad? I mean, tribes used to live quite well without money. Trading goods and time, making sure everyone had their basic needs met, supporting each other with their individual gifts. Supporting the basic needs, together. I wish we lived a few thousand years ago in a small indigenous village."

"Lila, that is all fine and well to day dream about, and I know it may seem hard sometimes, but the world is what it is. You can't change the fact that it takes money to buy food and shelter and other needs of life. We can't go backwards. It is what it is."

"Wow, that's a defeatist attitude. I personally believe that we *have* to shift things, sooner than later, and that the change is already upon us. But I know it is going to be very difficult to change these now deeply ingrained ways. Our planet needs us to change though," I said with a subtle shake of passion forming in my core.

"Well, my deer sweet child, I believe you are a little sage, sent to help us all." She smiled at me and grabbed my hand and kissed it, and then held my hand the rest of our short drive home. My shake simmered down, but I watched out the window in daydream of different times.

We decided to have leftovers for dinner, since we had a little of the two previous night's meals left. Before we ate, Mom asked, "What are you grateful for today?"

"I'm grateful for You, for your strength, and your softness," I said smiling at her, proudly. "I'm also grateful for Mrs. Varma, and her generosity and knowledge." Momma nodded with agreement. "I'm also grateful for Acarya, for his sweet love and protection." I blushed.

"Aww, that's so sweet. You two are very cute." She smiled a huge grin. "I'm grateful for *You*, and your incredible heart and mind, your passion for helping to heal this broken world, and me. I am grateful too for Mrs. Varma and her wisdom, and her gift of service for my healing. I am also grateful for this body and mind and soul that I am. I am grateful for this journey of health and healing, for all that is unfolding and the great lessons I am learning." She smiled at me, glowing with her gratitude and joy, and then brought her hands to her heart in prayer, bowing her head and closing her eyes. "Dear, God, Thank you for this blessing of nourishing foods. May we carry the nourishment into our hearts, to heal all wounds there, and fuel us on our heart's mission." It was the most poignant prayer I'd ever heard, and it resonated deep within me. I kept my eyes closed in silence for a moment. Feeling the words and their meaning, connecting to God in whatever that meant and whoever that was, which I didn't fully understand, but it was ok. Feeling the spiraling vortexes of energy all around and within. It was so peaceful and centering, and powerful at the same time. I felt a zingy sensation.

"Thank you, Mom. That was so nice," I said, finally.

We ate the delicious food, pondering our own thoughts and enjoying each other's company in silence for a bit.

Then I said, "Mom, I just want you to know it's ok to be sad or mad about Dad. I know you had to be my rock and you are so strong, but I just realized that I don't remember seeing you ever cry."

She began tearing up, and closed her eyes, blinking out a single tear down her right cheek. The way the thought came to and out of me so quickly out of nowhere, was as if it was *her* thought, that I was picking up on. She looked up at me with a look I had never seen her make, a mixture of confusion, sorrow, and a deep pain, mixed with relief. The look said it all. Then she shifted to a smile and wiped away the tear. I felt her heart relax a bit, release some tension, tension she'd been holding for years. She still had a lot of layers to let go of, but maybe it was finally starting to unravel.

After dinner, I did the dishes, while Mom took her evening bath. Then I did my homework and decided to read more of Dad's journal.

I hadn't looked ahead at all to see how many entries he had written, and I was curious suddenly to know how many more there were. Much to my dismay, the next entry was the last one. It wasn't even a long one…

"…I was back at the Forest's edge. I took my time, inching through the barrier of Love, feeling it all reverberate through me. I wanted to stay right there forever, and I would have, if a force hadn't seemed to push me from behind. I tripped forward, back into the Forest. I knew I had to get to the Tree of Life and figure out my mission, so I traveled in my mind again, through the twists of trees, following the flows of energy, back to the Mother. There it was, towering over everything. The Lovers, intertwined and dancing, were singing a song of Love, but a sort of longing sad cry. I mean, it sounded absolutely awful. I watched as they danced an awkward and sorrowful dance together. Pushing and pulling, wanting and escaping each other's hold. I felt their aching desperate desire. I came back down to the ground, back into my body, and searched for the answer, the key to this God-forsaken mission. What was I supposed to do? I had asked Whyla this many times, but she always had some vague response of healing the Tree of Life. The Tree seemed fine to me, and I couldn't figure out what I was supposed to do. I had this black powder still, and supposedly I was to feed the Tree with it. So I reached into my bag and felt the small box with a spiral carved on it. As I pulled it out, I noticed the spiral was glowing white. Just then, something else white and glowing caught my eye, there was something on the ground. It was a pine cone, an enormously huge one, and just inside one of the bud scales was a cracked open shell of a pine nut. It was huge, the size of my palm, and as I pried it out, I felt my whole body ignite with a flame inside. Holding this little seed, I could feel all the feelings of warmth and love and connection, just like walking through the protective shield, just like holding my hands against the trees. It felt amazing. I looked around, as I suddenly felt eyes on me, watching my every step. I wrapped it with a little leather piece of clothe that I had in my bag, and tucked it in safely. Then I ran, like lightening, away from the Tree of Life, away from the eyes and judgment. I ran to my hide out place. I pulled back out the Seed and felt all the feelings of Love and Connection filling me. Just feeling it on my palm was enough to absorb the Light. It was just like being in the Gateway. I was mesmerized and almost paralyzed by its power. Then I was woken up in a jolt from T, shaking and screaming at me. She said it took her 30 minutes to wake me up. I guess I was dug in pretty deep this time..."

I remembered back to the dream of receiving the seed and powder from him. I remembered feeling his fear, his cowardice. I held a lot of anger towards him. He was so selfish, so governed by his own physical desires, so blind to his own folly. It pained me to know that this was the last entry he ever wrote. The date, I now noticed was the day before his accident. The time frame of these dreams was so surreal, how I had dreamt of him only last week, the same dream he had experienced possibly years ago. How could this be? It was all too much for my brain to grasp, but

I knew that this mission was important. It was all too weird how we could be sharing these vivid dream experiences. I still couldn't believe that the Dream world was actually a real place, or that it might affect this World, or others. That was still too far out there for my mind to comprehend. But it was meaningful that we were tied together in the Dream space and I was determined to follow through with this journey, if for nothing more than my own peace of mind. So I turned off the light, closed my eyes, and drifted back…

…I was back at the Forest's edge, about to again walk through the invisible barrier that bursts open your heart center and expands your mind to encompass all forms of love, all in a split second of blissfullness. It truly was overwhelming and hard to describe. It was extraordinarily energizing though, like a rush of Adrenalin. I knew that time was of the essence, so I didn't wallow in the feeling. I went straight to my mission of searching again for the Tree of Life. The grid was back and I remembered the trick of using my mind to search by feeling the place within me. I followed the familiar speedy pathway through my mind and found the roots all leading to the center place, where they were. The couple made of energy, intertwined with their silver ribbons of existence, were dancing a gruesome and grotesque dance of pain and longing. Their cry was a lamenting and deeply sorrowful song. It was painful and stabbed deep within me. I felt myself becoming a form again, shrinking away from them, to the ground at the base of the tree, witnessing its immensity and power as my awareness shrank back into human form. It towered above me. I stood there, walking staff in hand, white glowing rope wrapped around my chest, with my satchel, its contents I was unsure of, this time. I reached in and felt the crystal shard, the box of healing resin powder, and the small wrapped bundle with the precious seed inside. I had all the components. Now what? My instincts told me that I should attempt to communicate and simply ask the Tree what I was to do.

"Oh Great One, I am here to help you. Please tell me *how* am I to help you, what am I to do."

There was no answer, only the lamenting howling and moaning of the Two in the nest above.

I called out again, "Oh Great Tree of Life! How am I to help you?"

I heard my words echo, through the Forest that seemed hollow and empty suddenly, and through my body that felt the same.

Still nothing but the sorrowful song.

I closed my eyes and tuned inward, connecting through my heart's spiraling sphere, feeling and witnessing now the spheres of energy all around. They were all slightly off access. It was subtle to even see, but the energy spin was irregular from it. It wasn't as blatant as Dustin Smith's failing energy had seemed, but it was still in a slow decline of speed. There was a leak of energy happening somewhere, or something subtly shifting the speed at which everything resonated. I couldn't figure out where the shift was coming from, but it was definitely a problem, or an effect of a problem. I sat down on the ground, laying my white snake entwined staff in front of me. I pulled the glowing white rope in a circle over my head and placed it over the staff, so there was a circle split in two perfect hemispheres. The crystal started to glow from within my bag, shinning through the thick suede. I pulled it out, shocked at how bright it glowed, squinting at its light. It called to be placed in the center of the glowing circle, bisecting the line of the white staff that had created two hemisphere. The crystal's tip arrowed toward the heart of the Tree's base, the point where the original Seed had held the spark of Life. The knowledge that from this point, from that Seed, all of Life came forth to flourish on the Planets, suddenly flashed through me in an inhale of visions of Seeds sprouting and creatures growing inside spherical eggs. The seed, and egg, was Love. The heart of this Great Tree was Love, and it *was* a great conduit of energy to the other realms. The Two Lovers lamented louder, as if stirred by my epiphany. It startled me and I looked around. Then I pulled out the carved box with a spiral on it, filled with the smoky black powder of Shilajit. It called to be placed below the crystal, on the other side of the staff, now creating a circle nearly split into quarters. Then I felt my heart start to beat with the drum beat of the Earth again, and heard a drum beat call from my bag. I reached in and felt the small leather wrapped bundle beating loudly with primal rhythm. It called for its Mother. I unwrapped it with a small sliver of fear, unsure what might come of me if this really was stolen from her inadmissibly. Yet I knew they needed to be reunited. As the leather unveiled her glory, the Seed glowed with an aura that brought a tear to my eye. It reminded me of the first time I ever saw a newborn baby, at church when I was young. The remembrance of the angelic glow of that few day old child, fresh from the womb, still brought tears to my eyes. This Seed possessed that energy, the energy of a newborn baby, pure and innocent, deeply connected to Great Spirit, the source of all. It was radiating this, and its energy sphere was perfect. As my hand touched it, I felt the ultimate feeling of Connection and the deepest knowing of Love pulse through me. It was breathtaking and I actually gasped for air. It was unreal and almost too much to bear. I burst out in a loud cry and tears streamed down my face as if they had never been allowed to flow, damned up with blocks. I let the tears flow freely and intensely, hugging the seed tight to my chest, pressed against my heart. As the tears subsided, and the waters leveled back into the basin of my soul, I felt myself sink into relaxation. Energetic roots formed from my spine and twisted slowly down into the Earth, as the top of my spine stretched up toward the star-filled sky. I sat there for I'm not sure how long, just feeling myself as an antenna, deeply grounded and uplifted at the same time, perfectly still in between. It was ultimate peace. I felt what it was to be Tree. It was in this place that the heart of Love could be protected. I felt the seed that perfectly molded to the inside of my palm, with its rhythmic pulse of life potential. It beat the drum of a thousand generations of heartbeats.

I knew I had to get it back to its Mother. I knew that it needed to be protected and nurtured. Perhaps this was what the Lovers cried and fought for. As I thought this, they cried louder. I felt it in my heart. This was the lost potential of their Love, the Seed that could have been, but was ripped away from them. A small tear fell from my left eye and landed on the seed. I felt it shimmy and shudder with internal energy, then it began to glow brighter. Then another tear fell on the seed, and it glowed even brighter. I started to cry, tears from my deepest places of conjuring. Pain and emotions from lifetimes, and generations of suffering and grief, were releasing. The Seed glowed with a light blue hue and the drumbeat within it grew to an overwhelming bang, pushing hard against the walls of its shell. I could barely hold it anymore, as its density was growing exponentially and my hands could no longer bare the weight. It was like a high powered magnet pulling for the ground below me. So I placed it just above the crystal point, within the white glowing circle, and it began to sink into the ground. Its density and gravity were so great, it began to bury itself into the rich Earth bed. The spiral on the box began to glow, the same blue color. I opened it and the dark powder floated out on a spiraling ribbon of energy, floating through the air to the precious Seed that now glowed with a bright blue hue. The powder wrapped around it, providing a blanket of nourishing minerals and healing Love from the Earth. I reached out my hands and covered it with dirt, holding my hands there for a moment, feeling a mutual blessing way. Then I felt an intense pulling, so strong it was nearly unbearable. The Seed was pulling me with it, trying to take me down into the ground. I pulled my arms back and fought with all my might, beginning to feel fear and anxiety overwhelm me. I screamed out, "Help!" There was no one to help me, no one to answer my call. I felt myself giving in to the pull, it was too strong, too undeniable. I felt myself letting go of form as I squeezed into the Earth, my feet dangling up in the air as my upper body slowly became the dirt around me. I felt myself letting go, knowing that this might be the end for me. Perhaps my place in this journey was to simply become the fertilizer for the next Tree. Then the thought penetrated my mind and I began to wrestle, freaking out and fighting for my life, pushing against the strong hold on me. Somehow, I managed to fight my way back out, covered in dirt and gasping for air. I was relieved and terrified. Was this really my mission? How could I just be a meal, whose bones, flesh, and blood was meant to nourish the next Tree of Life? Was I really just a human sacrifice? How cliche. How absolutely horrifying. It couldn't be true. I started to breathe quickly, feeling my heart beat faster and faster. I felt myself drifting away from the Oneness, the euphoric feeling of joy dissipating, and I dove quickly into a deep fear and anger. I screamed the loudest scream I had ever screamed, coming from all my scariest nightmares and darkest places…

I awoke with a soft scream purging out of me, remnants of the horror. I was sweating and breathing heavy.

"Lila, oh thank God. Lila! Are you alright?!" The rocking. The familiar frightened energy. The wiping of my face. It was all too familiar.

This time however, Mom sobbed out, "I can't take this anymore!" She was sobbing real tears of anguish and pain. I managed to see out the corner of my eye that it was 8:05, meaning she was probably trying to wake me for over an hour. I felt her pain and sorrow, her anxiety and fear, I felt her feeling of helplessness and confusion.

"I'm sorry, Momma. I'm sorry. I'm ok. I'm ok." I was so groggy, so out of it, I almost felt ill. It was a strange 'out of body' of feeling, mixed with exhaustion. I knew where I was but I couldn't feel myself. My body felt limp, yet I was still shaking with a stiff intensity, and I had tingling all over my whole body. Slowly, the feeling was returning, to my toes and fingers first, then spreading inward. I could barely keep my eyes open though.

"An hour and 15 minutes to wake you this time. What the heck is going on? Why are you so deep? How? I don't understand how I can't wake you up, the way I shake you and yell. It's frightening, Lila. It's like you're unconscious." She wept through her words, sharing her suffering. It was the most terrifying thing she could probably imagine, not being able to wake me up. I felt sorry and sad for her. She was sacrificing a lot too. Although for her, it was completely out of her control, she had no choice in the matter. I however, had choice, and I had a very big choice to make. I couldn't tell anyone about it either, absolutely no one would understand and agree with what I knew I had to do.

Momma was still rocking me, sniffing her nose frequently, and wiping her tears away. She felt relieved in some ways, but also felt completely drained and nearly defeated. It was all coming back to her now, she was thinking about Dad.

The seed of fear inside me was being watered with her tears, and my own tears too. I knew I had to extinguish this flow, if I was ever to succeed on my mission.

So I wiped my last tear away and took Mom by the cheeks with each hand, staring into her eyes, and said, "Everything is alright, Mom. Everything is ok." I smiled and wiped her tears away, trying to get her to smile too. She wasn't going to smile for me right now, but she did take in a deep breath and I felt her pain subside a bit. She pulled me in for a giant squeeze of a hug, one that was so desperate and nearly painful, that it was almost like she was trying to cage me into her heart, or punish me with her heart's pain. I allowed the near suffocation, knowing that she was releasing a slew of emotions with this one embrace. So we hugged for a few minutes, feeling all the feels and allowing our nervous systems to unwind a bit.

"Now hurry and get dressed. You're going to be late for

school," she said, hurriedly getting up and rushing out the door, without an 'I love you ' or anything. I felt her heart's pain, and a thin wall forming around my entrance. I knew it was what she needed for her own protection, but I also knew that the wall she built around Dad's entrance was at least in part to blame for her current health condition, probably the main cause. So I felt inclined to speak again,

"Mom, everything is alright, it's exactly as it should be. I'm perfectly fine." She finally smiled, but it was half-assed at best. I felt the words echoing through me and allowed them to reassure me as well. I *was* perfectly alright, and everything was as it should be. I knew what I had to do.

Chapter 6
Cleansing and Transforming

I arrived to school 15 minutes late, which was a serious feat of chaotic magic. Mom was probably barely on time for her appointment, the one where she should be told the Doctor's opinion of her fate. No big deal. I felt the stomach butterflies flutter a little. We were both in the hot seat.

Mrs. Avarie looked disappointed but also not surprised to see me walking in late, again. I had a pretty good week of being on time though, so she let it slide. I tried to figure out what I missed, what part of the Hero's Journey we were discussing now.

"The Ultimate Boon, what does this mean? It is the final step in the trial, the whole reason for all the previous steps, what the Hero has been working toward. It's what they were meant to do. All the previous steps were simply to prepare and purify the person for this step. So can anyone think of an example from a common tale or movie?"

No one was too eager to raise their hand this early in the day, and most of my peers didn't like to participate voluntarily.

I thought this might be a good chance to win some points with Mrs. Averie, so I raised my hand.

"Oh alright, go ahead Lila," she said sounding surprised that I would have any idea what was going on.

"When Frodo throws the ring into the volcano, in the Lord of the Rings?"

I said in more of a question form, not totally confident of my answer.

"Yes!! Thank you, Lila. It's good to know someone is paying

attention and understanding what we're talking about here. She was even late, folks. Can we all wake up a bit? Anyone else have an example?"

I returned to thoughts of the Dream. What was my Ultimate Boon? I felt like maybe it was simply to plant the Seed, but perhaps it was truly to sacrifice myself with it. I got chills all over. It was terrifying to think of going back to sleep tonight. I knew that this was the night, or at least the weekend.

"Lila," Mrs. Averie called out to me, as I was packing up to leave after class.

"Yes," I said, as I walked over, still fumbling my books into my backpack a bit.

"I wanted to say thank you for your response earlier. It was good to know you were not skipping a beat with all this tardiness and spaciness I've gotten from you lately. I really value you as a student. We had such a good year last year, and then all of a sudden you have been kind of all over the map. Is everything alright?" She looked at me with the most sincere and caring eyes and expression one could imagine. I was tearing up and I couldn't imagine spilling myself out to her right then and there, but I also for a split second imagined it.

Then I said, simply, "I'm sorry, Mrs. Averie. I'm fine, there's just been a lot going on, a lot on my mind. I'm alright though and I really want you to know that I really appreciate you as a teacher, and this class. I mean this subject we're focusing on right now, the hero's journey, it's really resonating with me and helping me a lot at the moment. I know that I've been absent minded and physically absent at times, but I'm here in my heart and I am hearing you. I really appreciate you, Mrs. Averie."

"Well, uh, good. I mean, thank you. I mean, you're welcome. I just wanted to be sure you're ok."

"I'm fine, Mrs. Averie. I feel some heavy weight, but I'm really taking it one breath at a time and am so grateful to be on this ride." I found myself putting my hands into prayer position at my heart and saying, "Namaste."

I smiled as I breathed in a reassuring breath and walked out the door to my next class, slightly laughing at myself. Who was I? I mean seriously, who am I? I was so comfortable saying Namaste and prayerfully thanking my teacher, while confidently walking out of the room without needing to explain my struggles. I was proud of myself. I caught my reflection in the window of the next building and thought I looked taller, more mature. In fact, my small breasts were actually looking kind of pronounced. Ha! Maybe I was actually going through puberty finally, I joked with myself. It wasn't like I was late, but many other girls had already gone through changes. I was feeling a bit curious and desirous of what it might be like. Certainly seeing models in magazines and actresses in movies didn't help a girl's self esteem, especially when her best friend-maybe-more-than-a-friend was constantly being hit on by already developed girls with big bouncy boobs in his face. So seeing that in the reflection also perked me up, boosting my confidence even more. I felt like I was glowing, and it felt good.

That's when fate slapped me in the face, as a door opened at lightening speed out of nowhere as I was walking by. Ouch!! I think I saw little stars.

"Oh my gosh, are you ok?" The guy asked. I never even saw his face, I had my eyes closed shut hard from the pain.

"I'm fine, I'm fine. It's cool," I lied.

He tried to contain his laugh as he walked away and his friends didn't even bother to hide their laughter. Jerk jocks. I was pretty sure I knew who it was. In any case, it hurt. Square in the nose. Seriously, God's painful joke to be like 'hey, you think you have it all figured out? You think you're hot stuff?...you still have more to learn. Pay more attention! Here feel this unending throbbing/stinging pain in your face, that'll do it.' Flipping Ouch! I rubbed my nose to make sure it was still in the same place and not bleeding. All good, just a nice wake up call to pay attention to where I was walking and not my damn reflection in a mirror. Seemed like a beautiful metaphor. I felt sort of tingly all over, and hoped that I wasn't going to pass out or something. Then I looked around to see if anyone else had witnessed it, feeling myself blush with embarrassment.

I saw Acarya at lunch and we chatted for a bit about all kinds of things. Including why my nose was red. I didn't tell him about my dream and what was really on my mind though, and it felt strange to withhold the info. I knew that he would start worrying about me and tell me to go see someone again. I didn't need to see anyone. A Psychologist couldn't help me with this. Or could they? I wondered, then dismissed the thought when he brought up that he had another Deer encounter this morning. I filled him in on the meaning behind Deer medicine and we smiled and laughed at the sweetness of Acarya's Totem animal representing gentleness. He *was* a gentle soul, and my heart was always nurtured by his presence. I felt more grounded and centered after we ate lunch together. Although, there was still a bit of a pit in my stomach, and all the confidence I had gathered earlier was gone in that instant of a smack to the face.

The rest of the day was admittedly, sort of a blur, again. It wasn't that I wasn't interested in the subjects being taught or that I didn't try with all my might to focus on the teacher, but I was so lost in daydream. My own inner world of things was overtaking me. I was bouncing between my Dream and the task ahead of me, Mom and her diagnosis appointment today, Acarya and his flirtatious side smile, the glowing white pure Seed of Love, Mr. Peen's words, Mrs. Varma's words, my father's betrayal, my father, the girl's draped over and around Acarya, elder Mrs. Pombokom pointing at me yelling, "Whytee!" Whyla, the spiraling spheres of everything. It was a lot. I was lost in it. I felt dizzy and flushed, like I needed air and I asked to use the restroom.

Splashing some water on my face, I calmed down to a restful

heart rate, but I was still feeling dizzy and strange, and actually a little sick to my stomach. Going pee, I felt a sort of cramping in my bowels, hoping very much that I wasn't catching a bug or having a reaction to my salad from lunch. It came on suddenly and then it sort of left suddenly, like a wave, and I felt ok again. I went outside and walked around the long way back to class, to keep getting some fresh air. The walk felt great, getting fresh air was just the ticket. I got back to class and guzzled water from my water bottle. It was pretty crazy how much I felt like I had never tasted water before. It was intoxicating: a cool, silky, naturally semi sweet, smooth, refreshing, perfectly amazing wonder of a substance. I was brought back, to being in the Water with Whyla, spiraling around in the silky smooth blanket. Water, the elixir of Life. It was where it all came from, how it was all sustained. I felt ultimate gratitude in my heart for it, and I nearly cried at my extreme love for water. This was how my day went. Kind of all over the map.

After school, I rode the bus home. Lina was being particularly gabby and filled me in on all the gossip of 8th grade. I could've done without it, but it distracted me from my real issues at hand, so I indulged her. Luckily, it was a quick ride to my stop, and she only had 10 minutes maximum to talk my ear off. It was a relief when I saw my house as we pulled onto my road.

"Wow, well thanks for filling me in. I hope you do get to hang out with Justin tomorrow at Rachel's house. Have a good time. I'll see ya."

"Wait, what are you doing tomorrow? You want to come?" she asked.

"Oh, no thanks. I have some things I want to do this weekend. Thanks anyways. Have fun! I'll talk to you sometime this weekend, I'm sure," I said. I couldn't fathom hanging out with that group of people, but I was happy for her if she wanted to. She seemed almost desperate for me to go with her though, which was kind of strange. Whatever, it wasn't my cup of tea and

I wasn't going to be guilt-tripped or peer-pressured into doing anything that wasn't totally worth my time. I had a lot of things and places I'd rather be than with the 'popular' crowd.

I walked home and just as I got to the door, a giant tree frog crossed my path. It startled me, but I smiled with glee. I loved frogs!! It was scared of me and rushed away, but its presence seriously uplifted me and reminded me to take in a deep breath. I made a mental note to look up Frog medicine.

Mom was inside at the table drinking tea, when I walked in. I had nearly forgotten about her appointment today until I saw her. Her expression was not reassuring. She looked like she was about to pass out, kind of pale and in shock.

"Are you alright? How'd it go? What did they say?" I felt by her expression and energy that it didn't go as well as hoped, but I needed her to speak.

"Well, they found another questionable spot, on my other breast, and they're suggesting the double mastectomy, with chemo and radiation. He suggested that I stop doing the Ayurvedic remedies and that we book the first chemo treatment for Monday. I have to admit, Lila, I'm not feeling good about this." She was about to cry, and her tears made me well up with them. My eyes had been filled with tears much of the day, but none had actually fallen, until now. The flood gates opened and it was like the faucet had been turned on full stream.

"So can you get another opinion? I know you said you thought you couldn't, but maybe you can, maybe in another town nearby? That's so much." I was sobbing, not because of the procedures and all that Mom was going to have to endure, but because I knew she was scared. My mother was absolutely my rock, and to see her afraid, was terrifying.

She wiped her tears and blew her nose. She offered me a tissue and I did the same. I took a deep breath in and she did the same.

"I don't think you should stop doing the Ayurvedic remedies. I really feel in my heart that all of it is beneficial and complimentary. Please don't disregard it just because your Oncologist doesn't know about it and is maybe threatened by it. He doesn't know about it, therefore he can't say that it isn't helpful. I really really need you to believe that your body can heal itself too. Please don't let him, and the system, take your power of self-healing away. I feel very strong in my heart and in my being that it is extremely helpful." I reached for her hand and looked her right in the eyes with intense seriousness, another tear rolling down my cheek.

She wiped it away and said, "Alright, sweetie, I won't stop the herbs and other recommendations, and I'll keep working with Mrs. Varma. I also feel that it is all helpful and that Dr. Brennan is a bit traditional in his approach and perhaps just doesn't know how beneficial it all really is. But I think I am also going to begin the other treatments as recommended. It's all going to be just fine, dear. I promise."

I felt her words, felt their weight and their Truth, but still there was an air of question. I felt unsure in my gut, a feeling that had in ways been present all day. There was a subtle vibration deep within me, a stirring of emotions and feelings from hidden depths. It was unsettling and unnerving, but also felt uncontrollable and very present, creeping more and more into my awareness.

"It's all going to be alright, honey," she said again and scooted her chair closer so that she could wrap me in a big hug. Being tight in Mother's arms was nearly every creature's sanctuary, and I was no exception.

Soon it was 5:00, and I went out to the backyard where Mom was actually pulling weeds and tidying it up. It looked like she had been out there most of the day.

"Wow, Mom! It looks amazing out here. You've done a ton! Don't overdo it, you need to be resting."

"Oh sweet girl, you worry about me too much, but I

appreciate it. I am absolutely loving being out here today. It feels very therapeutic to be outside, with my hands and knees in the dirt, listening to the Sparrows and Towhees sing to each other, and the Scrub Jays squawk back. Nature is really quite comical when you pay attention." She was smiling brightly, beaming with joy and peace. Her face even seemed to flow a bit.

"Well, just listen to your body and don't push yourself. I agree though, Nature is pretty funny sometimes, and very healing. Smiling and laughing and the fresh air, is all great for you too, I'm sure." I smiled and kissed her forehead.

"Well, thank you, 'Mom!'" she said sarcastically, but appreciatively, smiling at me. I knew I was being an overprotective and worrying motherly type figure, and that truly Mom and I were that for each other. Hearing her say it out loud though, I realized I was probably being ridiculous.

"Alright, have fun. I'll be back around 9:30. I love you," I said, realizing how much I still sounded like a 'mom.'

"Alright, sweetie, enjoy. Let yourself be a little kid again with her! Play and have fun!" She said, beaming with a genuine grin.

I smiled in return.

Mrs. Pombokom arrived precisely on time and we made our way to their cabin in the woods. It felt like a shorter drive this time. She was talking most of the time, about various things, a lot relating to new cool stuff she was hoping to instill at school, and some grant money that had a few options for use. I had a lot of moments of "oh, cool," "Yeah," and "wow," but truly I was pretty lost in my own thoughts again. Looking out the window in a car, especially on country roads in the forest, always triggered my mind to drift into daydreams and memories of dreams. I started thinking about how close I was to night time again. Would I be able to do it? What I knew I *had* to do.

We arrived and Dakota was outside playing with some sticks she had wrapped with a rainbow colored yarn and some feathers.

They looked like a mix between a walking stick and a magic wand. She came running as I got out of the car, so excited to see me.

She handed me one of the sticks and said, "here, it's your magic power stick. What's your magic power?"

"Oh, umm, I might have to think about that for a moment. What's your magic power?"

"I can make things become invisible, including myself, and make things disappear, banishing them to another realm," she said in a booming powerful voice. She definitely had a flare for the dramatic. It made me giggle, but I felt my inhibitions for being playful. I had already built my tween walls pretty high by this point.

Then I heard Mom's words echo through me, "play and have fun…let yourself be a kid again." It was admittedly pretty tempting to dive into character and just let loose a bit. It would certainly take my mind off of the things that I was obsessing over.

"Alright, my power is the ability to heal things. I can even make things come back to life," I said with a witchy demeanor.

"Ohh, awesome! Come on, I want to show you my fort!" She pulled my hand and led me toward the back side of the house.

"I love you, Dakota! Have fun!!" Mrs. Pombokom yelled out.

Dakota went running back to her and gave her a big hug, looked up at her and said, "I love you too, Mom, you have fun too." Then she ran back over to me eagerly, wide open smile from ear to ear. It was truly awesome to feel her energy, so pure and free and uninhibited, so full of joy and inspiration. She grabbed my hand and pulled me around the house to a structure made of about 25-30 large sticks, all placed around and on top of each other, creating a sort of dome. There were two logs inside for sitting on, with a third between them as a table. It had a little blue towel over it like a table cloth and a small mason jar of flowers. There was also a circle of stones, and inside the circle was a pile of logs as a fire place. It was cozy and adorable and although quite simple in many ways, it was well thought through and meaningful. There was a small structure I hadn't noticed at first, I was curious so I asked.

"What's that little area for?"

"Oh, that's a fairy house. Or a pixie house. Or possibly a small animal house, whatever wants to make itself home here," she said.

"Oh, that's clever and sweet. I bet all of the above would love to live there, or at least spend an evening there. I know I would, if I were a fairy."

She smiled at my comment and looked proud and happy.

"What about having some real tea here in this sweet little fort? I could make us some," I offered.

"Oh yes, please, that sounds lovely. I'll help you."

So we went inside the back door and made up a little pot of tea. They only had a few choices, which I found surprising, but we decided on some Herbal spiced tea. We took it outside and enjoyed the sun sparkling through the trees, warming our souls. This completely delicious cinnamon spicy warm tea totally hit the spot.

"Mmmmm," I let out, feeling my belly relaxing for the first time today. I was so grateful to be right there, right then.

"What a lovely way to end the week," Dakota said. Sipping her tea, like a grown up.

"I would have to agree," I said, wholeheartedly. It really was pleasant.

"Do you want to go for a walk? We have a really cool trail that starts right there. Come on, let's bring our magic wands, in case we need to use our magic powers." She handed me my wand stick. I loved that mine had a white feather, reminding me of my white feather plumes in Liluye's hair.

"Yeah, sure, I'll go on a quick walk. I didn't do much in P.E. today and I could use the movement in my body. It's so beautiful out tonight, almost a warm breeze on the air. The mosquitos are going to be out soon though, plus we better make some dinner soon too, so just a small walk." We finished our tea and set off on our little adventure.

I was entranced by the way the light was playing with the trees, bouncing through the leaves of the Oaks and Madrones, the needles of the Pine. Their shadows were dancing across the ground and each other. I closed my eyes and felt the breeze on my face, it really was unusually warm. Breathing in deeply, I felt everything around me breathing in too. Then we all exhaled together. I felt the Oneness here, the feeling that came so easily in the Dream World, but was so fleeting here. But I was feeling it. So strongly. It brought the biggest smile to my face, to realize that it was accessible here too.

"What's that up ahead in the trail?" Dakota asked, holding her stick out in front of her, creeping towards it.

We got closer and she slightly squealed, alerting me to be on guard and jolting me back into the present moment, out of a dreamy space.

"What is it?"

"It's a Snake!" She exclaimed, sounding quite afraid.

"What? Really? Let me see," I said as I moved in front of her, to protect her and to get a better look. It was just off the trail, all coiled up, in a little sunny spot. I couldn't tell what kind it was, but if it was a Rattlesnake, we needed to turn around and get away quick. If it wasn't, we might be able to get around it and continue on our journey.

"I will go invisible and make you invisible and we can go around it." She gestured with her wand.

I still couldn't tell if there was a rattling end to this snake's tail, or if it had noticed us yet. I felt a weariness though, a hesitation. It was also completely intriguing and mystifying to be in its presence.

"Alright, I'll go closer to the snake. You go on my right side, farther from it." I put my wand out to protect us, and my other arm in front of her, as if I could protect her if it decided to strike. We crept ever so quietly and carefully around it, and then I saw its triangular eyes, watching our every move. It was definitely a Rattlesnake. Luckily, he watched us carefully going around him and figured we were not a threat. My heart was beating out of my chest. Dakota stepped on a stick that cracked and made a startling sound, the snake pulled out his rattling tail and shook it wildly in warning, sounding like a perfectly timed Maraca. We maintained a slow creeping away and then just as we felt far enough to escape, we ran as fast as we could. After a moment of squealing, we laughed in shock and horror.

It was the end of the trail, it looked like, and I was terrified at the thought of having to go back past the snake again.

"We can use the loop, and head around the other way. It's not as maintained of a trail, but we can do it. Probably better than going back that way," Dakota said.

"Yeah, cool, that sounds good." Phew, an alternative route.

We headed through a fence, where there was a small passageway between, and headed around a blind corner into the woods.

There was a giant Madrone as we came around the corner, still slightly lit up with the warm evening sun. She was a majestic sight, grand and powerful, still and peaceful. I felt her exalted joy, beaming with love and appreciation for the sun. Such a simple existence.

I took in a deep breath with her and felt her spheres of energy dancing with mine. Oh, to be a Tree, *would* be incredible.

We walked the overgrown pathway, through grass as tall as me in some places. Other areas were clear and the red clay dirt of this region shined through. It made me feel more like a child, being dwarfed by the grasses around me. I felt myself sinking into the magic. Listening to the crickets beginning their sacred songs, and the birds beginning to quiet, it really was a wonderland…Earth.

"There's something jumping in the trail ahead. I think it's a big frog," Dakota declared. We got up closer to it and found it to indeed be a frog, a pretty good sized Tree Frog, brown and dark green. He was anxious to get off the trail, but he seemed to stop, turn and look right at us as he got to the edge. Then he turned around again and jumped into the tall grass. Frogs truly always made me smile, inside and out.

Dakota taught me a song about them that she had learned in school, and we sang it together as we skipped the rest of the way back. Suddenly, I had a flash back moment of skipping with my Dad when I was a little younger than Dakota, through the field by the park we used to go to. We were also singing a song together and laughing. Mom was behind us smiling. It was a very happy memory indeed. Sad how much I had blocked. Any memory of Dad was too painful for so long, I really had learned to just forget him all together. I realized how much joy it brought my heart to remember this moment and felt that joy spreading around my body, filling in little cracks and spaces. I beamed a giant smile and felt my heart pouring out joy. It felt so much like the light that beamed from my heart in the Dream. Then I realized that joy was a manifestation of connection to Great Spirit. Feeling joy, I felt connected. It was a funny epiphany that made me giggle, it was so simple.

When we got back to the house, Dakota helped me make dinner and we decided to watch a movie while we ate. She asked if I had ever seen "The Labyrinth." It was an old 1980's Jim Henson film. I had heard of it, but had actually never seen it.

"Oh, Lila, you'll love it! It's one of my very favorites."

The movie was really pretty brilliant, I enjoyed it tremendously. It was also enlightening, and inspiring. She was given a mission, and ultimately the mission was really about empowering herself to know herself and to not be afraid anymore, to know that nothing has control over her happiness. She also went through many mini-trials of discovery, such as "life isn't always fair, but that's the way it is," and to not have expectations of things being perfect or the way you think they should be, but rather allow the mystery to unfold as it should, and witness all that can be, all that you didn't know was possible. Another great lesson, "not everything is as it seems," don't be quick to judge something, you might not have any idea what it's really like. Overall, I was not only thoroughly entertained, but I was taught a lot of very timely and important lessons that were very relevant to my journey too. The Dream even felt like a labyrinth. Life was a beautiful series of connections and synchronicities.

The movie ended and it was about 8:30, so Dakota helped me do a few dishes and then got ready for bed. She was still all wound up about the movie, singing "dance, magic, dance" while bouncing around her room. I read her a book to calm her down and then left her to fall asleep on her own.

I hadn't been in the living room for five minutes before I heard the familiar door creak of Elder Pombokom's room. Her nurse had left around 7:15, and she told us she was asleep. I felt the hairs starting to stand up. She was a little bit unpredictable and I wasn't sure what would come of this interaction. I didn't hear anything, so I went back to reading my book I had brought. I still hadn't heard any noise whatsoever, but a presence suddenly presented itself to my left. I turned to look quickly and nothing was there. Weird. I turned to look back right, and there was Ky sitting right next to me on the couch, staring right into my face. It scared me into a startled jump and my heart started beating a million beats a minute.

"Oh, Mrs. Pombokom, you startled me. Let's go back to bed now," I said, trying to gather myself.

"The time is now. You cannot wait any longer. The blood will feed her," she said intensely, with wide eyes staring through my soul. I had no idea what she meant, but it was terrifying. Then she reached out and placed her hand over my heart and said,

"Trust." She moved her hand to my lower belly and said again, "the time is now." Then she released her intensity, as if the Spirit possessing her suddenly left, and she smiled a tender sweet smile. She reached for my hands and brought them to her lips to kiss the top of both of my hands. Then she looked me in the eyes again, and ever so sweetly said, "thank you. Thank you."

I felt tears welling in my eyes and my heart seemed to relax, alerting me to the fact that I had been holding tension around my heart, trapping it in a tight cage all day. I felt the beam of invisible light forging through. Suddenly, I could see Kylem's spheres of energy, and my own, and they seemed to be spinning in unison. I closed my eyes, Ky still holding my hands, and I felt our Oneness. I felt her strength and wisdom filling me. It was a beautiful feeling and one that was extremely empowering. It reminded me so much of being with Whyla. I felt the tears now flowing down my face. I lifted her hands to my lips and kissed the top of each of her wrinkled soft hands and felt their story flood through me. She had been through more than I could have ever imagined, and I could even feel her ancestor's stories filling inside me. I didn't need to know details, I felt the pain, suffering, strength and deep connection they possessed. She wiped my tears and then subtly bowed her head and closed her eyes. Then she stood up, which I helped her do, and she patted my left cheek and smiled. Then she turned around and hobbled slowly back to her room.

I sat there motionless, filled with a lot of conflicting feelings, but not a single solid thought. I was stunned. I was slightly shaking, but also felt extremely centered and calm. It was as if part of my being was still scared, still separate from connection, still questioning everything, but the core of me was as grounded as a Tree, sure of my path, One with everything. I knew that tonight would possibly be the night. I knew what I had to do. But I was also still holding on, still wanting the life I had imagined for myself. Why did it have to be me? The second I thought it, the answer flooded me. It was a feeling, not words, and I just knew. I wanted to be with Whyla though, I still had so many questions and still a lot of fear. Then I heard a replay of Ky saying, "trust," and I felt it reverberate through my bones. I closed my eyes and allowed the energy of the word to spiral around me, offering comfort to the insecure places.

Mr. and Mrs. Pombokom arrived only minutes later, and I knew that I was still showing all my conflicting emotions on my face. I gathered myself and found a smile.

Mrs. Pombokom talked my ear off the whole way home, giddy and excited about her dance class and date night with her husband. She had a lot more energy than I felt I had left. So I couldn't really add much to the conversation, but I was happy she wasn't asking me anything about me.

We got home and Mom had already gone to bed, leaving a few small lights on for me. I didn't normally do this, but a hot bath sounded so good. So I went to the bathroom and started to fill the tub with water, I even poured in a little of Mom's Epsom salts that she always boasted about. I felt still a slight shaking in my body, and knew that the bath would be just the ticket. I was also prolonging the inevitable, going to sleep.

I laid in the bath, with my eyes closed, replaying all the things from the day, from the past few weeks, from the Dream. I thought about Acarya. I thought about Mom. My eyes filled with tears at the thought of leaving them. I felt my ego fighting the Truth and throwing a tantrum inside me. It didn't feel fair. Then I remembered the wise words from the movie tonight, "no, it's not fair, but that's the way it is." I had a choice, to embrace the idea and face my fate with strength, pride, and acceptance, or to run from it like a coward and be caught in my emotions of anger and sadness. I knew what was the right thing to do. In knowing this Truth in my heart, I felt even another layer of the shackles falling away. My heart seemed to be beaming with light, and I opened my eyes to see if I was in fact lighting up the room with my heart space, like in the Dream.

Not only was I *not* shinning light from my heart, but I was freaked out to discover that my bath had turned pink. I searched for the answer, and then saw a small trail of blood flowing from me. The blood flowed out like a pathway, and then spiraled into a helix shape, spiraling around before it dissipated into the abyss of the bath. It was strange to witness and I felt almost out of body, hovering above this odd situation that was so foreign yet felt so natural and familiar too. No wonder I was so all over the map today, and had felt those cramps earlier. I guess Ky somehow knew, and that's why she touched my belly. Then I thought more about blood, how it resided within almost all biological creatures, how it fed us, nurtured us, protected us, how it connected us all. I felt fear, excitement, anger, and joy all at the same time. Then I just started crying. I allowed the tears to flow, and the pain from all my deepest places begin to flow out too. I sobbed out loud and felt the immensity of the release.

A soft knock on the door, and Mom gently opened it. "Are you alright, sweetie?"

I didn't even bother to wipe my tears and address her, like I normally would. Instead, I just continued to let the tears flow, closing my eyes. I cried out loud, releasing the sounds that represented the pain, that I had been holding for a very long time. The sadness was deep and it felt like I was barely scratching the surface. Yet it was utterly releasing and liberating to allow this flood. Mom came to the side of the tub and wrapped my upper body in a towel, kneeling beside me she pulled my head to rest on her shoulder. She just let me cry, holding me gently against her to let me know she was there to support me. She didn't wipe my tears or tell me it was alright. She just let me cry, knowing it was exactly all that I needed to do. So I cried, and I cried. Until I suddenly felt I was done, and I came to a stop, and I took in a really deep breath. Then I wiped my face in the towel and opened my eyes. It almost seemed like I was viewing through new lenses, things seemed almost clearer. Mom took my face and brought it up to look at her. She smiled a big smile and I slowly smiled back. We didn't need to say anything.

As Mom was leaving the bathroom, she went to a cupboard and pulled out a box and left it on the counter. I appreciated that she understood I didn't want to talk about it, but I also really appreciated her support.

I went to Mom's room after I got dressed. She was back in bed again, so I spooned up behind her, and wrapped my arms around her. She let out a sweet sounding, "mmmm," and touched my arm, hugging me back.

"I love you, Lila."

"I love you so much, Mom."

I could have stayed there forever, and nearly fell asleep with her, but then realized it, and motioned to get up. I kissed her on her left temple, smelling her face lotion that was a quintessential scent of my mother. I breathed her in, as if to take her essence with me. It brought a smile to my face.

"Good night," I whispered, and headed back to my room.

I felt lighter, refreshed in a way I hadn't felt in a very long time, maybe ever before. It was just so nice to know why I was feeling so strange lately and especially the last day or two. As I was getting dressed, a cloud moved and revealed the Moon's light, shinning extremely bright now into my room. I went to the window and saw her in her fullness, as if shinning just for me, smiling down on me with Love. I felt taller, my posture was different. I felt like a woman, and that made me proud. I closed my eyes and let my heart open to the Moon's Love and once again felt that feeling of Oneness, sacred connection to everything around me. I felt like the Earth, myself, full and fertile.

The sound of frogs outside then filled my awareness and I remembered the frog encounters of earlier. What did frog represent? I went to my book and looked it up, remembering I also wanted to look up snake medicine, after seeing the powerful Rattlesnake as well. First, Frog…

Frog
~Cleansing~
Sing Frog sing! Call the rains, Quench the dryness, Cleanse the Earth, Then fill me up again.

Frog medicine is akin to water energy, and the West on the medicine wheel. Frog teaches us to honor our tears, for they cleanse the soul. All water rites belong to Frog, including all initiations by water.

Water cleanses and prepares the body for sacred ceremony. It is the element we understand best in the womb. Frog, like ourselves, is a pollywog in the fetal waters, and only learns to hop after it experiences the world of fluidity.

The transformation into adulthood prepares Frog for its power to call in the waters of the skies, the rain. In knowing the element of water, Frog can sing the song that calls the rain to Earth. Like Frog, we are asked to know when it is time to refresh, purify, and refill the coffers of the soul.

If you were to look at where you are today, would you use any of the following words to describe your condition: tired, overloaded, harried, frustrated, guilty, itchy, nervous, at a loss, empty, or weakened?

If so, take a break and allow yourself to bathe in the waters of Frog medicine. This could mean a long, relaxing bath, disconnecting the phone, yelling "stop," or taking in deep, cleansing breaths.

The key is to find a way to rid yourself of distractions and to replace the mud with clear energy. Then replenish your parched spirit, body, and mind.

An ability of Frog medicine people is to give support and energy where it is needed. A Frog medicine person can clean negativity from any environment. Many mediums or clairvoyants use water on their hands when tapping into other realms of reality due to water's super-conductive nature.

Frog speaks of new life and harmony through its rain song. The deep tones of Frog's "ribet" are said to be a call to the Thunder Beings: thunder, lightening, and rain. The "ribet" is the heartbeat that comes into harmony with Father Sky and calls for the replenishment needed. Call to Frog and find peace in the joy of taking time to give to yourself. A part of this giving is cleansing yourself of any person, place, or thing that does not contribute to your new state of serenity and replenishment.

Wow. How were these always so spot on?!! I had chills once again, my hairs standing up on my arms. It was uncanny how the medicine always made sense with what was happening. I felt Frog deep within me, and wanted to "ribet" for myself. It made me smile to imagine myself hopping about, calling in the Rain of positivity, cleansing away the negativity. Powerful little creatures indeed. Alright, what did Snake medicine represent...

Snake
~Transmutation~

Snake...come crawling, there's fire in your eyes. Bite me, excite me,
I'll learn to realize, the poison transmuted, brings eternal flame.
Open me to heaven, to heal me again.

Snake medicine people are very rare. Their initiation involves experiencing and living through multiple snake bites, which allows them to transmute all poisons, be they mental, physical, emotional or spiritual. The power of Snake medicine is the power of creation, for it embodies sexuality, psychic energy, alchemy, reproduction, and ascension (or immortality).

The transmutation of the life-death-rebirth cycle is exemplified by the shedding of Snake's skin. It is the energy of wholeness, cosmic consciousness, and the ability to experience anything willingly and without resistance. It is the knowledge that all things are created equal in creation, and that those things which might be experienced as poison can be eaten, ingested, integrated, and transmuted if one has the proper state of mind. Thoth, the Atlantean who later returned as Hermès and was the father of alchemy, used the symbology of two Snakes intertwining around a sword to represent healing. Complete understanding and acceptance of the male and female within each organism creates a melding of the two into one, thereby producing divine energy.

This medicine teaches you on a personal level that you are a Universal being. Through accepting all aspects of your life, you can bring about the transmutation of the fire medicine. This fire energy, when functioning on the material plane, creates passion, desire, procreation, and physical vitality. On the emotional plane, it becomes ambition, creation, resolution, and dreams. On the mental plane it becomes intellect, power, charisma, and leadership. When this Snake energy reaches the spiritual plane, it becomes wisdom, understanding, wholeness, and connection to Great Spirit. If you have chosen this symbol, there is a need within you to transmute some thought, action, or desire so that wholeness may be achieved. This is heavy magic, but remember, magic is no more than a change in consciousness. Become the magician or the enchantress: transmute the energy and accept the power of the fire.

I was stunned. This was a powerful one, and I knew it would be. The two together, Frog and Snake, were interesting. The power of Water and Fire. This was the Ayurvedic combo that created the Pitta Dosha, Mrs. Varma said. Water and Fire, balancing the two forces of creation and transformation, for the purpose of wholeness and enlightenment. It felt potent and timely, and it was empowering. I laid there in my bed, feeling the words coursing through my body, feeling a louder than normal drumbeat within me. It was time. I grabbed the sandalwood beads and felt each bead as I listened to my breath, centering myself and sinking into my strength, finding my calmness.

I laid there for a while before I was able to fall asleep. Even though I felt empowered, I was still scared, hesitant and not ready to let go, if I was really being asked to. I cried a few more tears, thanking the Universe, God, or whoever might be listening, for the gift of my life. Crying the last remaining tears within me. And as I emptied myself, I was finally able to drift off to sleep…

Chapter 7
Liquid Gold

I was surprisingly, on a cliff side next to a massive waterfall, nowhere I had ever been before, but definitely in the Dream. It was breathtaking. Lit by the vast sky of starlight. Looking out at the expanse of land before me, bushier trees like Oaks and Madrones all around, and a rushing river flowing through it all. It was truly stunning. A tear actually formed in my eyes, and I took a deep breath in, trying to digest the beauty. Then I realized I was on the edge of a cliff, but there was nothing but cliff above me, below me, and to my left. A giant, rushing waterfall was to my right. I looked down to find my magic rope and discovered it was not there. My heart skipped a beat. I had my satchel and my walking stick, but no glowing white rope, which would be a big help right now. I reached in and found the crystal, but nothing else. Interesting, to say the least. I looked around and truly couldn't imagine where I could go from here. I looked down over the edge and felt a flutter in my stomach. I wasn't much for heights. I couldn't tell how far down the base was, so I picked up a rock at my feet and dropped it, counting, "1 1000, 2 1000, 3 1000, 4 1000. Wait did I hear a small splash? Shoot, that's way too far to jump into an unknown pool below a waterfall. I felt a little shaky suddenly. I really wasn't much for heights. So now what? I felt like sitting and just looking at the scenery. It was truly, but kind of unbelievably, gorgeous. The way the twinkling starlight reflected on the river below. The sound of the waterfall rushing, and wind dancing through the leaves and needles of the trees. It was a warm breeze, like that of a late August night. I took another deep breath in and closed my eyes, now aware of the scent of moist Earth and various plants, trees, and grasses. It felt like a while that I was just sitting there, watching the water splash off the rocks to my right, admiring the scene in front of me, breathing deeply. It was so peaceful. Then I postured myself into a meditational position and started to chant the sound of Om, it just happened, and it felt so right. I felt it ruminating through my body, clearing any fear or apprehension. I felt it pouring from my heart. I opened my eyes to discover that my heart was glowing bright again, and now the crystal I laid on the ground in front of me was also glowing a bright white light. I lifted the crystal and it felt strangely heavier, and charged with a static energy that shifted the energy of my hand, my right arm, and was making its way through my whole body. I felt electric, a subtle yet strong buzzing within. Then my spheres of spiraling energy appeared, bright white. I was lighting the space around me with a powerful energy. Suddenly, the light from the crystal beamed outward, far in front of me, and it was hard to hold it, vibrating intensely with energy. I witnessed it reach out to the rushing river down below and in front of me, and the starlight sparkling on the water seemed to suddenly merge with it, joining the beam of light coming from the crystal, ignited by my heart light. The starlight was being gathered, recruited, as if a magnetic attraction was taking place. The crystal light beam seemed now to be returning, enhanced with the sacred starlight. My arms were shaking intensely at the weight and pressure of holding the crystal with this magnitude of energy streaming back into it. It seemed as though there was too much energy to be contained. The crystal was now violently shaking and seemed as though it was going to burst open. I dropped it, unable to hold it's density and intensity any longer. Then my walking staff began to light up and stood up on its own. The spiraled snake on top suddenly burst into a bright white light beaming in all directions. I had to squint for fear of going blind from the light.

Then I thought about my glowing white rope, that I normally

carried wrapped around my chest, and somehow the thought of it began to manifest it. Then the light from the crystal burst into a million fractions of light. They began to twist and intertwine into threads, that intertwined into a rope, looking and moving like a Snake. The energy slithered to the staff and coiled up around it, finally reaching the carved snake on the top of the staff, and merging together. Their merging created a sound boom. A blast of energy that knocked me over, with a light that was so bright, it lit the back of my eyelids as I closed them tight as I could. Then it dimmed significantly. I opened my eyes and could barely see, my eyes stunned from the massive amount of light energy, blinded momentarily with a bright white spot in my eyes. As I began to see again, I became aware of the rope now coiled around my staff, still standing upright, still glowing but not as bright. I went to it and the rope seemed to be alive, a Snake of energy with bright blue eyes that glowed and seemed to look directly through my soul. It slithered onto my arm and up around my chest, and I felt guarded, protected by its energy, as if it provided an energetic barrier or force shield around me. I felt strong, stronger than I had ever felt in my life. I felt powerful. The acknowledgment of this power brightened my heart light, and it beamed out in all directions.

For a minute, I nearly forgot about my mission, I nearly forgot about *everything*, but it all flooded back into my awareness. I felt myself stand taller and embrace that I had a very big purpose here. Then the ground began to rumble again, and I knew I needed to hurry....

"Lila, breakfast!" I heard Mom's voice calling from the kitchen.

How was I awake? How was it already morning? I actually felt a small bit of panic as I realized I hadn't completed my mission still. I closed my eyes, trying to force myself back to sleep, but I heard Mom's footsteps coming.

"Lila, sweetie, I made us a veggie egg scramble, would you care for some? It's already 9:30!"

I was so out of it and confused, I couldn't totally focus my attention on her. I even reached down to my heart to feel for the coils of protective light, the rope of starlight and heart light, that was no longer there. It made me feel vulnerable again, unprotected. I wanted to cry.

Mom touched my forehead and brushed my hair back, resting her hand now on the very top of my head. Her energy replaced the lack of force shield, and I once again felt protected, my energy back contained within me. It was as if I was tied to the Dream through a spigot at the top of my head, and Mom turned it off. Somehow, intuitively.

I was out of it for a while, and don't even really remember eating breakfast with Mom. My body felt foreign to me, for so many reasons, and it was strange to be within myself today. I was kind of irritable too, and I slightly snapped at Mom during breakfast for asking me too many questions about how my body was doing. I felt vulnerable still, like I was an open book for anyone to read, and Mom was reading out loud. I just wanted to go into a cave today, or at least just spend the day in my room, by myself. My body felt tired and drained, my mind the same, and my heart was all over the map. Part of me wanted to go back into the Dream, to feel the Oneness that was so comforting, to fulfill my destiny. I was also afraid, and knew that tonight was in fact *the night*, and it filled me with anxiety. Another part of me was strangely at peace, still and quiet within myself. Overall though, I was just tired.

I got a call from Acarya, asking if I wanted to meet up in town today, and possibly come over to his place after. His mom was making some ghee and Ojas balls and a Chai tea concentrate, and she wanted to know if I was interested in learning how, and taking samples home. It all sounded wonderful, but I wasn't sure if I wanted to rally. Mom sounded so excited about the proposal though, that she sort of convinced me to go. So I got dressed and did my best to pull myself together.

I met Acarya, not far from Mr. Peen's place (who didn't appear to be home), and we walked the rest of the way to downtown together. He reached out for my hand and interlaced his fingers with mine. I felt that zingy feeling again, but also more stable, from our hand's embrace. He seemed to sense I was in a more fragile space than normal and didn't ask me any questions, but rather filled me in on his evening the night before. It was a normal uneventful night, but he was just trying to fill the silence and relieve me of needing to. Then he thought to ask how it was watching Mrs. Pombokom's daughter last night. It was hard to believe that was only last night, it already seemed like days ago. I told him about our walk and how we saw a Rattlesnake, only the second one I had ever seen, even though they're supposedly common around here. He told me a story of a baby one in his mother's garden when he was younger, but it didn't even have a rattle and they were only told it was a Rattlesnake by a neighbor who saw it. I also told him about the Frog. I didn't tell him what they represented and how the rest of my evening went. I didn't feel comfortable telling him.

"Have you had any cool dreams lately?" he asked.

I felt myself flush with fear to tell him anything. My hesitation was telling enough though.

"What have your dreams been like?" He now asked insistently.

"Well, it's kind of hard to explain. They've been more surreal and kind of intense lately."

"Yeah...and? Tell me about them..."

I felt myself almost getting sweaty and kind of lightheaded. I couldn't figure out what I could even tell him. It all felt so crazy and unexplainable.

He must have seen this all over me, cause then he said, "It's ok, you don't have to share them with me."

"I want to. It's just sort of hard to explain..."

"Well, maybe when you're ready to, or another time perhaps." He smiled sweetly at me and grasped my hand tighter. He was so courteous and insightful. I felt so protected and supported by him. We walked around, not really having an agenda or place we wanted to go necessarily, and I suddenly felt like I needed to just sit or lay down.

"Can we just go back to your house now? I feel a little funny today and I don't want to be walking around anymore."

"Sure, of course. Let's go."

He talked the whole way back to his home, making me smile and even laugh with his comical way. He was trying really hard. I appreciated everything about him, especially today.

When we got there, Mrs. Varma was outside in front of the house, working on her Dahlia bed. She had some of the most gorgeous flowers in the summertime, their house definitely stood out compared to others. It was not surprising to me to hear that they had trouble with Deer trying to eat everything. If I was a Deer, I'd hang out there too.

"Namaste, Madre!" Acarya spouted as we got closer.

It made her giggle and she replied, "Namaste, son," through a huge grin.

Then she looked up at me, "Hello, Lila! How are you, sweetie?"

"I'm good. How are you, Mrs. Varma? It's lovely to see you. Your yard is so beautiful, as always."

"Oh thanks, dear. It's a never ending story. Weeds grow extremely well here," she said with a sideways smile. "Why don't you guys get yourself some of my sun tea I brewed. I'll be making some lunch soon."

"Thanks, Mum. Sounds great!" Acarya said enthusiastically and motioned for me to follow him into the house.

Their house smelled of spices, as usual, but also of some kind of fragrance I couldn't pinpoint. Then I noticed a small device, lit up with a blue light, a kind of steam pouring out of it. It smelled absolutely incredible and was actually kind of intoxicating.

"What is that smell? Is it coming from this thing?" I asked Acarya.

"I'm not sure what Essential Oil that is, might even be a blend, but yeah, that's a diffuser."

"Essential oil, diffuser," I found myself repeating out loud quietly to myself, committing the words to memory. I was entranced. It seriously filled the house with the most delightful, uplifting, sweet and floral fragrance.

"We can ask Mum what it is when she comes back in." Acarya went straight to the kitchen, as he pretty much always did, and looked around for some food.

"Mum is waiting for us to make the Ojas balls with her, but I can make us up a fruit snack plate in the meantime. Does that sound good?" he asked with his head inside the fridge.

"Uh, sure. I could nibble on something. Thanks!" I said. He was so nurturing, like his mother, and he also had the metabolism of a Horse. Seriously, he ate more than anyone I knew and he was still thin. It made me giggle. Gosh, he was cute. His hair probably needed a haircut, but I liked how it was curling out of his skater hat. He turned around with an armful of things and set them on the counter, then went to a cupboard and grabbed a plate from their bright multicolored stack of heavy ceramic plates and pulled out a sage green one. It wasn't on the top of the stack, he chose it purposefully. I had mentioned once years ago that it was my favorite color. It made me feel acknowledged. He made up a plate of multicolored Olives, Almonds, Grapes, and Apple slices, with something that looked sort of familiar but I didn't know what it was.

"What's that one?" I asked, naively.

"Those are Dates. They're only my favorite thing. Girl, you should know about them," he said with his skater boy/Rastafarian/wanna-be-African American sass he often had. I smiled again. He was such a character. Seriously, he represented all the cultures together. He embodied the One.

He led me into their living room, the one that was more for meditation and lounging, rather than the formal looking one that was to the right when you first walked into their house. Come to think of it, I had never laid foot in that room. How strange to have a room in your house that you almost never used. But this room, this room was a haven, a sanctuary for comfort and relaxation. There were pillows everywhere and a giant sheepskin rug. The fire place was in there, although it wasn't the season for it yet, so there were candles of every size filling it. Pictures lined the walls, and beautifully colored tapestries of finely woven silks draped over ornate black wooden hangers. It was what I fantasized India to be like. Acarya sat down and placed the plate of food on a large round table-looking cushion that was adorned with a stitching patterned with intersecting flowers. It reminded me of the Flower of Life mandala. I don't know how I hadn't realized that before.

The plate was everything I didn't know I wanted and then some, and I actually found myself vocalizing my enjoyment.

"Mmmmm, Dates are *everything*!!"

"Mmmhmmm," Acarya said, this time sounding and even looking like a valley girl, or an African American woman, moving his head back and forth like an Egyptian, dramatic and sassy. I laughed out loud.

"Acarya, you crack me up!" I said, hearing myself sound super flirty without intention. He did seriously crack me up! He was right out of a sitcom sometimes.

"Girl, you know I love it when you laugh," he said going back to his Rastaman swagger. Where he got this, I have no clue, other than maybe music and YouTube. He loved Bob Marley, had a huge poster of him on his bedroom wall. I think he always tried to be like him.

"Well, you're really good at it," I said, side-smiling but not looking at him until I knew he was looking at me, then I slowly looked up under my lashes. I was totally flirting with him, I couldn't help it. He pulled it out of me. Then I remembered I needed to go to the bathroom, and politely excused myself.

It was good I remembered when I did, I was definitely not in the habit of dealing with a menstrual cycle yet. Strange how much I didn't feel like me. I really could only describe it as a feeling of being 'out of body.' I guess in ways it was like being Liluye, in the Dream, feeling my body but my mind was simply witnessing it, separate from it. It was like my body was a woman's, but my mind still felt in many ways like a child. I cleaned myself and replaced my pad, and flushed the toilet full of pink. It was strangely liberating and empowering. I looked in the mirror as I washed my hands and noticed I looked a bit different, I guess a little older. I looked tired though, and it instantly brought me back to the realization of my mission. Then I thought of Acarya, and all that I wanted to still experience with him, and I almost teared up. I didn't want to leave him, I didn't want to miss out on us. Then, a more mature part of me, wiped the single tear that did shed and stood up a little taller, feeling pride in being able to be of service to Great Spirit, and all of life. I stood tall and inhaled a deep breath of acceptance, then conjured a smile that was actually genuine, and walked out of the bathroom with my head held high.

Mrs. Varma was back in now and moving things about the kitchen, probably preparing for some cooking lessons with me. I went straight back to the meditation room though, to look for Acarya. He was still sitting there, eating and looking out the window, into the backyard.

"What are you thinking about?" I knew he was lost in thought, which he often was, although he rarely showed this side of himself.

"Oh nothing."

"I don't believe you."

"Well, if you must know, I was thinking about you." He looked down and smiled, shyly.

"Oh," I said, most certainly blushing.

"Alright, children, are you ready to learn how to make some Ojas balls and Ghee?" Mrs. Varma asked as she walked in. I wanted to inquire more of what Acarya was thinking about, but the moment was over.

We went to the kitchen where Mrs. Varma had laid out some ingredients and gotten a large mixing bowl and a small sauce pot.

"First, let's get the Ghee going, because it will take 15-20 minutes on a low boil, and we can prepare the Ojas balls while the Ghee is cooking. So literally all you need is unsalted Butter. I prefer Organic butter from grass-fed cows, this makes the most nourishing Ghee. Classically it's cultured, but that's vary hard to find here. It's important that it's unsalted though, as salt will increase Pitta, heat in the body and mind, and Ghee should be nourishing and balancing to all three Doshas. So all you do is place the sticks of butter in a sauce pot and turn it on a medium-low temperature to slowly bring it to a low boil. Then I will show you what to do and how to tell if it's ready. Now, let's start on the Ojas Balls. There are many different types of Ojas Balls you can do, and sometimes I prefer to use my food processor and make them with Dates. Today we are making Sesame Seed Ojas Balls, with local raw honey and Tahini."

"What's Tahini?" I asked, interrupting.

"It's actually Sesame Seed butter, here try a little."

It was hard to clear from my mouth, so sticky, but had a delightful nutty taste. I needed to clear my mouth and took a sip of the sun tea Mrs. Varma had made, it was so delightful and refreshing with a prominent mint taste but also cinnamon and some other things I didn't know.

"I like to dry toast my Sesame Seeds by putting them in a dry hot Iron Skillet and stirring them constantly until they're golden and begin to pop. Sesame Seeds are a very nourishing food, and they build strength in the body, supporting Ojas. Remember what Ojas is?"

The smell of the toasting Sesame Seeds was incredible.

"Yeah, Ojas is the body's immune system and strength against stress and stuff, right?" I replied, hearing myself sound like a teenager.

"Yes, that's right. It's our wellness reservoir and supports our energy, wellbeing and defense system. Alright, so then we just mix them in a bowl with the Tahini and some raw Honey. Raw Honey supports the immune system by providing local plant pollen enzymes, this supports against allergies and sensitivities. Honey, Ghee, and Sesame Seeds, all contain the elemental qualities of Earth and Water and are nourishing and grounding. We'll save some of the Sesame Seeds to roll the little balls in at the end. If we wanted to, we could also add some spices like Cardamom, Cinnamon, or Ginger. I really enjoy a little Cardamom in them."

"That sounds delicious, Mum," Acarya said, standing next to her and peering over the bowl as she stirred, while rubbing her back gently. I loved how he was with her. I figured you could tell a lot about someone by the relationship they had with their mother and how they treated her.

Acarya went to the spice rack and grabbed the Cardamom and Cinnamon. "I like both of these," he said smiling at us. We smiled back.

"Alright, so you can go ahead and sprinkle in as much as you think, but probably no more than a 1/2 tsp each. A little goes a long way with these two. But these are perfect choices for our season beginning to shift into Autumn, they are soothing to Vata, and Fall is the Vata Season. Our digestion can sometimes need a little support with the heavier foods we start to crave this time of year, and the changing weather, so spicing is important. Spices help our bodies to optimize digestion and the assimilation of our nutrients. All the culinary herbs and spices we use are not just for taste, they're for aiding with digestion."

"That's so cool," I said.

"Yes, it really is. Our friends, the plants, are great allies, with a great Dharma. They show us the connection we have to everything around us."

I heard her words circulating through me. …the connection we have to everything around us…Truth! It was here, plain as day for us to see. Yet, we were blind to it, naive most of the time. I even knew of this Truth, so deep in my being, yet here in the waking life I forgot so often. The Truth was there for all to witness and experience if we were merely open to it though. I felt so much gratitude suddenly for Cardamom and Cinnamon and picked up the jars to admire them. Their lids were still off so I could smell the intense sweet, spicy, effervescent aromas. "Ahhhhhhhh," I involuntarily stated.

"I know, aren't they lovely? Alright, so now that it is well mixed together, we just need to roll it all into little balls, then roll them around in some more toasted sesame seeds." She demonstrated one and then popped it in her mouth. "Then taste test to be sure it's delicious." She got a big grin and wide eyes. "Yes, those will do. They're quite yummy. Well done with the spicing, Acarya."

"Yeah, they're tasty? I am excited!" He said as he grabbed a little chunk and rolled it into a ball, coated it with seeds and also popped it into his mouth. "Yes, those are delicious!"

I rolled my first one, a little smaller than they had, and rolled it in the Sesame seeds. Then I popped it into my mouth too. So so good. I felt my eyes sort of roll back with pleasure.

"Those are amazing! Probably the best I have ever had," I said with utmost sincerity, still chewing.

"Wonderful! Now maybe you can help me roll the rest into balls and you can take some home, Lila."

"What a deal!" I happily set about to rolling and Acarya joined beside me. We rolled up the whole bowl and placed them on a large platter. I had only eaten the one, but Acarya had eaten a handful. I was really excited to bring some home to Mom, she needed the Ojas boost.

"Do you hear how the ghee is slowly stopping the crackle

bubble sound? It's been bubbling away over here, on a nice low heat, and now the sound is becoming quiet. You hear? That means it's done. Plus, if you come look at the bottom, there's a curd that has formed on the bottom that is just about to turn a golden brown. You see?"

She was stirring around and the bubbles on top made it hard to see, but I could sort of tell there was a coating of something on the bottom of the pot.

"The milk fat solids condense and sink, and that's the part we strain out. There, will you grab that measuring bowl with the strainer and cheesecloth in it, Acarya?" He handed her the things and we watched as she poured the melted butter, now turned into ghee, into the bowl lined with the strainer. The liquid gold was mesmerizing to watch.

"There, see, now all the solids have gotten trapped in the cheesecloth, and what's left is Ghee, our golden wonder liquid." She raised it up to reveal its full glory. It really was a beautiful thing, and it smelled amazing too, like a mild buttered popcorn. It made my mouth water and I reached out for another Ojas ball.

"Lila, I'm going to send you home with some of this too. You and your mom need to be having a lot of ghee right now."

"Oh, Mrs. Varma, you are so kind. I truly appreciate these gifts of wellness and love." I smiled at her and then took my hands to prayer position at my heart and bowed my head slightly.

She mirrored the gesture and said, "Namaste."

"Well, what time did you need to get home, Lila? Do you want to watch a movie now or something? Should I walk you home soon?" Acarya asked.

"Well, I don't know. I guess I should probably go hang out with Momma a little bit. Maybe we can leave kind of soon. But I'd love to come watch a movie another time soon," I said slightly blushing, imagining sitting nervously next to each other on his bed watching a movie on his bedroom TV. It did sound like fun, but I really needed to get home to Mom.

So after Mrs. Varma jarred up the ghee and put the Ojas balls on a plate (she said I could just return to her sometime), we headed out, back down the couple blocks to my house. Acarya had run upstairs real quick before we left though and came back seeming like he had done something to his hair or something. I asked if he had changed his shirt, but he said he hadn't. It seemed a little strange though.

We chatted about various random things on our way and Acarya was holding the plate of Ojas Balls, while I carried the ghee. We both used our outside hands to carry the stuff, and held hands with our other hand. I loved that this was so common place now, it felt so good to hold him, even if just his hand.

Chapter 8
Celebration of Life

We got home and Acarya followed me into the house. I told him that I could just take the plate of Ojas Balls, but he insisted on carrying it in. I didn't see Mom anywhere and called out for her. "Mom, are you there? I'm home." I noticed the house looked particularly clean and shiny.

"Is your Mom outside? The back door is open, just the screen door is shut."

I walked out and was totally scared and surprised to find the whole backyard full of people.

"Surprise!!!!" They all shouted in unison, some blowing little party favor horns.

"Oh my gosh! What??" I was so embarrassed and new I was bright red.

"Thanks, you guys!" I realized right then that my birthday was already on Tuesday, and this must be a surprise birthday party. I turned to Acarya, who had a look that told me he was in on it.

There were so many people, I was completely overwhelmed. Lots of friends from school, mostly Acarya and Alina's friends, but all people I had been in school with for forever. I found Alina in the crowd, and she winked and hollered. I waved to her, showing my embarrassment. There was even Mrs. Pombokom and Dakota, and Mr. Peen. I went running to Mom and gave her a big hug.

"Surprise!! I'm sorry if this was a shock, sweetie. I just really wanted to do something special for your birthday this year. You've been such a huge help to me and you just deserve to have some fun. So how about some music and dancing?" She went to a stereo that I recognized from Acarya's room and turned on some loud music and everyone started dancing and hollering in joy.

"Thanks, Mom. You definitely succeeded at surprising me! This is nuts!"

"Well Acarya helped a lot, and Lina did as well. She came over to help me decorate out here, has been here most of the time you've been gone actually. I have pizzas ordered that should be here soon, and ice cream cones for later."

"Wow, Mom, you didn't have to do all this for me. I don't know what to say."

I was in shock. I kind of wanted to just go lay down on my bed for a while and not see anyone, or have a mellow night with Mom, but this was over the top and I had to play along. I was grateful though, it was touching to think that all these people actually cared enough to come celebrate my birthday. I started to make my rounds, thanking people for coming and letting them say "Happy Birthday." It really was kind of embarrassing, I always hated being the center of attention. Yet, this much love surrounding me was also very touching and I was tearing up a bit.

Someone tapped on my back and I was surprised to see Dustin standing there, dressed in clean clothes and his hair combed, he looked nice.

"Lila, I, uh, I just wanted to say thank you. You know I never really thanked you for standing up for me that day. You kind of don't know what that meant to me. I didn't even know at the moment. It was truly the nicest thing anyone has ever done for me. I just want you to know, I got your back."

"Aw, it was nothing. I just finally did the right thing. You look really handsome tonight. Thank you for coming." I smiled. He smiled sweetly back, and I continued my way through the crowd, feeling happy and proud.

I got to Mrs. Pombokom and Dakota and they gave me a little sandwich hug, squeezing me in the middle. Dakota looked so excited to be there and was dancing around to the music with a huge open-mouthed grin on her face. I twirled her around and danced a moment with her.

"Come here, bestie! Happy Birthday!!" I heard someone say from behind me.

"Thanks, Lina. How long have you guys been planning this? This is crazy! I'm so embarrassed." We hugged and laughed and enjoyed an awkward moment of acknowledgement of the whole thing.

"Don't be! It's your 13th Birthday!! We have been planning this for a couple weeks now. Are you surprised? Isn't it fabulous?!!" She was dancing as she spoke, and was scanning the backyard, waving to others as she talked to me. I was dancing a little too.

"Yeah, I'm in total shock. I had *no* idea. You guys really got me. Well, thanks for all your help. I don't know what to say. This is so much."

"Just enjoy it! Live it up!! Dance!!! Woooooooo" She started dancing even crazier, joining others. It gave me a chance to sneak away.

Mr. Peen was chatting with Mom in chairs in the back left corner of the yard. Next to them, I noticed there was a table of snacks and drinks, and there were streams of lights hung up. This party was planning on going into the evening. I felt my self, I guess an obvious introvert, pep talking myself into it. 'It's ok, it's fun! You're going to let loose and enjoy yourself.' Then I realized this may be the last time I would see all these people, might be the last time they would see me. It really was my celebration of life. I felt another layer of tension simultaneously form and release in me. I turned around and there was Acarya, watching me from the side line, with a look of utter admiration. We motioned towards each other, our side-smile flirty expression, sort of dance walking to each other.

"So, were you in on this too?" I smiled up at him.

"Maybe," replied Acarya, coyly.

"Well, you guys got me. I had no idea. It's a lot to take in actually."

"I told them that a small party of a few people was more your style, but they insisted on it being a big bash." He knew me better than anyone and I truly loved that about him.

"Happy Birthday, Lila. I want you to know..." He looked shy or nervous, but was interrupted.

"Lila, come dance with us!! Sorry, Acarya, I'm stealing her away." Alina grabbed my arm and pulled me backwards. I gave Acarya the 'here we go' look of concern, and he returned it with a look of 'it's ok.'

Looking around the space, so many people of my life in one place, it truly was overwhelming. I nearly felt myself going to a place of panic, and then I took in a really deep breath, closed my eyes and felt the love overflowing out of everyone's hearts and minds. When I opened my eyes, I saw everyone's heart spheres of energy glowing bright and connecting to each other, in the Flower of Life. There was only one energy that was 'off,' and that was mine. I tuned inward, closing my eyes, and felt the love of Whyla fill my heart, and felt my energy shifting, uplifting. I actually laughed out loud, and cried a few tears at the same time, maybe finally having digested the immensity of emotions, and all the love that truly did surround me. Then the music hit my body and I just began to dance. I started jumping in the air, kind of gentle at first, but growing quickly into a crazy wild energy release. I felt the emotions fleeing me. I felt myself becoming free.

I danced harder than I had ever danced in my life, still witnessing the spheres of glowing orbs all around us, including my own which was glowing brighter than anyone's now. It was truly incredible to feel, to witness, to be a part of such a web. Just letting sound vibrations move the body, mind and soul, was such a gift. It wasn't even my style of music, kind of techno but funky, definitely Acarya's music playlist. But hearing and even feeling the base in this way, and feeling my bare feet on the grass, I felt more connected to this body than I ever had before. I felt my feet connecting to the Earth in a completely new way too, feeling her heartbeat, in my pulse. I felt like Liluye; strong and unafraid. I released any last inhibitions and freed my body to the rhythm, completely letting go. I flashed visions of the last few weeks with Mom, visions of the Dream, visions of Dad. I was releasing my fear, dancing it out. I was more centered than I had ever been. I always had good rhythm, which I got from my father, and a memory flashed of us dancing together at a wedding when I was only maybe 5 or 6. We were laughing and smiling bigger than any memory I had recalled of us yet. It burst my heart open even more and I laughed out loud again. Then I felt a warm, caring hand on the small of my back and melted slightly in my knees. It was Acarya, come to join in the dancing. I looked up at him, and we looked at each other, a look I wish someone had captured with a picture, for us to see ourselves objectively. It was a look of completely mutual admiration and love, with me sweaty and teary-eyed, my Irish curls like a wildling and my cheeks bright pink with warmth. Acarya his normal cool-guy self. It was the picture of us, and the moment was precious but fleeting. Consumed by the music again, we both went back into our own worlds of dance.

An 80's song by Michael Jackson came on, "Bad," and everyone in the joint rose to their feet. There wasn't a single person there who wasn't movin' and feelin' the groove, feeling like a badass in their own unique way. Acarya was playing with his hat and twirling just like the legend himself. He'd obviously been practicing these MJ moves. I giggled a little, but everyone else was thoroughly impressed and whooped and hollered at him. He was a better dancer than I gave him credit for, and he really was the cool guy. Everyone loved him.

I then saw Mrs. Varma had come, she was dancing near Mom,

Mrs. Pombokom and Mr. Peen. The 'oldies' were really getting their dance on and I decided to go dance next to them for a moment. They all greeted me with various sweetness and we danced together beaming with joy. These were all the adults I looked up to the most right now in my life, the ones who I felt supported me the most. I was feeling the love and I gathered them up in a big group hug and squeezed tight, closing my eyes, as if I could gather up all the love and support and tuck it away for when I needed it the most. Mom touched my cheek with her palm, like she often did, and I felt her love pouring into my face.

"Thank you," I said, looking up at her.

"Thank *you*, for being *you*. I love you, Lila," she replied back. I teared up again with the immensity of emotions inside me.

The next song was a U2 song, "In the Name of Love," and somehow it seemed that everyone in the place knew the words. We all belted out the chorus together, "in the name of love, want more in the name of love, in the name of looove, want more, in the name of love!" We had gathered into a large circle and a lot of us were linked in arms. I saw again our spheres of energy spiraling around us with the brightest glow, all in a giant circle of white light. It was overwhelming and powerful and I felt almost light headed at the intensity of the energy all around me. It was joy, pure and true.

After joining together, belting our hearts out, we laughed and hugged, before we started dancing again to the next '80's song Acarya had lined up. I needed to go sit down after the last love fest moment though. I got myself some water and went to the chairs over in the corner of the yard. The adults were still dancing, loving this era of music. Their expressions told of their nostalgia. I loved seeing Momma so happy, having so much fun. She was singing all the words and really dancing hard. Made my heart feel so happy to see her smiling so much. I felt a sense of comfort in knowing she could still find joy, mixed with a sense of sadness that I hadn't seen her this happy in a while.

I needed a moment to my self and I needed to use the bathroom, so I snuck back inside. After using the bathroom, I opened the door and was startled by Acarya, who was waiting right outside it.

"Sorry, I didn't mean to scare you," he said laughing. He had a sweet but almost nervous energy. "Do you want to take a short walk?" he asked.

"Yes, that sounds great. I need a break from the crowd." I smiled at him.

We went out the front door, feeling like we were sneaking out, and Acarya grabbed my hand and started us in a skip. We were giggling like we were escaping being caught or getting in trouble, and we were giggling because we just didn't skip like this enough, it was really pretty fun. We went out the front gate and ran a little ways past the house, around the other side of Mom's car. It was twilight now, getting dark, easy to hide in shadows. We were still laughing, checking to see if we were followed or caught. Then I turned back to him and he grabbed my face with both his hands and planted a passionate, long awaited, kiss on my lips. I stood there for a moment, stunned, still closing my eyes.

"I'm sorry, I didn't mean for that to be so intense. I guess I've been wanting to kiss you for a while," he said. I was still a little in shock and a little loopy feeling, flooded with feelings and sensations that were overwhelming. Then I felt an urge from within that seemed to be fulfilling a major purpose or goal, and I reached up and wrapped my arms around his neck and kissed him again, even more passionately. He hesitated for a split second, caught off guard, then embraced me back with his arms wrapped around my waist, pulling me closer. He smelled of Sandalwood, the same as the beads I received from his mother, and it was both comforting and intoxicating. We didn't know how to French kiss really, but we just planted massive pecks on each other, moving our heads around and feeling the intensity and passion behind the pressure. Tasting each other for the first time. He tasted better than I imagined, and I felt a flood of sensations go through me, starting at my lips and melting down my body, wobbling my knees when it got there, which shifted our footing. We both started laughing again, feeling ourselves between two worlds, the childhood world of innocence and the insane world of adulthood. We left it at that though, and he grabbed my hand again. We giggled our way back to the party, using the side entrance to the backyard, by the garage.

Justin and Alina were walking towards the corner of the yard, in our direction, his arm wrapped around her shoulder. We all smiled at each other, the boys did their cool dude head nod, and Alina and I were both blushing very obviously. She made a look of "Oh my God!" but subtle so he didn't notice. I was so happy for her, it was everything she had been wanting for forever. Then I realized I felt the same level of giddy happy, which I truly didn't remember feeling ever, but it was also vaguely familiar. I squeezed Acarya's hand tighter and looked up at him, he looked back at me and smiled his signature flirty side-smile, and my knees felt weak again. How cliche. How perfectly fantastic. Love was utterly wonderful.

Mom and I then found each other in the crowd and she was smiling so big, so sweetly, witnessing our hand-holding and our love. Her look said everything; that she was happy for me, that she was approving, that she was also happy because I was so happy. That was the last piece needed to brake down the last bit of blockage from my heart shinning in full glory, the last bit of fear that I had built walls for. I felt my heart burst open. If I had been in the Dream, my heart light would be shinning brighter than anytime before, probably blindingly so.

"Would you like some lemonade?" Acarya asked.

"Sure, that sounds lovely."

He went to go get some and I noticed that Mr. Peen was heading over to say something.

"Happy Birthday, Lila. I hope you're enjoying this party as much as we all are." He laughed, "I haven't had this much fun in years. I don't know if I ever told you what my people's name means. Nisenan translates to "the people," or also sometimes "from among us." It signifies a lot of things, but one of those things is that we are all from One family. I am truly grateful to you for reaching out to me, an old sad man, and making me feel like family. I can't even tell you how much that means to me. Your father would be so proud of you, Lila."

His words hit me like lightening. I nearly forgot that he knew my father. Yet his words also brought a deep peace I didn't know I still needed. Without a word, I just reached out and hugged him tight around the waist. He hesitated a moment, then put his big warm hands around me, embracing me back. I felt his love, he was like the Grandfather I didn't have.

He was apparently getting a little emotional, cause he sniffed his nose and backed away saying, "alright, you're making me feel like the big softie I am. I better be getting home now."

"Thank you for coming, Mr. Peen."

"Oh please, call me Sam, and truly, thank *you!*" He smiled and walked away, making his way through the crowd.

Acarya arrived back right after he left. "Is he leaving?"

"Yeah. He is truly a wonderful man. I want you to know that you reaching out to him, and being there for me when I needed a job, was a really remarkable thing to do, Acarya. Not just for me, but really for Mr. Peen. He probably needed it more than we did."

"He just seemed like he needed a friend or two," Acarya said, and winked.

"I think that's what we all need sometimes, but it's an easy thing to say, and another thing to actually do it. You're a pretty great guy, Acarya Varma." I turned toward him and looked up coyly.

"With an awesome taste in music," he said starting to dance

again, this time in his exaggerated almost Bollywood style. I laughed out loud, and he grabbed my hand to come dance again.

We danced for what seemed like hours, and the strands of tiny white lights lit the backyard full of people, laughing and having a blast. Mom and Mrs. Varma talked for most of the night, looking as though they could be best friends, lost in their own world, laughing regularly. It made my heart so happy. Not only because I always hoped for Mom to have a best friend like Mrs. Varma, but also because I knew how healing it was for her to just be laughing.

"Hey, your party was Lit, Lila," A boy named Kyle said as a big group left.

"Ha, Thanks. It was definitely a surprise," I said, smiling at Mom and Acarya and Alina, who were all standing there.

"Truly, thank you, guys. I would never in a million years have thought to have a party like this. I wanted to run away at first, honestly, but this was beyond what I ever could have imagined. I had the best time ever," I said as I came in scooping them with my arms for a group hug.

"You seriously got me too, I had *no* idea. How did you keep it such a secret?"

Alina replied, "It was really hard, but so much fun to keep it a genuine surprise party. I'm so glad you enjoyed it. It was the best night of my life." She looked dreamy and lost in thoughts of you know who, it made me smile. "Well, that's my mom, so I'll see ya at school on Monday. I love you, girl." She came in for a hug. "Happy Birthday!"

"Thanks, Lina. Love you too!" I called out as she ran to her car.

Acarya slyly grabbed my hand as Mom and Mrs. Varma were saying their good-byes. He pulled me to face him and it looked as though he was going to say something, but he held back. Then he said, "Happy Birthday."

"Oh, yeah. Thanks," I said back, shyly. We were both so awkward it was painful, but our mom's were both right there. Then he took my hand and brought it to his lips and kissed it. It was sweet, but my lips longed for his again, and the thought made me blush again. I wanted to tell him that I loved him, that he meant the world to me and that I appreciated him so much. Instead, I just went in for a hug. I wanted to hold him forever, and I truly didn't know if I might see him again. I didn't know what might happen in the Dream tonight. The thought of not seeing him again brought a little tear to my eyes. I concealed it though, for fear of being caught and having to explain myself.

I breathed him in and exhaled my fear. The thought of him, and our love, would keep me strong tonight. I stood tall again, even a little taller than before, and said, "Thank you."

"You know it was nothin', girl. You know we'd do anything for you," he said in his cool kid voice he got, and wrapped his arm around my shoulder. We walked out to the car and I felt the butterflies return. Even though I knew I wouldn't probably be getting another kiss, the memory of our kiss was enough to light me up inside.

We turned to each other when we got to the car, and we smiled so big we started laughing. We didn't need to speak in words, we already understood the chaos of emotions that we were.

When our laughter subsided, he took my hands and this time he kissed the top of each hand gently with eyes closed. I felt the energy inside my hands activate. Then he formed our hands together into prayer pose, and he looked down at me and whispered with loving sincerity, "Namaste." It activated my heart and my belly, like an ignition in an engine, as if he was sent to me to turn on my energy centers.

"Namaste," I sincerely agreed back. I absolutely did acknowledge the light inside him.

"Aww, Namaste," Mrs. Varma said as she walked up, semi startling us out of our moment.

"Namaste, Mrs. Varma. Thank you for everything today." I was truly grateful to her, for the nourishing foods and taking the time to teach me how to make them, and just for her caring nature and all she always did for Acarya. He was great, and she had a huge part in that.

"Oh sweet girl, it is always my pleasure," she smiled and answered, in her beautiful British-Indian accent.

I decided to just hug her, despite the cultural barriers to such, and I wrapped my arms around her tight. She was surprised and made a "oh" sound, then wrapped her arms around me too. It made Acarya smile.

"Well, I hope you can get some sleep tonight, that was quite the party and a bit stimulating for your Vata. I would make some Chamomile tea and light a candle when you go back inside, turn the lights off and try to calm those nerves," she said lovingly but with authority and know how. She had no idea how truly lit up my nerves actually were, how nervous for bed I actually was. Although, I hadn't thought about it until right now as she was reminding me. I felt a tremor of terror rush through my body. Then Acarya touched my hand again, and I intertwined my fingers. He knew me better than I did and he probably sensed my vibe. I looked up at him and said 'I love you' with my eyes, for whatever reason unable to tell him with words, the truth that was written in my bones. It was the only moment of the day that I felt regret for. I wanted so badly to tell him, but the words never came. His eyes told me he understood and that he also loved me, just as deeply. I felt that Love uplifting and soothing my anxieties, and our hands grounding my nervousness. He was my rock, and I was beyond grateful for him.

"Have a good night, Lila. Sweet dreams," he said as he kissed my hand one more time and got into the car.

I watched them back out of their spot and start to drive away, doing everything in my power to harness the stability of Acarya's loving energy, and hold onto it. Mom put her arm around me, witnessing my desperate longing, unaware of the deeper meaning behind it. "Come on, let's go make that tea. Shall we?"

I had a million things running through my head, and it almost always came back to visions of us all dancing and singing our hearts out. The energy of those moments were so powerful. I think we could have lit the whole neighborhood with our energy if you could have captured it.

"Mom, that was probably the Best night of my life. I truly can't thank you enough. I also can't believe how you guys pulled it off as a surprise, I truly had no idea."

"Oh, I'm so glad, Lila. I wanted to do something special for you. This was a combination of Alina and Acarya's ideas, and I just sort of let them do the planning and the invites. I'm really happy you had a great time. You and Acarya are a pretty cute little couple too." She nudged my arm. I started to blush again.

We made some tea and continued to chat about the night. She filled me in on her conversations with Mrs. Varma and Mr. Peen, which were all pretty deep. It made my heart so happy to hear Mom speaking about the sacred ways of life, the need to make life sacred.

Then she says, "Oh, I forgot to tell you that Mrs. Pombokom wanted you to know there won't be a need for you to babysit this next week. Her mother in law is on her death bed. She refused to eat today, and I know from my work, that means it will be within the next week."

I felt a flop in my stomach. Somehow learning of Kylem's mortality coming to an end, made my own end seem that much more real. I felt a subtle shaking in my core. Mom touched my hand and looked at me with concern. "Hey, it's ok. It sounds like Elder Mrs. Pombokom is just ready. It's just her time," she responded to my look of fear and shock.

"Yeah, I know. It's just hard to say good-bye." I looked up at her caring, sweet eyes and felt mine filling with tears.

"Oh, sweetie. I'm sorry. I didn't think you would be so affected by this news. Come here." She pulled me in for a sort of side hug.

I just started crying, releasing tears of every sort, purging an over abundance of feelings.

"Oh, honey. It's alright." Mom stroked my hair and slightly rocked us, holding me closer and tighter.

She had no idea of the magnitude of things I was crying for, and I wouldn't burden her with them even if she asked to know. But being held and able to just release it all out, through tears, was the most healing thing I could imagine right now. It felt so good to just cry, in her arms.

"I love you so much, Mom," I managed to say through my blubbering.

"Oh, my love, you have no idea just how much I love you."

She kissed my forehead and then my right temple. I felt her love seeping into my head and melting down my body, my nerves responding to it with relaxation. She started humming the lullaby she used to sing to me when I was little, and I felt the tears returning. This time the tears were for the good times, a deep gratitude for all that I had been able to experience. Then Acarya flashed in my mind, and I felt a deep sorrow for the loss of all that could still come. I didn't want to leave. I didn't want this to be the end. If not tonight, then I didn't know when I would have the courage again. I was so full tonight, so much love to charge and fuel me on the journey ahead. I knew it was time.

"Honey, I bet you are just exhausted and overwhelmed with hormones. I nearly forgot it's your first period too. How are you feeling?"

I wiped my tears and gathered myself, "I'm fine, Mom I think you're right, I'm just a little overwhelmed and very tired. I should probably just go to bed. Can we just stay here one more minute though? Your singing and cuddling is my favorite medicine." I felt the tears returning, it was like a valve was stuck on.

"Oh my dear, sweet Lila. I will rock you and sing to you any day, any time." She pulled me close again and this time she actually sang the words, something that was truly rare these days, since Dad left. It both shattered and cured my wounded heart.

I wanted to stay there forever and felt myself actually starting to fall asleep, but knew that I couldn't yet and I jerked out of it and sat up.

"Mom, thank you, for everything you have done for me and all that you are. I am forever grateful to you. I really do love you more than anything."

I took her hands and, being inspired by Acarya, I kissed the top of both of her hands. I felt their pain and suffering, their relentlessly hard work and their sorrow. I felt my lips full of love and kissed her hands one more time, this time filling her hands with joy. I felt the power I contained and it filled me with a new sense of courage, a renewed sense of purpose. It was time.

"Have a good night of sleep, honey. I love you more than all the stars in all the galaxies." Then she kissed my forehead again, this time directly above the point between my eyes, the place where Mrs. Varma told us to focus during meditation. I felt an activation of energy inside me, and raised my head back up proudly.

"Good night, Mom."

"I am going to go to church in the morning, with Mrs. Varma. I'm going to check out the Unitarian church with her. Would you like to join us?" Mom asked as I started to walk away.

"I think I could use some extra sleep tomorrow, you go ahead and go without me. Sounds great though, I'm glad you two are doing that," I said.

"Yeah, I'm looking forward to it. Alright, I won't wake you then. You can enjoy sleeping in for once." She smiled at me. "Good night, Lila."

"Good bye. I mean, good night, Mom. I love you so much." She sort of giggled, just assuming I was extremely tired. I felt my body flush with Adrenalin, knowing I could really be saying good bye. My heart was now pounding loudly inside me.

It was hard to not break down every few seconds as I was getting ready for bed. The last time to brush my teeth. The last time looking in a mirror and seeing this reflection of this person I was only beginning to know. I regularly went back to anger and frustration, "why me?" Then I thought about our kisses from earlier, and how much I loved Acarya. I cried tears of sadness and longing, that turned into tears of gratitude and a deep, unconditional love. Unconditional. Just thinking the word brought me to a place of inner peace. No conditions, no swings of emotions, no judgements, just simply being. I felt my zen coming back and the love I felt and even saw in the circle of people in my backyard tonight. "In the name of love…" I could do this. I could release my own needs and selfish desires for this mission. If it was true, if it was indeed real, I could potentially heal all hearts and make Love the presiding emotion. What a powerful gift for the world. What an honor that I was chosen for this mission. I inhaled strength and courage and finished my evening washing rituals and looked, for the last time, at myself in the mirror. "It's been real, kid. See you on the other side." I laughed at my ridiculous humor and then felt Acarya's love in my heart. He would have appreciated that line, he was likely even responsible for me saying it. Then I had a lightbulb moment, that their love was truly inside me. That all those who care for me had actually given me the gift of love, which was stored within me. I could access this Love. It was my heart's light. This realization was essential for what I needed to do.

I got in bed, but my eyes were wide open now, fear and anxiety were slightly back and trying to take over again. I looked over and saw the golden wood beads of the mala, sitting on my desk and felt the urge to go grab them again. I put the necklace on as I got back into bed, and the smell reminded me of Acarya, making me feel instantly more safe. Then I took in a deep breath while hearing Mrs. Varma's soothing voice saying "deep breath in, full exhale out…allow yourself to take in peace…release out tension and worry...breathe in Love," lulling my body into relaxation. Then I remembered some of Whyla's last words to me..." You can only succeed, if you see yourself doing so, and you wish it with all of your heart."

I closed my eyes and a kaleidoscope of images flashed before me. Images of Life; flowers blooming, babies laughing, birds flying, a creek trickling, children playing, horses running, dolphins spinning, waves crashing, lovers kissing, a sunrise, a sunset. Every moment of my life flashed in an instant too; dancing with Dad, laughing at the river with Mom, playing with my best friend as a child, my first kiss with the Love of my life. Life was precious. It was fleeting but remarkable, a brilliant and beautiful mystery. It was absolutely worth dying for. I felt pride and strength and courage, ready to take on this mission. My last tear rolled down my cheek, and I finally fell asleep...

...I awoke into the darkness, hearing myself breathing and the breathing getting heavier, I honestly didn't know where I was and my heart started to race. Before the panic set in though, I recalled the Sandalwood beads (Acarya flashed in my mind), and breathing deep (Mrs. Varma flashed through), and I thought about Love (and saw a vision of Mom and Dad dancing in the kitchen and laughing together, I don't even know when it was). Then I heard Whyla's heart song, the painfully beautiful melody of everything, and I felt my heart light up. Shinning into the darkness, dim at first, but quickly growing in the remembrance of Love, my heart showed me that I was in a box, underground. There was dirt and roots and nothing else. I took in another deep breath, trying to keep my calm, mentally wrestling with panic. There didn't appear to be anywhere out, and the air felt thin. It was a serious struggle to not freak out. I closed my eyes and thought a million things, including, "how do I crawl out of here?", "is this the end, I sit in a carved out box under ground until I slowly die of starvation, thirst and lack of air?" None of the things I thought were helpful or beneficial to my nerves. Then I looked down and saw that I had the leather bag, but not the rope and not the walking stick. I reached into the bag and there was only the crystal. As I reached for and touched it, it began to glow. I could feel its energy like a magnet. It pulled my arm up, pointing its white light laser into the ceiling of this underground dirt box. I nearly felt stuck with my arm up, which almost brought on another level of panic. Until I remembered that the mind was in control here. I remembered that it was my mind that usually had me feeling trapped, not my circumstance. So I closed my eyes again, and allowed the crystal to pull my arm straight up. In minor fear that it wouldn't work, I clenched my eyes, as I thought, "I am above the ground, I am out of this hole, I am just fine." In a nauseating motion, I was forced through the ground, thrusted upwards, through an infinite web of microscopic threads, up into the dense forest. It took a minute to catch my breath and I looked around to see that I had no idea where I was. It was a dark forest, dingy and damp, crawling with bad feelings and creepy vibes, nowhere I had been so far. In this dense labyrinth of trees, everywhere looked kind of the same, but the difference was the feeling. Intuition was the only way to distinguish between the spaces.

This was a dark place, a place of fear and hatred, a place of loathing. It felt like mud, or quicksand, dragging my energy down. I could barely carry my weight forward. In the darkness, a light shined, or something reflecting a light perhaps. I pulled myself forward, with all my might, trudging through thick and painful bramble, sharp and clawing. I felt my legs slicing open and I began to moan. It was involuntary, and I gasped in fear of being heard. I looked around, checking to see if there was anyone or thing watching me, because it felt like everything was caving towards me. I bore down on my tongue to withstand the pain of the unforgiving thorns, not wanting to make another sound. It was agony. There was nothing more anguishing than trudging voluntarily through thick sheaths of needles trying to attack you. There was also nothing more empowering. I witnessed myself grow in size from the mere acknowledgement of my strength. I knew that I was empowered by something so far beyond me that I was a mere vessel of it. Then I didn't feel pain, I didn't feel anything but complete surrender and a revelation at the idea of *not* feeling. I laughed a "ha" in epiphany, and moved with ease, dancing my way through the pain and suffering without care, toward the shiny light ahead.

As I got closer, my focus lay on the light, that now seemed to be reflective and moving. I squinted to see more clearly, and much to my surprise, it was a small trail of water shinning some source of light from the heavens. It reached my feet, feeling cool, yet also slightly warm, perfectly pleasant and inviting. It was pouring towards me, growing with volume.

I remembered my first dream of Whyla, running through the waters until my feet gave out and she was there to catch me and fly me through the waters, and then the air, of the mountain-encircled bay. I felt the welling of energy I needed and called forth, letting out a giant heart song, to signal to my dear friend and guide. As the welling grew and intensified, all within a split second, I felt myself struck down, hit in the back of the head by something hard. I fell to the ground, seeing the legs of a man. Then it went black....

Chapter 9
Quiet

'I'll just leave a note here for Lila, even though I told her that I would be going to church today. I don't want to wake her, she clearly needs her sleep. I really am excited to meet with Mrs. Varma, and I think church is a great idea for me right now. Curious to see what the difference is between Lutheran and Unitarian.' I thought to myself.

Mrs. Varma arrived and I grabbed my purse and coat and headed out to join her. It was such a beautiful day. A cool September day, just like the one we… then I remembered what day it really was. It was 5 years to the day. I felt a jolt like lightening hit my heart and make me gasp for air. Anjana saw me and looked to jump in concern at my body's response. I opened the car door, shaking slightly, and she asked if I was alright.

"Yes, I'm fine. I just remembered something that was alarming to me, to my heart, I guess. It's nothing. I'm fine. How are you this morning?" I was going to go on to ask, but was interrupted.

"Are you sure you're alright? It looked like you were having a minor heart attack, or that you saw a ghost or something." She looked extremely concerned.

"No, no. I'm fine. I just realized that today is the 5 year anniversary of my husband's passing, well its actually the five year anniversary of his accident. Then he was in the coma for 3 more months, as you may remember. Oh my gosh, I'm so embarrassed that I'm talking so much."

"Tihana, This is all very good for you to talk about. I'm so sorry, love. Certainly, don't feel bad about speaking about it," She assured me.

"Thank you, and don't feel too sorry for me, he was an alcoholic. He had been sober for a few years. It's why we moved here, to start a new life, when Lila had just turned three. But he had fallen off the wagon, right before the accident. She was about to turn seven.

He had gotten really weird, having these dreams he couldn't tell me about, but was lost in daydream of them all the time. He wrote about them in a journal even, but I couldn't bare to read them. I gave the journal to Lila recently, she's been sounding like him when she describes her dreams. It kind of terrifies me, actually." I suddenly realized I was saying way too much and didn't even know how much I had just said. She was *really* easy to talk to.

"Uh huh. That's so interesting that they both have similar dreams. How did Lila take it when your husband passed?" she asked, sounding like a therapist.

"Well, she seemed fine for a long time, but also kind of numb, unshaken, like she maybe hadn't actually processed it. Then she was quiet for a while, sort of withdrawn and solitary. Then she started having dreams, and has been in a completely wonderful but oddly out-there space since. It does seem she's gone through a metamorphosis of sorts lately."

"Well, I think I can say the same for my son." She looked at me with a 'wink-wink' expression. We both started giggling.

"Aren't they adorable? I just can't be more happy for them with their love," I said, daydreaming of my middle school boyfriend, my first love.

"I couldn't help but push Acarya last night to tell me that they actually kissed last night, their first. He was so funny and spaced-out, I had to know what was going on. For a moment, I thought he was on drugs. Ha! He was fairly quick to tell me though. In our culture back home, this would be greatly frowned upon before marriage, but we are in America now, and I know how much they truly love each other. True love is rare, you know," she said with a dreamy look.

I just smiled, and felt all kinds of feelings, but mostly warm fuzzy happy feelings of joy for my daughter having had that experience, for having found love.

We got to the Unitarian church in only a few minutes, it was really pretty close, definitely within walking distance. Right as we got there, I noticed Mr. Peen heading in the door.

"I didn't know Mr. Peen also came to church here," I said.

"Oh good, do you see him? I invited him to join us, last night at the party," Anjana answered as she pulled into a parking space.

"Oh that's very nice. Yes, I believe I just saw him walk in," I said.

"He is such a sweet man, and I think he spends most of his days alone. You know there are very few of his people left, only maybe two who still know their language. Wouldn't it be strange to be endangered, or basically extinct? It breaks my heart."

"That would be so strange, and it is very sad. He actually knew my husband. They attended AA together."

What was wrong with me? I couldn't even help myself, speaking so many secrets.

"I didn't know that." She seemed to be pondering all that I had just said.

"He really is a very caring man. I am so proud of our children reaching out to him, and helping him out. Did you know they took a lesson from him? Learning of the Nisenan ways and history," I said, proudly.

"Yes, Acarya told me some of the things they learned. It is very fascinating for sure. They are under the assumption that we come from the stars, that we came on UFOs essentially, to this planet. That all of our ancestors are aliens. I found that part fascinating. It perhaps correlates with some things in the Bhagavad Gita, a sacred Hindu scripture," she said. All of which was a bit of a shock to my system.

I hadn't heard this part at all, the fact is, Lila hadn't shared much of any of the details with me.

"Wow, that's interesting. I hadn't heard that part," I replied.

"Isn't that fascinating and quite cool?" She said.

I didn't know if cool was the word I would use to describe it. Truthfully, it made me feel very uneasy. It was definitely *not* what I was taught was the origin of humanity on Earth.

We gathered our purses and made our way inside. Mr. Peen was near the back, Mrs. Varma saw him and led us over to him. We all nodded and said 'Good morning,' smiling brightly as we greeted one another. Those moments with the youth last night seemed to give us all more of a bounce today.

"Good morning, ladies. I trust you're doing well this morning." He seemed to smile directly at me, and I wondered if he remembered what day it was too.

"Well, ladies first." He gestured his hand to usher us into the pew beside him. There was a woman I recognized from the grocery store down the street, she worked in the deli. I couldn't recall her name, but we smiled at each other as I sat beside her. We were just in time, as the pastor was about to get up to speak. He looked young, maybe only in his early to mid-thirties. He was wearing nice khaki pants and a button up moss green shirt, but no tie, no robe, no symbol that he was the minister of this sermon. There was a guitar next to him though, and he had a laptop. He stood up with his guitar and started playing, truly incredible acoustic music that actually raised the hair on my arms. The way he presented himself, I honestly couldn't tell how old he was, now I was starting to think closer to 40. Then he started to sing, it was not a song I had ever heard, but it was beautiful and the words were of a mountain stream, peaceful and symbolic. I realized my mouth was slightly open and I shut it quickly. Embarrassed, I glanced around, to see if anyone had noticed.

Mrs. Varma leaned in and said, "uh huh, I told you that you'd like it here," and she sort of giggled to herself. I felt myself blushing.

When he finished his song, he set his guitar down and put his laptop on a podium that was fashioned out of pine branches, rustic and local.

He started to speak, "Good Morning, Everyone. Welcome. Our first reading this morning is from the book "The Prophet," by Khalil Gibran. 'Then said a rich man, Speak to us of Giving. And he answered: You give but little when you give of your possessions. It is when you give of yourself that you truly give. For what are your possessions but things you keep and guard for fear you may need them tomorrow? And what is fear of need but need itself? Is not dread of thirst when your well is full, the thirst that is unquenchable?

There are those who give little of the much which they have- and they give it for recognition and their hidden desire makes their gifts unwholesome. And there are those who have little and give it all. These are the believers in life and the bounty of life, and their coffer is never empty. There are those who give with joy, and that joy is their reward. And there are those who give with pain, and that pain is their baptism. And there are those who give and know not pain in giving, nor do they seek joy, nor give with mindfulness of virtue; They give as in yonder valley the myrtle breathes its fragrance into space. Through the hands of such as these, God speaks, and from behind their eyes, He smiles upon the Earth.'

Isn't that beautiful? Isn't that powerful? Have you been someone who gives from your heart? Willingly and without need for exchange, and without resentment? But simply rather do the thing so that the other is boosted up? It is so important to check in with ourselves and ask, 'Am I being a good giver?' If we can all reach out to each other in times of need, there will eventually not be any need. We can all live here harmoniously. It's not only possible, it's necessary. More so than ever, because we are approximately 5 billion too many of us. That's right, the optimum population of this planet for humans is around 3 billion maximum, and we are now over 8 billion. So that means we must rally together and find a way to make it work, for *everyone*.

In Galatians 5:13, in the Bible, Paul says, "You, my brothers and sisters, were called to be free. But do not use your freedom to indulge the flesh; rather, serve one another humbly in love." Isn't that beautiful? 'Humbly, in love.' Serve each other, humbly, in love. It brings a tear to my eye.

So, one of the people that we need to be a good Giver to, someone we need to serve in love, probably the number One person actually, is ourself. We have to give ourselves time, to do our sacred work in the world, then to rest and heal, to learn and to integrate what we learn. We have to give ourselves care, nourishment, and loving protection; not just with proper nutrition and a roof over our head or shoes on our feet, but with words, actions, situations and the places we go to. We have to give ourselves the acknowledgment that we are trying really hard but that we are innately flawed as humans. So we can be humble, and not expect perfection from ourselves. But we have to give ourselves a try too, a try to make ourselves the best version of ourselves we can be. If we are not actively assessing ourselves and where we need to grow, than we will possibly be broken, misshapen, and sad, taking each other down with our energy. In order to build a society that is giving, we must individually *be* giving. Giving first ourselves a chance at joy, then reaching out to our neighbors, seeing how we can help them. Allowing ourselves to be of service to Spirit, to our highest Selves. When we are of service, our egos release control, and our souls find each other. So I invite you to see how you can find joy and spiritual bliss this week, giving of yourself to others and to yourself. See if you can start a movement with those around you, a pass it forward if you will. See if you have a better week than you did last week because of it.

Another sacred scripture in line with this thinking, this time from the Bhagavad Gita, when Krishna describes to Arjuna, 'They are forever free who renounce all selfish desires and break away from the ego cage of "I," "me," and "mine" to be united with the Lord. This is the supreme state. Attain to this, and pass from death to immortality.' Wow, right? There it is. Let us also this week try to be witness of how much we use the words "I, me and mine." Let us aspire to use more words like "us" "we" and "our." So I leave you with my favorite quote, from the great Sage Gandhi, 'Let us be the change we wish to see in the world.'"

Then he put his hands into prayer position at his chest, closed his eyes and bowed softly to us all. I felt the words ring so true for me. I knew I needed to give myself more time for relaxation, I also knew I needed to be more giving from a space of unconditional love, especially at work. I considered myself someone who was giving all the time, but when it came down to it, I think the only person I was truly giving to was Lila. Everyone else I hoped or expected something from in return. I needed to treat everyone in my life as though they were my daughter, including myself. It was a revelation. I loved the vision of being like a fragrant tree, just gently offering of my lovely scent into the breeze, not needing anything in return except the joy in having given my gift. I believed those really were the ones who God spoke through, those who knew of God's will and plan. I felt a renewed sense of purpose and took in a deep satisfying inhale. I felt refreshed. I felt my own personal story and the heaviness of it lifting away. I didn't feel sorry for myself, which I realized in that moment, I had been.

It was such a lovely sermon. Nothing I had ever witnessed before, wholesome and unpretentious. I loved it. I had to speak to the minister and tell him how much I appreciated it. So I made it a priority after to find him and tell him.

As I got closer, I could see that he looked really good, but he maybe was even older than I thought, and I immediately looked to see if he was wearing a wedding ring. It was ridiculous of me.

He wasn't wearing one though and it actually gave me slight butterflies. His dark curly hair reminded me of my high school boyfriend, and his bright green eyes were absolutely stunning.

"Hi, I'm Tihana. This is my first time here and I just wanted you to know that I really enjoyed your sermon. It really was just what I needed to hear today, and well I didn't know what to expect but it was really lovely. I'm sorry, I'm sort of blabbering on, I will, uh, let you go." I felt myself starting to sweat. What was wrong with me? He had really kind of put a spell on me.

He laughed a little and replied, "Tihana, you said? What a beautiful name. I'm so glad you enjoyed the service today, and I'm glad it was relatable." He smiled and reached out to touch my hand. His touch felt like magic, a light and gentle yet powerful energy. He was very gentle in every way. I felt little goosebumps forming on my skin.

"Thank you, Jonathan. A lovely service as usual," Mrs. Varma said and put her hands into prayer and bowed slightly in reverence. He did the same and then said, "Namaste, Anjana. Will we see you at Meditation circle tomorrow evening?"

"Well, of course you will, you know it's my favorite group to be a part of. Tihana, would you like to come with me tomorrow?" She put me on the spot and my eyes lifted wider, showing my insecurity around meditation.

I surprised myself though and instantly blurted out, "Yes, that sounds fun!" I couldn't believe myself, I was like a giddy school girl. I just wanted to see this man again.

"Wonderful, we will see you tomorrow at 5:00 then," Pastor Jonathan said and smiled, a genuine and peaceful energy with it.

I smiled and felt myself blushing slightly, and turned quickly to conceal it.

Mr. Peen was waiting just outside and we all walked towards the cars together. He thanked Mrs. Varma for inviting him and said he would love to come again, that it was just what he needed today. Then he asked politely if he could speak to me privately for a moment. My heart started to race a little.

"Mrs. Hickey,…" Mr. Peen said.

"Please, call me Tihana," I replied.

"Tihana, I just wanted you to know that I am thinking about you and your family today. I know what day it is and my sincerest condolences. And…I wanted to say I'm sorry. I've wanted to say that I was sorry for a long time. You know it is kind of my fault that your husband isn't here," he said with his gaze shifting in different directions, showing his anxiousness.

"What? What are you talking about?"

"I should have been there for him. I was angry with him, for what I realized later were personal reasons. You see, I was his sponsor, with AA. I was the guy he called that night, and asked me for a ride home. He had asked me for a ride home every night that week though and I was tired and didn't want to go back out and get him. It was only 10:00, but I was pissed he called me again. I was pissed he was being so weak and had fallen off the wagon so hard. I felt helpless and that I couldn't change him, and that made me angry. I realize now that it was my ego that told me these things and prevented me from being a good Sponsor, and a good friend, that night. I should have gone to pick him up and bring him home. You would still have a husband, and your daughter would still have a father, if I had been of service that night."

"Oh, Mr. Peen…"

"Please, call me Sam."

"Sam, please do not blame yourself. It was by no means your fault that my husband chose to drink and drive that night. He could have called *me*, his wife. He made that stupid choice himself, because of *his* ego. He was in a weird place and he couldn't find another way to deal with it. I wish he could have made different choices, but he didn't. And that was none of our fault."

He looked like he was going to cry and that this was the first time he had allowed himself to believe that it might not have been his fault. I don't think he was fully convinced yet, but he was digesting the idea.

"Seriously, please. Don't at all put that on your shoulders. I'm sure he would have just done it sooner if it hadn't been for you trying to help him. That was the hardest thing I have ever witnessed, the couple of weeks before the accident. He was in most ways… a lunatic. I always knew why he went to alcohol; to numb himself. But I didn't know the depth of his inner turmoil, until that time." I started to cry, tears of every emotion running down my face.

Sam handed me a kerchief.

"I miss him, you know. I really do. Life is as it should be though. There's a piece missing in many, many ways, and also there is now a peace that couldn't have been if things were another way. The things that happen to us, happen for a reason, or a million reasons, and the lessons learned are the important part. If we dwell on how things could have gone, or what we think *should* have happened, we will drive ourselves crazy and miss the present moment completely. I really hope you can forgive yourself for ever thinking these thoughts of blame, but truly, please don't carry that any longer," I begged.

He reached out and hugged me, and I felt our connection, even if it was through the act of loving and missing another person. The tears returned. It was like hugging a teddy bear, and I didn't know how much I needed that.

I pulled away after a moment and wiped my eyes again. He looked at me and smiled.

"I'm really thrilled that Lila is learning of your ways and the philosophies of your people," I said, still gathering myself.

"M'am, you have no idea how amazing, no, I don't even know a good word for it…it means more to me than *anything*, that those kids are interested in hearing about my people and honoring their ways of life. That they care to learn. It truly was the miracle that a man prayed for on what he thought was his deathbed."

I imagine he was speaking in third person and was referring to himself. He gave a bit of a head nod.

"You have yourself a wonderful day, Mrs. Hickey, uh Tihana, I mean." He smiled and went in the way of his old truck.

"You too, Sam," I called after. I stood there a moment, just taking it all in and absorbing all that just took place, and feeling a plethora of emotions, but couldn't pinpoint a single one. I felt sort of stunned and numb mixed surprisingly with a sense of peace. I turned around to walk back to the Varma's car, seeing Anjana watching curiously, awaiting my return.

"I'm sorry, I didn't realize that was going to be so long. Thank you."

"It wasn't long. I am curious to know what you were speaking about, but I know it isn't my business."

"Oh, he knew my husband is all, and he remembered that today is the five year anniversary of his accident."

"I really want to get you in for some healing body work as soon as possible, Tihana. I'm sure that this is stirring up some of the old stored emotions and pain. A great time to release those stored feelings and thoughts, and to nurture new feelings. Maybe this week?" Anjana said with sincerity, and urgency.

"I would really love that, but I need to see what is happening with work and my appointments and I kind of need to be deciding what to do about my condition. My Doctors are all waiting to hear what my path is, of course they want me under the knife as soon as possible. I just keep feeling this hesitation in making a decision. It's probably just fear or denial, but I feel like I maybe also need a second opinion," I finally said out loud.

"Oh yes, you definitely should always have a second opinion with things like that. My husband may know someone. I'll ask him."

"Oh, thank you." It went silent for a moment, we were just

looking out the window, thinking our own thoughts.

"SO, I'm sorry, I just am feeling all kinds of guilt now, and I kind of need to confess something. I am suddenly aware of the fact that our house is actually more peaceful now without my husband. I mean, he was a loud guy and got really angry at times, about the world and injustices, but also about stupid stuff. He was just intense. I mean, he was a really good man and he made us all laugh, and he was the life of the party. But not having a constant party in my house, is really actually nice. I haven't allowed myself to confess this until now. I sort of just told this to Mr. Peen, but I really just told myself at the same time. Is that horrible?"

"Oh sweetie, no, that's not horrible. You're being honest and it is probably absolutely warranted. What you are describing is called Rajas, the subtle reflection of Fire and the energy of intensity, chaos, passion, action, and turbulence. This is one of the three Gunas, or energetic influences. There is also Tamas, which is the subtle energy of Earth and is dull, heavy, and dark. The last is Sattva, which is the subtle energy of Ether and is of the qualities of purity, clarity, and gentleness. It is said that disease cannot arise from the energy of Sattva, only from that of Rajas and Tamas. That is why we seek all things that are peaceful and serene and nourishing to our senses. This is what you are describing. Your husband sounds like he had Rajasic and Tamasic tendencies. You are now needing and seeking Sattvic ways and things, to heal and nurture your nervous system, and your soul."

"Huh, that is really quite interesting, and I think it makes some sense, a lot of sense actually. Ayurveda is much broader than I thought in how it paints a picture of life," I said, marveled.

"Oh, Tihana, you have no idea how much more there is. I haven't even shown you one full drop of water in the very full bucket." She smiled over at me. "But Pastor Teddy is a nice gentle soul, a wonderful example of Sattva." She gently elbowed me, smiling even bigger.

"Teddy? I thought you said Jonathan."

"Yes, Pastor Jonathan Teddy. Isn't that fitting? Sweet and gentle like a teddy bear."

I got chills up my arms again.

"You like him don't you?" Anjana asked me straightforwardly, with a grin.

"I, I mean, he seemed like a wonderful man. I think today is a strange day, and I just need to spend some time alone, healing myself and finding my bliss." I knew she was reading right through my words. So was I. It was all too overwhelming to even think about.

"Well, he is a wonderful man. I went to tea with him one day, because I wanted to get to know him better. We have been doing the meditation group together for about a year now, and it's lovely. He was married before too, when he was only in his early 20's, he's close to 45 now. He was studying ministry in the Christian faith, and then went to Cambodia to do mission work and learned about Buddhism and meditation and it changed his life. He leads a very simple life, teaching guitar lessons occasionally, and tending to some land just outside of town that his father passed down to him. If I were single…," she nudged me again.

"Well, I can't lie, I did feel a little like I was back in high school again. I haven't felt those feelings in such a long time. It was strange though, he seemed so familiar, like we've met before." I pondered where I might have seen him or known him from.

"Well, maybe you have in another life," she said so casually, like it was genuinely possible.

"If you believe in reincarnation, which I do. It's the idea that goes with the philosophy of Karma. Karma being the series of life lessons we are given and spend our lives trying to learn. It takes lifetimes to learn all the lessons, so you get recycled back into the wheel of Karma, and time. Once you reach Samadhi, enlightenment, you are freed of the bondage of lessons and you transcend the wheel of time. So basically, we are always going to have suffering as long as we are not actively trying to learn our lessons, and move past them. If we can simply see life as a series of tests and lessons, not being attached to the details of life, but rather seeing the big picture, we can move ourselves faster on the wheel. This is the purpose of Yoga. Yoga means "union," and it refers to the union of our soul, or Atman; that which is the 'eternal self' beyond the ego, with God, or Brahman, the collective or cosmic spirit, Great Spirit of all. I go to a Yoga class on Tuesday mornings, you should come with me." She sounded like she was speaking another language, and it was mesmerizing. I felt the loftiness and daydream of this amazing spiritual life she led. I would love to spend my days doing these wonderful practices. It must be nice to not have to worry about money, or working to pay the bills. I felt some envy for her life right then, and it prompted some resentment that was hiding just under the surface. I knew if I didn't gather my words wisely I might reveal my true emotions.

"That sounds lovely." All my thoughts about Doctor appointments and decisions, my breast, came back into my awareness. I felt suddenly warm, flushed with anger and overwhelm. I rolled down my window to get a little air. I needed to call my boss today and get back on the schedule, but I needed to figure out my Doctors appointments first, and it was Sunday so no one would be in their offices. Plus, I kind of needed to make my decisions of my course of action before I spoke to anyone. I really felt overwhelmed.

"Are you alright? You look concerned." She was so good at reading energies and expressions, attentive and genuinely caring.

"Oh, I'm fine. I have a lot on my mind is all. I still don't really know what I'm going to do as far as my medical path with cancer, and I need to figure it out asap because I have to get back to work and multiple Doctors are waiting on my decision." I wasn't planning on blurting it all out there like that, but it just happened.

"Oh Tihana, I wish I could take this suffering away for you.

Not easy things to decide and I am sorry you have to make these decisions. I know it's not my place to say or influence your decision, but if it were me, I would probably take another week to meditate and tune inward and ask my body what it needs to do, and I would also get a second opinion in the meantime. Making decisions hastily and based on one person's perspective sounds daunting and warrant for mishaps. Just my opinion. It might take some stress off if you just went back to work a few days and could focus on one thing at a time, getting some bills paid and feeling useful. It would probably be a good distraction. Just try not to overdo it, we want to be rejuvenating your body and grounding your energy through all this upheaval," she semi-lectured me.

I heard her wise words and they did offer me some relief, but I still held a tinge of resentment. Why did I have to be dealing with this?

"Thank you, Anjana. I do appreciate your thoughts. Yes, it probably would be good to work a little this week, and see if I can see someone else for another opinion. If I can work it out with my schedule, I would also love to attend meditation and Yoga with you."

We were pulling up to the house, as I said this and she looked at me and smiled, then said, "this too shall pass, including this life. Deep breaths and gratitude. Focus on having a heart full of love. I'm really grateful you came with me today, I hope you enjoyed it." She was beaming with a grace, and I felt all my tension soften.

"Thank you, truly. You are like an angel sent from God." I held her hand in my hands and looked in her eyes. She received my gratitude and I felt our hearts hug.

"It is an honor and a pleasure to have you in my life, Tihana. You and Lila are sweet gifts from God too." She placed her hand on top of mine and smiled sweetly.

I waved as I went inside and yelled out, "I'll call you this evening or tomorrow about the classes this week. I think I'll call my boss here soon and figure out my schedule."

"Sounds good, dear. See you soon." She waved and drove away.

I got into the house and it was eerily quiet.

"Lila? Are you up?" It was already nearing 11:00, she should be up. I put my purse down and looked around, not seeing any signs of movement in the kitchen, and my note still where it was on the table.

"Lila?" I walked back to her room, and opened the door. She was still sleeping, looking absolutely peaceful. I walked over closer and just watched her sleep for a moment, remembering all the moments of watching her sleep through the years. My favorite was around three years old, when she was at her most wild and unruly moment of youth. She was so feisty with me most of the time, but when she slept, her bouncy strawberry blond curls draped every which way. She truly looked like an angel. She always was a deep sleeper.

I hardly recognized her, no longer a child, practically a woman sleeping in my daughter's bed. I smiled at the thought of what she might be like as a mother herself, watching her baby girl sleeping and growing. It warmed my heart to think of it. I decided to let her sleep a little longer, and let her get up on her own. It was the weekend, it was the day after her birthday party, and it was her first period. She could use some extra rest.

So I went to the dining table and decided to call my boss. After a long but fairly painless conversation, he understood and granted me my choice of work days, so I chose Wednesday, Friday, and to be on call for Saturday. It was so amazing how easy it was to just ask for what I wanted. I was pleasantly surprised that he went for my request so easily. Made me think, 'I could get used to this.'

I called Anjana and told her that I wanted to join her for

meditation and yoga and that I also wanted to have another consultation, as well as some healing body work on Thursday. She was thrilled, but not as much as I was.

I felt empowered, a new sense of my Self; worthy of standing up for, worthy of asking for what I wanted and needed, worthy of having what I needed and wanted. I took in a deep breath and felt a sense of peace that I hadn't felt in a long time. It felt amazing. I realized then that I had something else that had been missing for a very long time. I had a sense of faith, a deep trust that everything was going to be ok. I felt it in my whole body, helping me feel relaxed and at ease. I closed my eyes and took in a deep breath, suddenly aware of the sounds of birds outside, and my heart beating in my chest. Life was beautiful, life was absolutely unbelievable. Every breath was a precious gift.

Chapter 10
Reunion

I heard a loud ringing in my ears, a high pitched squeal. I opened my eyes to find surprisingly that I was bound with rope. I was lying on the ground, with my face in the dirt. The back of my head hurt, throbbing intensely. I looked around and couldn't see anything or anyone, except dirt and brush and the trunks of trees. It was still very dark. I listened but couldn't hear anything, actually it was eerily quiet.

I didn't want to cry out, but I also didn't know how to get out of these ropes and I didn't want to wait for whoever put me in them. Then the white feather, that was tucked into my braid, fell softly on my face. I felt Hawk medicine in my heart and I let out a quiet but intentional Hawk call, a short whistle of sharp high pitch. I waited, then I did it again.

Then the return call, just one, and the familiar sound of air flapping under wings. It was Catori, I could feel him, but I couldn't see him yet. Then I closed my eyes and felt my heart beating quickly. I took in deep breaths, feeling now how easy it was to control my breath when I put my mind to it. All the breath work and meditation was helping, my mind was able to clear quickly, my body responded to my breath control nearly immediately. As soon as I relaxed, I felt my heart remember, I felt the connection to the Earth below me, and everything all around me. When I opened my eyes, there was a grid again, everything was energy, and my heart was glowing, but not as bright as normal.

"What happened?" Screeched Catori. "You don't have much time."

"I don't know what happened, or who did this to me, but I am stuck in these ropes and I don't think that I can get myself out of them. Can you peck at the knot and see if you can free it?"

He flew down to my back and began pulling and pecking and clawing, wings flapping around. He was trying to be quiet, but was also getting frustrated. Then finally he loosened the bind enough that I could wiggle a hand free and then free the rest of me.

"Now hurry...," he cried, frantically flying away and screeching his mighty Hawk call.

"Hey, how did you get out of those ropes?"A voice yelled from behind me. I whipped around to see that it was Mikasi and he was coming back with a rabbit hanging by his hind legs.

"Uhhh, I have to be going now, there's not much time."

"What do you mean? Stay a while," he said with a sweet voice and creepster vibe.

"My mission is time sensitive. I must go, now," I said with urgency and irritation.

He looked weak and scared. I could feel his fear.

"No, wait,... take me with you," he said.

My heart started racing, which I took as a sign that he wasn't meant to come, that I was supposed to do it alone. My mind was racing with a million thoughts. I was angry with him and hurt by him in so many ways, but the growing bump on my skull was kind of a topper. A small part of me also wanted to run to him like the little girl I was when I saw my Daddy last. He might not even know who I was. This could be my last moment with him ever though, so I figured there was no time like the present to let him know. Then I remembered that I was back in the past here, and didn't have the seed or the box of Shilajit. Suddenly, the ground began to tremor and a wave of energy whirled through the forest, knocking us both to the ground.

"What was that?" I asked, not meaning to vocalize the thought.

"They've been happening a lot lately. It still hasn't been light in a while either. Since, well, never mind."

"What?"

"I don't know. I have no idea why it's dark now," he said, lying through his teeth.

"Oh yeah? No idea why the source of light went out?" I prodded him and walked closer in intimidation and inquiry.

"No, I, I have no idea." He fidgeted.

"Wow, a liar *and* a thief...and an addict. You're a real winner." I turned to walk away, leaving my words to echo through him. Then I heard the words, and felt remorse and sorrow. It was harsh, even if it was true.

I turned around to make amends, and he was standing motionless, staring at me with a look of horror.

"How do you know so much? Who are you? Do I know you?"

"Well, considering you're my father, yeah, I'd say you maybe know me, and I should know a thing or two about you," I said with a newfound insolence.

He was motionless again, and then he nearly collapsed, his knees wobbling.

"Lila?" He looked at me tearing up.

"It's Liluye. Now, I really don't have anything to say to you, but I need the box of black powder and the seed, please." I reached out my hand and felt myself mimicking the teenagers I had seen, with a self-righteous pride. It felt great. I was uninhibited inside this woman's body, she seemed invincible to me.

He came towards me with open arms for a hug.

"Whoa there." I blocked myself with both hands out in protection and jumped backwards.

"Oh, Lila, it's so wonderful to have you here in the Dream too. This has been a long one and I keep waiting to wake up, but I am loving this epic dream."

It then dawned on me that he didn't know. Was he stuck here, in a dream, in the past? How was this even possible? It was mind warping.

"What year do you think it is?" I asked.

"What? That's funny, you're joking right? It's 2013. I have to admit, it is really weird to see you as a grown woman. I know this is just your dream character, but you are way more mature than I gave you credit for. I still don't get how we are sharing the same dream though. Oh wait, I get it. You're a projection of my imagination, right? That makes sense. You're probably the Forest's decoy sent to steal the…" he clutched his satchel around his chest, protecting the precious contents inside.

"No, I am the last remaining hope for the entire galaxy, apparently. You failed at the mission. Now you must give me the Seed and the Box."

"How do I know you are not just trying to trick me?" he asked with hesitation and fear.

"Do you want to know what else you didn't do? You didn't make it to my eighth birthday," I said.

He looked confused.

"That's right, Dad. You failed to make it home from the bar one night. You crashed into a giant tree, wrapped the truck around it. We worried all night and no one could find you until the next day. That was five years ago, to the day."

It felt strangely good to tell him what he had done.

"I don't understand. This doesn't make any sense. What are you talking about?"

"We are in the past here, but I am turning thirteen in two days…if I live through this mission, that is. I am willing to do what it takes though."

I turned around, not wanting him to see me getting emotional. Angry and sad at all the time we'd lost and how much I used to admire him. Scared at the thought of actually sacrificing myself soon. I felt all the doshas out of balance. This thought reminded me of Mrs. Varma and then of Acarya. I felt my strength return and turned back around.

"Now, give me the seed," I demanded, with a fierceness I didn't think I had and a deep seriousness.

"I don't believe you. It can't be. I mean. How would I be here then? I thought if I died..," he said, confused.

"If you die here, you die there too. But perhaps it isn't the other way around. Maybe if you die in the real world, but you're already a part of being here, you surpass death because of the weird time warp that's here. You are here in the past. Maybe you fell asleep first, before you crashed."

He looked like he had just been hit by lightening, as if it struck a truth deep inside him. His eyes were wide with epiphany.

"It can't be true. It's just been a long dream. There's no way," he said in disbelief.

"I wish I were lying, oh I can't even tell you how much. Every day I wish that you were still there with us. I wonder what things would be like if Mom wasn't working so hard and so stressed and sad, I imagine she wouldn't be sick."

"Sick? I, I,...I'm so sorry, Lila." He looked sincerely sorry.

It hit me like a power punch to the gut, but then also seemed to melt a piece of ice deep within. A large tear rolled down my face. I didn't expect him to say it, so fast, but it was obviously exactly what I needed to hear.

"If what you say is true, than I imagine it has been very difficult for you. I don't want to believe what you say, but I imagine you wouldn't be this upset about it if there wasn't some merit to it. You do seem a bit older than the last time I spoke to you, yesterday. Did you lose that tooth? Never mind, uh, I am just trying to comprehend the fact that I may have missed the last five years of your life." He looked genuinely hurt by this.

"It's hard to accept your apology, although I appreciate hearing it. You did bash me over the back of the head though." I felt at the knot still growing.

"Oh my gosh, I did. Are you ok?" He touched my head and turned it to get a better look at the bump. I felt the instinct to pull away. I still didn't trust him, and I was still pissed at him for so many reasons.

"Lila, it's me, your Dad. I'm here for you. You don't have to be afraid anymore." He reached his arms out for a hug. I was hesitant but felt myself walking towards him. He wrapped his arms around me and I closed my eyes. Even though we were in different bodies, I felt our energies the same as I remember them, his hug the exact same tight squeeze of ultimate comfort. I felt at home there for a moment, and another tear fell. Then I tried to pull away and he grabbed tighter. I relaxed into it for a moment, remembering how tightly I would squeeze his neck when he kissed me goodnight as a child. I felt another bit of the iceberg melt inside. Then Catori screeched from a nearby tree and I was jolted back to the here and now. I pulled away.

"Dad, I have to go. Now do you have the Box and the Seed?" I put my hand out again.

He looked at me and then brushed a rogue hair away from my eyes. He was staring at me as if he was trying to see Lila through Liluye, but I was no longer the child he once knew, and I was not Lila in this place.

He went through a million emotions and thoughts in one moment of subtle expressions, and then he backed away and reached his hand into his satchel. He grabbed first the Box with the spiral carved on top and handed it over to me. I opened it to be sure the black, shiny powder was still there. It smelled of sweet and pungent Earth. I reached my hand back to him, now inquiring about the Seed. He hesitated and put his hand over the bag, a gesture of protection and the desire not to give it to me. It looked like he was calculating an escape.

"Give the Seed to me…Now!" I demanded.

The ground rumbled again, and we stumbled to keep our footing.

"Look, if you don't let me complete this mission, there is a real chance that you will be destroying *everything*, including me." I said.

That seemed to strike a chord and he reached into his bag. He was holding it inside the bag, and I could see the physical reaction he had to touching it, it seemed to bring him peace. He closed his eyes a moment and relished in the feeling, trying to absorb it and take some of it with him, no doubt still debating if he should just take off running with it. I stepped closer, crackling sticks below my feet, alerting him. He seemed guarded, ready to defend the Seed.

"Look, this is how you can complete your mission. This is how you redeem yourself and stop hiding out in your shame. This is how you can change the image I have of you in my mind."

He thought about my words and suddenly looked sad, realizing that he was not my hero anymore. He pulled his hand out of the bag with the small piece of leather wrapped around the precious seed, and handed it to me.

"I'm sorry I failed you, Lila. I absolutely never meant to hurt you. I'm sorry I didn't realize how much my actions would affect you." His words went straight to that iceberg again, and severed off a huge chunk. It felt nearly like the blow to the back of the head, except the aftershock was not pain, it was liberation and a new meaning to the word peace.

I cracked a bit of a smile, and came in to hug him again. It wasn't the best hug we ever had, plagued with too many emotions, but I was glad I reached out to him one last time. I pulled away, without looking at his face. Turning around with my head held high, I went in the direction of my fate, and I didn't look back...

Chapter 11
Between Realms

Lila was sure sleeping a long time. It was nearly noon. I got a lil cramp in my stomach at the thought of something being wrong, and walked towards her room. My mood of peace and gratitude was shifting with every step. I knocked quietly first to see if she was awake and changing maybe, and leaned in to see if I could hear any movement sounds or talking. But there was nothing. I opened the door and looked up to see that she was lying in the same position, it didn't look like she had moved even a tiny bit. I felt my heart start racing and my breath quicken.

"Lila? Wake up, sweetie. Lila?"

I tried to sit her up and shake her, the whole feel of it seemed like routine now, or deja vu.

"Lila!! Lila Rose, honey wake up." The tears started to roll down my face as I rocked my lifeless baby girl.

She was more limp than usual though and I felt compelled to check her vitals. She still had a pulse, but it was slow for sure. She was breathing, but also very slowly. Then I noticed her lips were turning slightly purple. I laid her back down gently, and ran to the phone. Pressing 9-1-1, squinting through tears and panic, the number programmed in our brains since we were small children as who you call for help. I felt both extreme fear and a small desperation of hope.

I noticed her lips return with a little color as I laid her back down with proper open airways, and I just watched her breathing, holding her hand while humming her favorite lullaby. I must have shed a million tears, waiting for the ambulance to arrive. Visions of all the times I was able to rock her awake. This time, everything felt different. She was barely here.

I thought about Michael, and how many times I could barely get him to wake up too. They had an illness. They had something wrong with their wiring, that kept them stuck in sleep, stuck in their own minds. What kind of hell is that? The worst kind, if you ask me. I was so sad she had to succumb to the same horrific fate that he did. I felt in my core that she would be fine though. I would do every damn thing in my power to make sure of it.

The ambulance arrived and they whisked her off, strapped to a gurney, with an oxygen mask over her face. Through it all, she still didn't wake. A small part of me had I guess hoped that they would be able to wake her right then, and not have to take her away.

The next hour was a blur as I frantically drove to the hospital, was finally allowed in to see my child, witnessed them watch her blood pressure increase due to dehydration and hook her up with an IV, all while seeming mildly panicked that she was remaining unconscious through the whole thing. Their mild panic made my panic level skyrocket. My heart seemed to be one continuous thump, it was so fast.

After the first hour though, things seemed to settle. They had her hooked to an IV drip and oxygen and were monitoring her now slow and steady vitals. It was the hardest thing I had ever witnessed, seeing my baby girl in that hospital bed, all hooked up and truly lifeless. I thought it was hard with my husband, but this, this was an entirely different feeling. This feeling of helplessness was a knife in my side. My role of caretaker, the one who could always help her and hold her to make it better, was stripped away. All I could do was pray.

"Dear, God. Oh I know I have been asking for a lot lately. I know that I have been distracted with my own needs and fears. But now, more than ever before in my life, I need your help, for her. Please wake her. Please, oh please, God, wake her up. She is everything to me. I would take her place in a heartbeat if that was an option. Seriously, is that an option? Oh God, please, if you can hear me, give me a sign that she is going to be alright," I prayed intensely.

Just then, Lila called out, as she sometimes did while she was asleep. It wasn't coherent, but it was a sign of some movement in her brain. I took it as my sign from God, and felt a bit of hope returning to my heart.

...Catori screeched and flew forward. I ran after him, feeling myself channeling one of my four legged friends, charging forward with immense speed and agility. The Forest was my body, the pathways, along the roots of the tall trees, were my veins. I felt my heartbeat in the center of the Earth, pounding rhythmically, getting louder and faster. The drum was calling me. I ran as fast as I could with all of my might, charging towards my destiny. A small part of me also feared being followed and there was a bit of a feeling of being chased. I ran faster and so intently that I nearly ran off a cliff.

Catching my footing a split second before I tumbled down a steep and treacherous rocky slope, I stopped to catch my breath and calm down. I turned around for the first time since I left him, to see if he had followed. There were no signs.

'What now?' I thought.

I couldn't possibly go around this canyon, it was too vast, too steep to go down too.

"Squawk, you have forgotten all that you already know," Catori screeched from a branch nearby.

"I am in the past, I don't know things yet."

"Oh, but you do. Don't you?" He squawked again. "Time does not exist here in the same way that you know it to. Your mind creates your experience, and whatever you learn, you cannot unlearn. You are only limited by what you allow yourself to be limited by!" He screeched.

I felt his words digesting, and I started to remember. Wait, where was my walking stick? I looked down and realized that I still didn't have my glowing rope of starlight either. I knew they were necessary for the mission ahead. I couldn't recall when I received the walking stick though. I had just always had it.

"Catori, I can't recall when or how I received the walking stick. Do you know?"

"Screech, you must fashion your walking stick from the coils of all that you have shed. Those things that burdened you, will become the pillar you stand from later. It is out of the challenges of life that we may find the way to be at ease. Screech!" Then he flew away, back into the Forest.

I once again felt his words within me. I was so grateful for his guidance and support, it filled me with a sense of stability and hope.

I turned to my right, feeling that there was something nearby. I looked over to see a branch, broken and fallen to the base of a tree, basically propped right perfectly for me to walk over and simply reach out for it. As I got closer, I realized that it was in fact my walking stick, except the spiraled snake wasn't on top of it. I picked it up and felt my connection to the branch immediately. There was an energetic attraction, as if small magnets were inside it and my hands. I pulled it to my heart and had a flash of images of all our adventures together so far, including the epic dream sequence of creating the rope out of starlight.

I walked back to the cliff side and looked out at the vast majestic view. It was breathtaking, and I hadn't really allowed myself to stop and just take it in. I took in a deep breath of gratitude, and exhaled out a bit of worry. As I did this, the stick in my hand began to shift, and a small scale shape formed. I breathed in again and this time concentrated on releasing out my anxiety more intently. The large stick shifted and transformed in my hands. I closed my eyes and held the branch tight, this time going into a meditative state, searching my brain and body for all the pieces of pain, suffering, challenge, doubt, and fear, and allowed these thoughts and feelings to wrap and coil, manifesting into a snake. The snake grew as I remembered all the challenging times and all that I had persevered through. The realization that these feelings and moments were the source of my strength suddenly lit the snake into the familiar glowing white-blue light. The snake slithered around my body for a moment before wrapping around the branch, forming a spiral at the top that glowed brightly for a second and then all went dark again. My walking staff was complete, and I felt its tremendous strength. As I myself felt lighter, taller, stronger, and supported.

Using it to brace myself as I stood back up, I looked out at the horizon and saw the ominous tree in the distance. Just as I looked at it, it flickered a light, and within seconds the ground shook again. I knew that time was running out.

"I need the rope though," I said, thinking out loud. I stood strong, with my feet connected to the Earth, holding tight to my magical staff, feeling the weight of the bag over my shoulder, and I closed my eyes. I remembered and visualized the dream on the side of the waterfall, gathering starlight that glistened off the healing waters, meeting my heart light that glowed brightly. I felt how it spiraled through me and up the coiled snake staff. I felt how it connected me to the light. Then my eyelids began to glow and I opened my eyes to see that the rope was back around my chest, alive like a snake wrapping and coiling, gently, but assuredly. My heart was also glowing a bit, not bright, but noticeable, enough to remind me of the power within. I felt my strength intensify, my will grow, and I looked out at the horizon, at the distant looming unknown. I closed my eyes again and remembered that everything was within my mind's power here. I thought about being at the base of the Great Tree of Life and in a swift dizzying moment, I was there...

"Tihana, oh Tihana," I heard a familiar voice call to me from behind. It was Anjana and Acarya, running towards me as I was just leaving Lila's room to go find something to eat. The look of concern and worry in their eyes instantly brought my fear back into my stomach, and I was not hungry anymore.

"How is she?" Acarya asked, frantically, with a shaky voice.

"Well, she seems stable now, but she is still unresponsive. They want to start doing tests and possibly a MRI to look for the cause of the coma. They're worried there may be something wrong with her brain." I started to tear up.

"Oh Tihana, come here." Mrs. Varma came towards me with open arms, and as I hugged her, the tears began to pour again.

"She's going to be just fine, I feel it in my center," she said.

I looked at Acarya who appeared to be in shock. I reached out to him for a hug too, and he felt limp, lifeless like Lila felt.

"She is going to be fine. I believe it in my heart as well. She is going to be just fine," I said to reassure him, but really the words were for me to hear.

"Truly, Tihana, I know this may sound too esoteric or out there, but I truly have a really good intuitive sense about things, and my feeling is actually really good about this. I really consider myself to be a channel of healing abilities and part of that is knowing when there is something *really* wrong or only slightly wrong. I have to be honest, your illness is also actually in the category of only slightly wrong. Sometimes things haven't sunk in that deep, taken over to a point of it being *really* bad. Other times it has, and those times I suggest more of a pain management approach, and to simply make amends of any loose ends. But your cancer, feels similar to this situation with Lila, it is only temporary, a means of learning and healing. I have absolute faith that it will all be alright, even better than alright, in the end."

Her words were hard to comprehend fully, even though I was hearing them, I wasn't really understanding anything today. They brought me some comfort though. I came in for another hug, and whispered "thank you."

Just then, a nurse came to get me from the hallway, to tell me that Lila's behavior had changed.

I went running behind her, back to the room. Lila was moving around, writhing in snakelike ways, twitching randomly. She would yell out something, then she would lay still, and then the whole charade started again. It lasted about five minutes, and even though it was the longest five minutes of my life, it was a glimpse of hope. She was just dreaming. I knew that she was, but I also had every fear, worry, and doubt that she was just gone. She was so lifeless before, it was the most terrifying thing ever, to see her so lifeless. I would take this strange behavior any day, over the lifeless nothing from before. When it was over though, I felt my heart beat calming down from the running beat it was in. I was getting marathon level exercise just from the stress of witnessing my sweet girl going through all of this. It was so intense. I let out a big exhale and the nurse did as well. We both looked at each other with a look of absolute relief and nauseating exhaustion, having witnessed such an episode.

"I know it sounds crazy, but I think she is dreaming. Her father had the same...condition...and we ended up pulling the plug on him after three months in here, but now I am questioning if he wasn't in the same situation. My daughter told me a bit about her dreams recently and I let her read her father's dream journal. I wish I had had the strength to read it. I have a feeling there's a connection, and maybe even some answers in that journal," I said.

The nurse looked at me with even more shock than she had a moment before. "I'm going to go get the Doctor and just let her know what happened here." She scurried out of the room.

Mrs. Varma and Acarya were just behind me, somehow they had bypassed security clearance in the excitement and were just there in the room, having witnessed the whole thing and heard my proposed explanation. It was such a relief, that they were here with me. I just turned around and started crying, knowing that they were there with me allowed me to be less strong. They both hugged me tight, a group hug of deep healing, and so much shared love for Lila. I wiped my tears quickly, for fear of missing something else that may happen.

"Look at her. Now she's so peaceful, so serene. A total juxtaposition. What a cruel and hideous joke this all seems. Why, God? Why are you forcing me to witness this again? Why?" I pleaded out loud.

"I know you're not actually looking for answers right now, and I hate to even speak, but everything in me is telling me to tell you, that perhaps the question you should actually ask God is, 'What am I supposed to learn from this? What is my lesson?' If we can see everything we experience as a lesson, we will be utilizing our lessons for a more rapid growth, and this is the purpose of life," Anjana lectured. I agreed, but it was harsh timing.

"I don't particularly want to hear that right now," I said with anger. But then I really heard her words, and mine. "I'm sorry, I didn't mean to be rude. You're wise and kind, and I appreciate you two being here." I looked in both of their tender and caring eyes.

"We are all here only for a fleeting moment and that fleeting moment is precious. If it doesn't weird you both out, I would like to sit in prayer and offer Lila some guidance from the Spirit world," she said with a calmness. I didn't know if what she said was possible, but the idea of it made me both uneasy and relieved.

"Yes, that sounds lovely. Thank you, Anjana. Thank you for

your support," I said, tearing up again.

Poor Acarya seemed shell-shocked still and hadn't said much of anything since they arrived. I touched his arm and conjured what I could of a smile. I didn't know what I would do without them here. Thank God for those people that show up in life right when you need someone. They are angels, in my humble opinion, and we should always be on the lookout for them, and be grateful for them.

———————

…Staring up at this great mountain of a tree, I felt like the size of an ant or smaller. It was overwhelming, and its energy was palpable, as if I could reach out to the air and feel the Tree's exhale. It was intimidating and frightening, and absolutely powerful. Then I winced my face in disapproval of those thoughts and cleared them away. It was a nurturing, and serene, and perfectly still, Tree. It was harmless. I was being silly. Although, my gut was never wrong.

I stood there a moment, wondering what my next move should be. Should I prepare the ritual of seed planting again? Would I be pulled in with it again? Was there more for me to accomplish before I did this? Was there another way?

I pondered these questions and a hundred more, then scanned around, looking for an alternative plan. Suddenly, a flash of light came from the Tree, shot through my body, shaking me and everything around, violently. I would have fallen but I braced myself with my magic staff. As the ground settled, I felt a compulsion to reach out to the great Tree, my hand guiding my movement forward, to offer some comfort. It was so massive though, that I could barely get to the trunk, its gnarled root structures acting like a royal guard. As I climbed over the last root bump, I finally touched the magnificent trunk in front of me, the being that had been haunting me for weeks.

My hand was dwarfed by the unfathomable size. Even a small fragment of bark was larger than my head. Yet as I touched it, as small as my hand was against it, I could feel its pain and suffering. I could also feel that my hand's energy was acknowledged by it. It even seemed to make a creak sound, as I touched it. I felt our connection. The connection between my palm and this magnificent life giver, created a ribbon of energy that streamed right to my heart, lighting it again, brightly. Then my heart's energy went back through my hand into the massive Tree. I traced the ribbon of energy, slithering and spiraling around and through the great Tree of Life. My eyes were closed, but I could see clearly the path of energy, with my mind. I followed it all the way up to a point, about half way up the mountainous trunk, where the energy suddenly stopped and was attracted, hovering like a moth to a flame, curious and obsessed. It was painful, but pain like heartache, pain like loss. I just observed it, felt it, and held energy there. Then I thought, 'What is the antidote for heartache and loss?...Love!' The second I thought it, a light switch seemed to turn on, and a bright beam of light shined through the spot. For a moment, I naively thought that I had just fixed the problem, and I opened my eyes and let my hand go. The light went out immediately. I put my hand back on quickly, but the energy stream and awareness of the insides of the Tree was gone. I concentrated back on my heart and felt it light up, holding the word and feeling of 'Love' in my heart. I felt the energy stream return and grow and slither back down my arm into the trunk and back up to the spot. This time, I noticed that there was a branch broken in the spot that I was attracted to like a magnet, and it appeared as though something had done it, a giant blunt force from above. I couldn't quite tell what was going on, so I decided I should maybe get a closer look. I opened my eyes and pulled my hand away again, looking up at the vastness of branches above me. It was daunting to think of climbing it, but then I remembered I could just close my eyes and go there with my mind. In one swift, dizzying moment, I arrived. It was definitely an interesting scene, and did appear as though something had broken the branch. I didn't know if there was something missing or what, but I felt like there was a hole where something used to be, in front of the broken branch, making it an even larger hole. I looked around and saw that there were cones dangling in various places, the exact size of what seemed to be missing from the hole in front of me. I looked down toward the ground and couldn't even see the ground, I was so high up. It made me wobble in the recognition. It was surprising that even here, even in this strong and fearless body, I was still afraid of heights. 'Seriously?' I looked down again. 'Yup, seriously.' I had to recover for a few breaths. Then I held the branch at the broken point and tried to feel my energy connecting to it again. This time all I felt was loss and sorrow, and I couldn't seem to get past it. It was starting to build up an anger and frustration, because I couldn't help the situation, because I didn't know what to do. Then I allowed myself to just sit for a moment on the branch I had landed on. I tuned inward and asked, as I had done before, "How can I help you, Great Tree? What am I supposed to do?"

A voice from within, my own voice, my voice as Lila not Liluye, answered, "Forgiveness."

I felt a tear roll down my face and I knew that Mikasi had done this. How was I supposed to forgive him? It wasn't my place to, it was the Tree's place to. Then the familiar wailing of the ominous dancing characters above, cried their mourning song. I felt compelled to go talk to them. So I closed my eyes and imagined being up in their crow's nest, and once again, in a whirl, I was there.

They gasped at my abrupt arrival, and wailed and moaned, and the tree responded with a light flicker which reverberated across the ground again. I hushed them and motioned for them to calm down.

"It's alright, I won't hurt you, you are alright." I gently reached my hand out, like I would do for a new dog I met, being inquisitive but gentle. I felt like they would respond to subtleties or gestures more than my words. They reminded me of squirrels, fast and erratic, swirling around each other, frightened of me. One was more feminine with long shiny silver hair, the other more masculine, but they both wore robes of flowing sheer 'fabric' of various green hues of energy. Their skin glowed with a green iridescence and their eyes glowed a dim white light.

"Shhhh, it's ok, it's alright. I'm a friend." I reached out my hand again, and once again they felt threatened and scurried about. Then I just sat down, crossed my legs and closed my eyes. I concentrated on deep breaths and calming down. I allowed myself to drift into meditation.

Before I knew it, they were investigating me, curious of me, poking, prodding and assessing. They began whispering questions. They whispered a million questions at the same time, in an intense barrage. It was everything in me to just stay centered and calm. I kept my eyes closed, and concentrated on keeping my face relaxed. Their questions were vast and varied, some common, some crude. The ones that seemed to stand out to me, among the literal millions of questions that they purged out at rapid speed, were:

"Why are you here?" "What do you think you can do?" "Who are you to be on this mission?" "What have you done?" "Am I dying?" "What did you do?" "What is going to happen?" "Why did you do it?" "When will it stop?" "Are you dying?" "When will the pain stop?" "Why are you hurting me?" "Are we dying?" "When will you stop hurting me?" "Is she dying?" "Is this the end?"

I felt a welling up inside, as much as I tried to resist their energy, I was susceptible to their fears and mind tricks. Their energy leaked in slowly despite my best efforts to not allow it. Soon I had reached my point, I couldn't handle it anymore.

"Enough!" I yelled.

They hushed and seemed frightened of me, clutching to each other, wide-eyed.

"Now tell me, what must I do?"

"You must fix it. You must heal her," they said in unison.

"Fix what? The broken branch?"

"You must return the missing piece, heal the wound, make whole again." They both spoke together. Their speech was a combination of speaking normally, soft whispers, and harsh fast tones. Somehow I could make out what they said each time, but not without every hair on my body standing on end. It was disturbing and weird.

"What is the missing piece?"

They just moaned, their incessant cry that filled the Forest and my heart with ache.

"How do I heal the wound? What do I specifically need to do? What is the missing piece?"

"Love!!" They shouted, and then started to sing and dance with each other. "Love, Love, Love." Their dance was for a moment joyful and playful, uplifted and light. I partially smiled.

I felt the power of the word moving around me and inside me. As the energy of the word Love reached my heart, it lit brightly, shinning into the dusk around us. It empowered me from my core. The Tree responded with a dim glow, but even a dim light, in this darkness, was illuminating. The dancers twirled each other and laughed, making sounds like children.

Then I felt an attraction to my satchel and reached inside and pulled out the precious Seed. It was glowing dimly too. The Dancers gasped and held each other in comfort, then they rapidly and with intensity and anger in their eyes came at me. They were made of energy though and they couldn't actually touch me, they just went straight through me, like ghosts. They clawed and scratched anyway, screaming a high pitch cry. My heart started beating rapidly again, in fear. The light in my heart went out, like a switch had been turned off, and the Tree flickered again, causing a pulse wave through the Forest again.

The Dancers backed away, showing more signs of fear and anxiety, clutching once again to each other and continuing their melancholic moaning. I held out the Seed, and laid it on the ground in between us. It looked like an egg in this nest-like space, glowing dimly with its own fragile strength. You could feel its essence of innocence and unlimited potential, it was *filled* with pure Love.

I asked, "Is this the missing piece?"

They twirled around each other, again like squirrels, and chattered a lot of sounds that were unrecognizable as words, but held a multitude of emotions. I felt their mixture of confusion, fear, anxiety, sorrow, joy and desperation.

"Where did you get that?" One asked.

The other asking, "Did you steal that from us?"

"No, I didn't steal it. It was given to me. I want to return it." I reached my hands out, with it, in offering.

They wailed and moaned and twirled about again, as if they were almost afraid of it, but also just wallowing in their self-pity that it was taken from them.

"What do I do with it? How do I give it back?"

They didn't answer, only repeated their annoying squirreling. Now recognizing that I was beginning to get frustrated, they were getting more anxious.

I checked in with myself and took in a deep breath, closing my eyes, and exhaled long and slow, feeling it calm my heartbeat, mind and nerves again. I held the Seed to my heart and I asked in my mind, "Great Spirit, the core of everything that is, please guide me, tell me, what am I supposed to do?" Without words, I just suddenly knew. I carefully wrapped the seed back up and put it back into my bag.

"I am sorry you two are so distraught. I know it is confusing times, but you will be ok, everything will be alright. I know what I must do. Thank you for all you have taught me. I love you, and I forgive you." I felt the words leave my lips as if they were an entity, a bubble of energy that floated to them and popped in their face. They were taken back, and for the first time, they were nearly silent.

I turned around and thought about being on the ground, and in a flash once again, I was there, back at the base of the great Tree...

"Mr. Peen, what are you doing here?" I asked, surprised to see him in the hospital lobby, but strangely comforted by his presence.

"Mrs. Varma called me. Am I overstepping bounds? I should go."

"No, no, it's good to have you here. I am just in a bit of shock right now over everything."

"Yeah, I didn't know how to help, so I've just been sitting here praying to Great Spirit to protect her. I have to admit, I haven't spent a lot of time lately in communion with God, so I am not sure how much I am affecting things." He said with his head lowered down.

"You *are* helping. It is helpful for me at least, it gives me some peace of heart and mind, knowing that I'm not the only one praying." I smiled at him and touched his arm.

"Well, I also wanted to offer some insight, some things that your husband told me the night before his accident, when I brought him home from the bar," he said, and I felt my heart flutter.

"Yes?"

"Well, he was telling me about these dreams he'd been having and how he was scared because he was starting to not be able to control them. He said he was scared that they were taking over him and he was afraid his mind would be lost there forever if he stopped fighting against it. I didn't really know what he meant, but he said something about how it was hard for you to wake him up sometimes, that he'd be asleep for half a day and not know it."

"Yes, it's true."

"Well, I don't know if there's a connection here at all, but I wonder if Lila has the same thing happening."

"Yes, I believe she does, you're right. I've sort of mentioned this to the neurologist."

"I also want to say again, that I am truly sorry I wasn't there for your husband that night. I know that there's no way to change the past, but I would give anything to change my choice that night. I believe he was suffering from a real mental illness or biochemical imbalance, or maybe…Mrs. Hickey? I came here to also offer another perspective as well. It's one I think about all the time. My grandmother used to have dreams about a place that sounded so much like what Michael would describe. A place with mighty trees and talking animals, and an energy that was deeply powerful. I always dismissed this connection when he would speak of it, but now that I hear about sweet Lila, well, I have to wonder."

"What? You mean to tell me that your grandmother, my husband, and my daughter may have all had the same dream? I am ashamed to admit this, but I haven't brought myself to read my husband's dream journal and Lila seems to know that I don't want to talk about hers. It was just too painful and too much to comprehend, if it was a genetic thing or something that they suffered from…but now, I feel extremely guilty. I told them to turn off his air machine. I pulled the plug on him." I started to sob at the idea that my husband was just in a coma because he was in a dream. He might have actually woken up at some point. He hadn't shown much brain activity in over a week though. The thought that I killed him was overwhelming and incomprehensible.

"Tihana, you certainly aren't at fault for your husband's passing. Please don't blame yourself." His hand was on my arm now, just exactly as I was to him earlier today when I told him it wasn't his fault.

"Well, aren't we just a pair?" I said and wiped away a tear that had rolled down his cheek, then I wiped away my own tears.

I took in a deep breath and cleared my throat and said, "I need to release my guilt, I need to let go of him. It is in the past, and Lila needs my love and energy now. If I don't release all the emotions I have around him, I fear it will cost me my life. I believe it is manifesting into the cancer that I have growing in my breast."

I couldn't believe it when I said it. It was only the second time I had said it out loud. The first time was to Lila, but I was so detached from it then. Now it felt real, and the weight shrunk me a few inches.

"Oh, Tihana, I'm so sorry, I didn't know," he said, alarmed.

"No, it's alright, I'm going to be fine. It's treatable and I didn't even mean to bring myself up right now. This is not about me. My point is simply, that there may be a connection with everything, that's all."

"Well, that's definitely true, we are all greatly and deeply connected. There's nothing that doesn't fit in the great wheel of life, even all the things we can't explain and wish wouldn't be. It's all part of the bigger puzzle of Great Spirit."

This brought an unexpected deep peace to my heart, and I closed my eyes as it reverberated through my body.

"Thank you. Your presence soothes my soul." I touched his hand.

"Tihana, it's Lila, come quickly," Mrs. Varma called for me from the hall where Lila's room was. My heart started racing and I ran faster than I knew I could.

<hr>

...I looked up at the giant Tree that loomed above me. It was more majestic and magnificent than I could really understand, but I felt Her. I felt a presence that was the most powerful and most gentle, the most wise and most simple, absolutely pure. There was an aura of energy that emanated from her great cylindrical frame. It produced the overwhelming feeling that this world had, that was intoxicating, and was what had my father trapped here, in his addiction. The energy was love, pure unconditional Love. My heart light turned back on, brightly, and the rope around my chest lit up even brighter, and began to slither around me, as if it were alive again. I watched it as it slithered down my body and across the ground, along the exposed tangled roots, and around the great Tree's trunk. The ground trembled gently but intensely, a building up of energy. I felt compelled to touch Her again, so I climbed up the root structures and wrapped my whole body around the base. The snake-like rope coiled around the tree at about my waist line and I could feel it charging up my core, like a battery. I could barely stretch myself to wrap around this great Tree, and I covered only a small percentage of its enormity, but my whole body pressed against Her intently connecting. Suddenly, a flood of memories of my life in the real world came through my mind. It was strange how they felt both foreign and familiar. I saw Mom cradling me and singing. I saw Dad and myself running through our favorite meadow by the park, laughing loudly. I saw Acarya and me kissing our magical first kiss. I saw JoJo the cuddly cat purring as I snuggled her. I saw a flash of all the people I've ever known as they laughed or smiled, and my heart felt more full than I had ever experienced before. My heart literally felt like a balloon, expanding and growing. It was strange and disconcerting, it really seemed like I could explode. Then Mikasi came into my mind, and for a moment I felt a shift away from Love, but the Love was too overpowering and it wrapped around him too. I felt the energy of forgiveness, a sense of sympathy and compassion. These feelings grew into another snake-like energy stream that slithered from my heart into the mighty trunk, this time knowing right where to go. I saw in my mind, as the coil of energy wrapped around the broken branch and once again lit a bright light through the hole. I felt a shifting of energy there and felt myself crying, or the energy of crying. There were no tears or other physical expressions, but the feeling within me was that of a painful releasing of sorrow. But the suffering transformed into a feeling of emptiness, which then turned into a feeling of peace. I felt then a sensation in my right breast, a sharp pain. I redirected my awareness to my own body, and felt the Love in my heart slither over and fill the hole of pain in my breast. Mom flashed again into my mind, and I saw us hugging, embraced in a desperate and deep hug. I remembered the moment, it was the day the machines were turned off on Dad and he had just slipped away. I felt our pain and longing heartache. Then I focused on our hearts, connected together in that hug. With everything in me, I transformed the feelings of pain and suffering into first emptiness, then peace, and then into Love. I felt the pain in my breast disappear, and knew somehow that Mom was healed. All it took was deep energetic concentration of forgiveness and love. Was healing always that simple? A massive tear fell from my left eye at the thought of Momma being well again.

I continued to hug this amazing being. The magnitude of Her power was unfathomable. I felt my breath slowing, and the connection between us deepening. I didn't want to let go. Then I felt the snake rope slither over me, encapsulating me into the circle. The starlight of the rope was so nourishing and warming. Then, the epiphany: the Light *was* Love. That which was responsible for all of life in a solar system; a sun, a star; emitted not only Light, but also Love.

It struck me like lightening again, and I felt my heart light multiply in magnitude, feeling the amplified awareness of the Love wrapping around me. I felt myself as a channel, a conduit for this tremendous energy. I also then became aware of the fact that the Tree was having a hard time absorbing the Love. Why? Was there still a place of energy leakage? Was there still a wound? I looked again with my mind's eye, and went first up to the place of the broken branch, but found it to be closed and healed, as if it had happened a long time ago, nearly a scar now. It didn't seem to be this place that needed healing still. It was something else. Then my awareness was returned to the top of the Tree, to the Nest, to the sounds of the Dancers that were still wailing and moaning. My body remained entangled in starlight Love, embracing the great Tree of Life, but my mind now climbed up into the Nest again.

I could feel their confusion and sorrow, their desperate longing still remained. They were dancing together, but with tortured lament and a more painful expression again.

"Why are you still so sad? What do you need to be happy? This Tree is wrapped in Love now, and the broken branch wound has been healed. Why are you still crying?"

They squirreled around each other, now in more of a dance form than before, a modern dance version of two upset squirrels. I'd almost find it humorous, if it wasn't so emotional and slightly terrifying, raw to say the least.

"What must I do?"

"You know what you must do!" They said in unison.

"I thought I did it already though, so I guess I *don't* know." But the second I said it, I knew that I did already know, I was just in denial. I didn't want to perform the Seed ritual. I wanted to believe that I didn't need to sacrifice myself in order to complete the mission. I wanted to believe that the healing was all that was needed. I knew this wasn't true though. It was time for the final part of my mission…

————————

I stood there, watching my daughter's eyes rapidly moving behind her eyelids, witnessing her body twitching. It was intense and excruciating to witness her like this again, and not know how to help her, not be able to wake her up. I closed my eyes and just started praying. As I did, I became aware of my own sensations. I was so preoccupied with how Lila was that I had basically checked out of myself. Now I was aware that there was a pain in my stomach, maybe from hunger, maybe from a need to use a bathroom, maybe just muscular tension from stress. I took in a deep breath and tried to relax a bit. Then I became aware of a sensation in my right breast. I was already a bit sensitive to this breast these days, but this was a new feeling. It was almost tingly, like when you sit strange for too long and your foot falls asleep or something. Then there was heat, and a pulsing sensation. I was scared for a moment. Was my stress making the cancer more aggravated? Was it spreading? Could I actually feel it becoming worse? Then the heat subsided abruptly and I felt one sharp moment of intense pain that made me hold my breath and wince. This got Mrs. Varma's attention, who got up and came over to me to see what was wrong. She reminded me to breathe, and as I took in my next big inhale, I felt Lila's energy, like a giant hug from her. It made me smile and tear up instantly. As I exhaled, I felt a major release; a release of fear, of anger, of worry, of longing and loss, a huge release of pain. I opened my eyes and held my breast in a mixture of belief and disbelief. I didn't feel anything there anymore, all the sensations were gone. I looked at Anjana with the tears now streaming down my face. She looked back with a compassionate and curious expression, also tearing up.

"I can't help but feel like a major shift just happened in my breast. It didn't seem good at first, but now I feel absolutely nothing. Usually there's a slight heat and a subtle ache, but that's not there now," I said in astonishment.

She looked at Lila and smiled. I looked at my angel sleeping in the bed in front of me. She was perfectly still now, looking peaceful and serene again. Something had majorly shifted within me, and it felt guided by another source.

"Thank you, God!" I yelled out silently, in my mind and heart. I didn't know what had just happened, but everything in me told me it was good.

Anjana was now holding my right hand and also had an arm around my waste. I felt loved and supported, held and nurtured…for the first time in so long. I looked at her with a look of all that I wanted to say to her, 'thank you' mostly. She looked back with a look that told me 'no words are necessary.' I was so grateful to have a friend in this crazy moment.

Acarya was glued to Lila's side, he hadn't moved much since they arrived. I was so grateful for his love for her. It truly warmed my heart like nothing else could, especially in this moment, to see someone love my daughter that much.

Then Lila's hand grasped Acarya's tighter and she started to move again, a slower movement but involving her whole head, moving back and forth, as she moaned a little. Then she made a sound that undeniably sounded like the word 'Love.' We all looked at each other and couldn't help but smile. I closed my eyes again, to thank God, blinking out a little flood of tears. I felt a small glimmer of hope, something I honestly hadn't felt in a while. I continued to pray and visualized her waking up, wrapping our arms around each other and saying, "I love you."

Chapter 12
The Final Dream

As I opened my eyes, I squeezed the massive Tree a little tighter. I suddenly *became* the great Tree and could see far off in every direction all at once. I witnessed a millennium of memories of the land, shifting and remaining the same, a thousand years of life in one stream of a time lapse. It was overwhelmingly beautiful and almost painful, passively having no control over what happened. I needed to retreat, and I pulled myself away, pulling my energy out of the Tree, and the glowing starlight rope of Love with me. It coiled back around my chest.

I walked back over the tangle of roots and stood a few feet away, taking in the sight of this magnificent being once more. I picked up my magic walking staff and stood there a moment, not thinking, not feeling, just observing, baring witness to this moment, to this ultimately significant being in front of me. Then the thoughts and feelings of fear and anxiety flooded back, and I was nearly overwhelmed, but I knew what I had to do and I was actually ready now. I closed my eyes and took in a deep breath, feeling my strength and the humble power of being in service. Then one last flood of memories and visions of all those I love and all that might still come to be, flashed through me, charging me, filling me with power, might, and purpose, and flooding me with tears.

Then I fell to my knees and placed the staff in front of me, circling it with the glowing snake rope of starlight Love, the radius large enough for me to be encircled too. I knelt down in the center of the glowing circle, just below the staff, and reached into the leather bag. Pulling out the brightly glowing crystal first, I placed it in the center of the circle. It was pointing towards the Tree, and as I placed it on the ground, it began to glow even brighter. I reached into the bag and grabbed the spiral box with the black life-giving powder inside, and placed it in front of me, below the crystal and horizontal staff, also center in the circle. The spiral lit up with a white-blue glow. Then I felt the Seed ignite with energy and it made my eyes involuntarily close. I reached into the leather bag, one last time, and pulled out the small suede wrapped bundle. It filled me with a feeling of unconditional Love, the second my hand touched it. It was intense and overwhelming, but the sweetest most precious sensation imaginable. It was truly only comparable to the moment I first saw a newborn baby, so soft and sweet like a peach, I could have just taken a bite out of them. Then I bounced back out of it and realized I was being overthrown by its tempting power and glory. I grew more serious and my strength magnified at the thought of inheriting addictive tendencies like Dad. It motivated me to override.

I closed my eyes again, inhaled and centered myself, once again thinking of all those I loved and cherished, reminding me of why I was here. I felt stronger than ever, more steadfast and focused than I had ever felt in my life. I held the Seed in front of me with both hands, and offered it out to its Mother. Then somehow and from somewhere, sacred words filled my mind and begged to be spoken.

"Great Tree of Life, I am here to help continue the legacy of Love. You are the Giver of Life, but you have nearly given all that you can give, and now a new generation must begin to grow in your loving shade. I willingly, with devotion, give of myself to you, oh mighty Seed of Life. Accept my offering of Love. May it be a blessing to the thousand generations that follow. I pledge my life to the everlasting Light of Love that ignites all of Life, so that the next generations may know an even deeper and more full understanding of Love."

My heart light glowed brighter than it had ever before, and I was nearly blinded by the entombment of white light. Then, without hesitation, I placed the glowing Seed in front of me and began to dig, digging with pure abandon and single-visioned obsession, my fingernails filled with cold moist Earth. I dug until my nails began to bleed and tears filled my eyes. Some were tears of sorrow for the life I knew I wouldn't be able to continue. Some were tears of absolute joy, at the thought of all beings knowing unconditional Love, if the mission was completed. Then I picked up the Seed, its pure white now marred with dark dirt. The box with the spiral on it glowed even brighter. I opened it and the powder whirled out as if picked up by a strong and directed wind. It twirled its way to the Seed in my hands and wrapped around it with grace and beauty, dancing a tight bundle of magic protection around it. I felt my hands fastened tightly to it. Tied together now. I knew there was no going back. I was also filled with more Love than I had ever been before, and my heart nearly grew outside myself. The light was beaming now with more vibrancy and brightness than it had ever before, truly nearly blinding, and the crystal responded and glowed brighter too, channeling my heart light into it and beaming it out to the Tree. The Tree began to tremble and shake and then a bright light shined through every crack and crevice. I could barely handle the shaking, and intensity of brightness, and the overwhelming feelings that filled me. A scream involuntarily consumed me and I burst out with a louder yell than I knew I could make.

Just as I raised my hands to thrust in the Seed to the ground, someone grabbed my hands and the Seed. I opened my eyes to see Mikasi, Michael…Dad…looking at me with desperate Love and intensity.

He said, "you have your whole life to live. This is my mission to complete." With that proclamation, the spiral of Shilajit powder unleashed its hold and wrapped around his hands instead of mine.

Then he said, "I love you, Lila, I always have and I always will, the same as I will always love your mother. Take care of each other. And please know I am so sorry for not being there. I wish for nothing more, than to have been there, and to be there still. I love you so incredibly much."

Then he shoved me out of the circle, sending me tumbling sideways. It was so bright, I could barely see, but I squinted and just barely made out the silhouette of him thrusting the Seed into the ground. The Earth began to rumble, and I scrambled to my feet and backed away from the glowing bright circle. Then I witnessed, as the Earth swallowed the last remains of my father. He didn't scream, he didn't look scared. He actually looked proud and strong, with his head up. I felt a hundred emotions, but gratitude, shock, and pride were the dominant ones. I couldn't believe what just happened.

In one more motion, he was underground, along with the crystal and spiraled box, the glowing white snake rope of shimmering star light, and my magic walking staff of challenges. I ran to the spot, and cried harder than I had in the real world when my father was pronounced dead. My tears created a small puddle that soaked the ground around me. I cried tears of gratitude at his sacrifice for me, tears of great sorrow for losing him, and tears of pride for him finally completing his mission. I cried tears of Love, for the man that gave me Life, and allowed me to continue to live.

Then the ground began to rumble again and I stood up and backed away. A small seedling appeared, in the place that swallowed my father. It quickly grew to have a branch, and another, and another. It grew rapidly into a Tree as tall as me. I approached it with wonder, and it seemed to witness me, to acknowledge me. Then time moved quickly to hasten its growth, and it surpassed me. I could feel its youthful yet wise and excited energy and desire to grow and give. I felt the energy of Love reaching out in all directions. Then it seemed to burst with energy, and grew to be enormous, reaching the same height and even a little taller than its predecessor. The glowing rope slithered out of the ground and around the base, becoming a part of the Tree. It lit up the Tree in a tremendous glow, a light that permeated the darkness of the skies and lands all around. My heart was overflowing with Joy and Gratitude, and the tears were streaming down my face, my heart light was lit as bright as the Tree.

The sounds of mild confusion and fear from the Dancers above grew louder and caught my awareness. I closed my eyes and thought about being with them in their nest.

In a swift blur, I was there. They were clinging to each other with fear and anxiousness. I stood between them and held out my hands as if to hold theirs, even though I couldn't actually touch them. Concentrating on sharing the Love in my heart, I transferred a peaceful calm to them. They relaxed, and we all bore witness to the birth of this new and absolutely magnificent Tree, the new Tree of Life.

It towered above the old Tree, and soon our necks were cranking up in attempt to see its peak. When it finally stopped growing, it brought another tear to my eye at how unbelievably brilliant, bright, healthy, and happy it was. Its life-giving power was unfathomable but could be felt in every cell of my body, and I assumed every other living organism around. It truly was more than I could ever describe and fully comprehend. I was humbled and in awe.

The Dancers went silent with stoic expression. They looked at each other, and then the masculine one reached out his hand for the feminine one and they glided gracefully, like ballerinas, holding hands, floating in the air up to their new home. I watched as they settled into their new Nest of Joy and began to twirl around each other with beautiful blissful movements of happiness. Their song now a melodic tune of bird sounds, laughter, and joyful praise. It was stunning to witness, and my heart glowed even brighter, so bright it began to blind us all. My Joy was literally about to burst my cells open. Then I realized it was done. Our mission was complete.

The feeling of ultimate satisfaction, pride, and accomplishment, mixed with overwhelming gratitude and Love, overcame me, followed by the most centering sense of Peace one could imagine. I felt ultimately connected, to Everything. I closed my eyes, and felt my heart beating as One with the heartbeat of the planet. I felt myself *as* the planet itself, and I breathed One breath with her.

Then very suddenly and surprisingly, I was back in the water. It was still dusk, but there was a glow on the horizon now that hadn't been there before. I felt a flutter of excitement at the thought of getting to see Whyla one last time. My heart was still glowing bright, lighting up the water around me. I closed my eyes and welled up my heart's song and poured it out into the great sea. My song had changed though. It was more serene, more peaceful now. I twirled around my heart song, feeling the bliss, and connection to it, and to everything. Then her song's fibers reached me, and my entire body got chills. I had never heard her song so full of Joy, it was glorious to behold. I twirled around in it, wrapping the melodic strands of Love all around me, smiling bigger than I ever had. My heart was expanded. All the feelings that filled me as a child were back; pure bliss, wonder, excitement, and a truly undeniable and simple joy. I started to laugh and cry at the same time. The most freeing sensation.

In one swift motion, Whyla lifted me from below, and my legs reached around her. I felt our connection, and I hugged her tightly.

She glided through the water as I rode on top of her. I looked out to witness a sun about to rise, a bright glow filling the bay and the surrounding mountains and forests. Then I noticed, far off in the distance, the Great Tree of Life, lit up brightly, radiating the Light of unconditional Love. It was magnificent, undeniably powerful. Then I thought about my father, how he had just sacrificed himself for me, and tears welled up in my eyes again.

"He finally found his bravery and his purpose. You should be very proud. All of life, has you two to thank. Without your perseverance and dedication, without your steadfastness to the mission, and your selflessness… without your bravery, your father would not have been able to do what needed to be done. You have allowed the full expression of Love for the next 1000 generations." Whyla's words sang through me, nourishing all of my wounds. I couldn't imagine what this journey would have been like without Whyla and her wisdom. She was my protector and guide. I hugged her again, tightly, wrapping my whole self around her. Then she lifted out of the water and we began to fly. I became aware of the other songs spiraling through the water. That we were not alone. There were more, and soon we were all flying around the bay, singing our heart songs with full abandon. Rejoicing. Spiraling around each other, I noticed that the way the water was dripping off these amazing creatures, dancing through the air, was forming a shape. It was a shape that looked remarkably familiar, a pattern deeply ingrained in me. Then I remembered, it was a helix, like the sacred matrix that made up DNA, the building blocks of life.

"Now you must go back, the seed of Unconditional Love Awareness has been planted, but it will take time to sprout and grow in your world. The depth of the darkness there was beyond a point of immediate shift. They need your understanding, your words and actions. Your mission is only just beginning." The words held so much weight, even though they gracefully spiraled to my heart. It filled me with all kinds of contradicting feelings and thoughts; excited and nervous, prideful and irritated, loving and guarded. I wanted to stay here with Whyla, in the Unconditional Love, forever. My mission was complete, I had already done what I needed to do. I also didn't know how to help the people of my world. The systems of power and greed were so deep, money had ultimate control over Humanity's hearts and minds. How could I change that? Would people even want that to change? How would the people in power ever let that happen, even if there was a model and collective desire for it? How could I possibly make a difference? These questions and a million more flashed through, as I doubted myself and this new mission.

"Liluye, do not be afraid. Remember what you have just overcome, all that you have already done, and all that you have learned. Your heart is open, your mind is free, and your spirit is One with Spirit, with *Everything*. Feel that, trust that, learn to be guided by that. You will always have the right words to say and know the actions to take, if you live in this guided space of faith in the connection of things, guided by Love. You are now merely a conduit of this sacred and divine energy, that fills you and flows out from you. You must teach others to find this Truth, to remember their true nature…as part of the Everything, belonging to the Great Web. We are all beings of Love and Consciousness. We are all of us, everything, reflections of Great Spirit. Our power and potential for Love is limitless. We are only limited by the barriers we create and the shadows we choose to hide in, away from Love. When we step into the Light of Awareness of other beings, Awareness of our actions and words, Awareness of the Connection of Everything, we choose Love. You know these Truths. These Truths *are* You, Liluye…Lila. You embody them, and will lead with them," she assured me.

Then all of a sudden, a bright light shined from the distant horizon, the first sunrise I had witnessed here, possibly the first one there had been here in a pretty long time. It warmed me with a feeling I had never felt, a warmth from my core beyond the feeling of Love. It ignited a fire there, a flame of passion, a flame of motivation, but a still and centered flame. I was overcome again with the feeling of deep, pure, absolute Love for Everything, and a surreal, uplifting, expanding, and overwhelming sensation of Peace. I was truly filled, charged with a great purpose.

Then the spiraling matrix around me lit up with a bright glow, overwhelming and intense. It made me squint from the brightness, and I closed my eyes, soaking in the magic, absorbing the power of absolute Love and Connection. Then I noticed that a spiraled ladder was forming, from the ribbons of heart songs pouring forth from the great and graceful Orcas flying and spiraling around the bay. The whales were creating me a portal to return, a gateway back. I wrapped my arms around Whyla one last time, tears streaming down my face, and then reached up and grabbed the helix shaped ladder of bright light. It was so bright as I climbed up towards the sky, I closed my eyes and trusted my arms and legs to know where to hold, trusting myself to know, trusting the divine energy around and within me…

When I opened my eyes, the lights were still bright and intense, but now I was dazed and confused, and I couldn't focus on anything. Feelings were different, everything felt heavy, and I had no idea where I was. I was no longer in the Dream though, that was certain. My whole body started to shake, and I began to cry. It was all really overwhelming. Part of me wanted to go back to Whyla, desperately and longingly. I closed my eyes and tried hard to return. Then I heard the most soothing voice I had truly ever known, in my existence, and my heart lit up, remembering the Connection, remembering the Love. I opened my eyes and saw what I thought was an angel at first, then the haloed glow dissipated and I saw my mother's face.

"Lila? Lila, are you there? Can you hear me, Lila? It's your Momma. I'm here for you, sweetie. Wake up, love," she said sweetly, but with emotional undertones, like she was crying.

A tear rolled down my face, as I realized that I was back. I opened my eyes and saw my mother's beautiful face again, overcome with delight and gratitude now. I smiled slightly and then closed my eyes again. Exhausted from the journey, I fell asleep, for possibly the first time in weeks.

It took a few days for me to talk about what actually happened. I guess there were tests ordered for me and an appointment with a specialist, for them to check out my brain. I didn't want to, and thought numerous times about ways to get out of it. Then again, I was sort of curious what they might find. Perhaps my brain *was* different. The part I thought was different was something unmeasurable though. My consciousness had expanded, beyond what I knew possible. I could look at someone and see from their eyes, knowing the details of their perspective. I didn't embody them, I could just 'put myself in their shoes' and clearly imagine seeing from their eyes. I could also feel their feelings. This included animals, and not surprisingly, trees, and other plants. It was really quite bizarre, but also amazingly beautiful. I felt like I was seeing through the eyes of God. Although God was redefined now to encompass all the known and unknown, all that is and was, and will be. We were all unique reflections of God. Everything a small piece of the great puzzle.

I eventually told Mom about the Dream, about how Dad had actually completed the mission, how he sacrificed himself for me, for us all. I don't know if she believed me, or if she believed that it was really another realm. At least not then, but there were things that happened that she couldn't explain. She told me that right before I woke up, she felt a release of fear and anxiety, a subtle but profound shift in her body and mind. She figured it was faith coming in and giving her a boost, or possibly that she was given a sign from God that it would all be alright. But at least eight other people she talked to, described a similar feeling at that same moment, in different places and for different reasons.

Acarya and Mrs. Varma said they felt something shift strongly in them, as if a wave of energy went through them.

"Massive warm fuzzies," Acarya called it.

It was incredible to be back with him, with our whole future still potentially there for us. A gift I wouldn't take for granted. He couldn't be any cuter, either. Doting on me, so complimentary, and so noticeably protective. I loved it, and I loved him.

My mother would also come to discover that her cancer was miraculously in remission. She told me that her breast at one moment (while I was still unconscious) was suddenly very hot and throbbed for a minute, then became almost cool, and felt better than it had in months. I think she knew then that she was healed, but she wouldn't know for sure for another few weeks, when they would do an ultrasound and find that there was nearly nothing left of the tumor. You see because there is no wound that isn't first caused by an emotional or psychological pain, and once that is healed, the physical body responds with healing. The body, mind, and that which connects us to everything, the Spirit, are all energy, responding to other energy, gathering matter and experience. You hear that? We are energy! God is energy. We *are* a part of God. Everything is God. It is a beautiful miracle, as simple as it is complex. Each and every being is simply seeking to Be. To be here, in balance, connected, with a desire of belonging. So Humans, can we please get with the picture? It's about Love. It's about simply being together, in harmony with the planet around us. We all have our place in this manifestation of Love. Every living creature, fauna and flora, has it's place in the great actualization of being. We're all here together. Our purpose isn't just for us or right now though, it's for everything else too, for generations to come. We simply have to steward peacefully together, in accordance with balance for the land, the animals, the plants, the waters, the air. Then people will live in balance, our world will live in balance. It starts with us. We each have a part to play. Caring for our own wounds and needs, and finding our sense of connection to Source and to each other.

We are in need of hero's right now. Wisdom seekers. Way keepers. We are in need of a wake up to this new way of thinking, of seeing, of feeling, of caring. A new way, of togetherness. This may mean we need to dismantle the means in which we are separated. We must eliminate the means of prejudice and judgment, because we are all equal...we are all earthlings, here to live life. We were all babies once, yearning to be held, and nurtured.

The task is to love all beings equally in our hearts. See our 'enemy' as a dance partner instead, someone we can learn to appreciate, and move and flow with. Someone we can have compassion for and eventually learn to love. This is the shift that I pray we see unfold. That we all feel we belong, that we truly feel Love in our hearts, and that we act in accordance with Love. Our planet will heal, based on these choices we make. Choices that are for the good intentions of everything, not the best interest or greed of a few. We can work together, and we must. We are one planet, one tiny speck in space, and it's one unbelievable place. Don't you think?

Do me a favor, and close your eyes, take a deep breath, clear your mind, then keep reading. Think of your favorite place to visit, go there for a moment. Think of your favorite view that takes your breath away. Think of your favorite animal, how awesome or cute or strong or smart it really is. Think of your favorite tree, the shade under it or how beautiful it looks in your favorite season. Think of all the ways this planet inspires you, provides for you, and how this is true for all the other creatures that have privilege of life on Earth. We are here to live in balance with it, to preserve it, to nourish it, to love it. We are here to be a part of the great circle, not to dominate it. We are not here on our own, we are here as a whole.

I think about the translation of the Nisenan name, 'from among us', and it seems to prove this point. We are here together, you, me, us all, The People, chosen to be here now. From among us, from around this place, here we are, this is us. It's pretty simple really. So how's about we get our act together and make this planet wonderful for all? Learn to live in harmony, in all the ways possible. Listen to the wise ways of the First Nations people who lived in harmony with nature for thousands of years. Listen to the ancient Sages that learned the ways of inner peace and enlightenment. Listen to the scientists and convert our energies of our most brilliant minds to the betterment of our world and the ways in which we can make all the waterways, airways, soil, plants and creatures, happy, healthy and well, rather than the reverse. Revere our healers, and focus on healing our inner wounds and traumas and forgiving those pains that have separated us from our true nature; connected and loved. Focus on healing in all the needed ways, so we can come together in our best versions of ourselves. Yeah, maybe its a dream, but a dream worth living for, a world worth living in. I believe it's possible. The question is, Do you?

Alright, I guess I'll wrap up this blog post for now. Get off my soap box. Wether you believe these events took place, and that my dreams were of a real place or not, that miracles and profound healing took place, is neither here nor there. I simply hope it inspired you, to feel your connection to life, and to find out how you can do your part. We have a lot of good work to do here, and we're all in this together. We got this, Earthlings. We can make this world loving and peaceful, healthy and happy, together.

So I end with a prayer, the only prayer I ever make now…Thank you, Creator, for this incredible gift of life. May all beings know peace.

I also end with a question to ponder…What part will you play in the refolding of things for the betterment of all living beings?

Works Cited

Gibran, Kahlil. *The Prophet*. New York: Alfred A. Knopf, 1968.

Halpern, Dr. Marc. *The Principles of Ayurvedic Medicine*. California: Harmon is Health Press, 1995-2020.

Haye, Louise. *You Can Heal Your Life*. California: Hay House, Inc. 1984.

Johnson, Richard B. *History of Us; Nisenan Tribe of the Nevada City Rancheria*. California: Comstock Bonanza Press, 2018.

Mitchell, Stephen. *Bhagavad Gita; A New Translation*. New York: Harmony Books, 2000.

Sams, Jamie and David Carson. *Medicine Cards*. New York: St. Martin's Press, 1999.

Tunseth, Scott. *Understanding The Bible; A Study Introduction*. New York: Augsburg Fortress, 1990.

Ywahoo, Dhyani. *Voices of Our Ancestors; Cherokee Teachings from the Wisdom Fire*. Boston & London: Shambhala Publications, 1987.

Credits and Acknowledgments

First and foremost, I thank Creator, Universe, God, Goddess, Great Spirit, for this incredible gift of Life. It is truly beyond words, beyond understanding, beyond dreams. I am forever grateful for my being and perspective, all that I am and have been taught and given, that has brought me to this place in existence, with the ability to share these gifts and lessons with you. Many great Whales have visited my dreams, since I was a small child, and I owe those spirit guides a great debt of gratitude as well. Without those dreams, this book would not have been.

Dhyani Ywahoo's book, Voices of Our Ancestors, literally jumped out of a recycle bin at me, changing my life forever, a major catalyst in the creation of this story. Speaking to the Venerable Dhyani Ywahoo in 2018 after I wrote these books, was a life changing conversation. She had read about 90 pages and offered such sweet thoughtful words of encouragement and approval. She also told me that "an empath's job is not to take on the darkness, but rather to shine the light." Such incredible wisdom in her words and teachings.

I also believe that Twyla Niche, who seemed to embody Whyla the Whale's character, may have influenced this entire book. Twylah's granddaughter, Jamie Sam's book and deck of Animal Medicine Cards have been essentially supportive in my connection with Spirit and in the unfolding of this serendipitous book as well. In any and all cases, I believe this book was divinely created. I witnessed it become itself, just as I witnessed the creation of my children within my womb, I was merely a vessel to channel that light into manifestation.

*Edit: post-initial writing of this…my sister, Natalee, ended her young life here in January 2023. I wrote this book in 2018…but didn't get it published until 2024. After 'the incident.' The moment that re-set time in my immediate world, with ripple effects in other's worlds, that are still rippling outwards. She did the unthinkable after immense mental pain and suffering, a culmination of trauma, loss, unknown mental illnesses, heartache at the nature of the world, and a desire to know if there was more after this life. What she did sent ripple effects of concentric circles of Love at a massive scale. A wave of awakening and lightening and radical loving and healing and learning and opening and connecting and weaving. She said that "everything is meaningful, everything is important, look for the signs, look at the symbolism. Everything is symbolic." I believe wholeheartedly that my sister influenced this book, in more ways than I can comprehend in this dimension. And I am forever grateful to her for her love and wisdom and light, and the gift of her whimsical beautiful hilarious incredible brilliant and just wonderful self here on Earth. For the time we got to have her, and for the real wake up call she gave. She is missed beyond measure. I cry for her every day. At the same time, she still exists, and she continues to show us and prove to us constantly. Blowing our hearts and minds wide open…another story to come of that someday…stay tuned. But the main take away message is this…we must all work together to make this world more livable, loving, and nourishing for all, including for the Earth itself. Where everyone can be free to be themselves, and face and heal their shadows, and feel that they belong. And a need to look at how we're making life a stress battle of basic survival, separate and alone, when we could be making a beautiful life, together.

I also want to thank my teacher, Dr. Marc Halpern (and faculty and staff), from the California College of Ayurveda. The following are authors and/or teachers that directly influenced my knowledge and life perspective… Dr. Marc Halpern, Mary Thompson, Dr. Frawley, Dr. Lad, Amanda Lyon, Brenda Krulikowski, Kim Kinjo, Carol Prentice, Amadea Morningstar, Light Miller, Maya Tiwari, Louise Haye, Kathy Keville, and many others.

I want to also thank Richard B. Johnson, his wife Kay, and Shelly

Covert, of the Nevada City Rancheria Nisenan and the non-profit organization California Heritage: Indigenous Research Project for their time, knowledge, and support of this book. I am honored to represent a bit of their people's story. They are currently still in a fight for their federal recognition as a people, told that they went extinct after attempted annihilation, although they certainly did not. They still exist. I stand with the Nevada City Rancheria Nisenan, and support their native sovereignty. May they be recognized and acknowledged, and healed of their deep lineage wounds and traumas.

I want to also acknowledge Amma, the hugging saint of India, who is doing the work my soul wishes to do, and although I haven't been able to meet her yet in person, she popped into my head regularly while I wrote this book. I also want to acknowledge the Dalai Lama, who has always spoken for my heart, and who I deeply respect for his healing words of Love unto this world and his lightheartedness.

I owe a great amount of gratitude to my 7th and 8th grade teacher, the late Mrs. Barbara Hinman, who taught me and many others, of Dr. Carl Jung's teachings of the Hero's Journey Quest, and that life is about a journey of self discovery and symbolism and learning lessons.

I also want to thank my 4th and 5th grade teacher, Mrs. Sue Madigan, who planted the seed of my love of writing books, and instilled in all of the children she taught, the importance of loving our Mother Earth.

I also want to thank Ryan for believing in me and my vision, and for the endless hours of conversing about the meaning of life and the philosophies of man. I wouldn't be who I am and have the perspectives I have without you. Thank you.

To my daughter, Jade Hawk, for the infinite lessons you continue to teach me every single day. Life is brighter with you in it. You are probably my number one inspiration for this book. And your spirited baby sister, Sage Vera, who has since made her debut in this world. You are both beacons of light. Everything I do is for you two, and for a better world for you to grow into.

To my sister Natalee...all that I said already...and As above so below. I truly believe you sacrificed yourself in an act of ultimate Love for you, for us, and this planet, guiding us all everyday on this journey, from the next realm now. I miss you everyday. I also see signs from you every day. There's no words for my love for you, for the gift that was and Is you. I really do imagine you had a significant part in the creation of this book. Since you've shown us that time is under different laws there, and you've been guiding us for a while now. Thank you for your part. I love you more. For eternity. Seester, who saw so much. Until we dance together again…

To my parents and other four amazing siblings, thank you for supporting me to discover who it is to be me, for all of your love, and being major catalysts on this journey. Embracing Ayurveda and all my other alternative ways was a process of opening and acceptance, which I am forever grateful for. I love you all so very much.

Thank you Larry Litton, for your generosities and support in making this book a reality.

To my besties, chosen family, thank you for your endless love, and showing the importance of community, honesty, sisterhood, and growth. Life wouldn't be as colorful and wonderful, as fun, funny and sweet, without you. You know who you are…

To the new love gifted to me, divinely guided to me, I am humbly grateful. Chris, you are an inspiration to me. WAY! Life is an ever changing mystery puzzle and I'm so here for it.

To all my other friends and family, aunts, uncles, cousins, you also all know who you are…thank you. I love you.

Last but maybe most important, thank you to my grandparents and ancestors before you. Thank you for your lessons, your love, and your lineage of grit that enabled me to exist at all. I feel you in my veins and bones, and I honor your dream of life moving forward. I vow to do my part in the making of a loving planet, so that all beings may know peace.

About the Author

J ess Hartley was born in Alaska, and raised between there and rural Northern California, where she gained her deep love and connection to the Earth. She is an Ayurveda Practitioner, healer, and herbalist. When she's not playing with her girls or helping people heal, or bringing more people to the science of Ayurveda, she can be found modern dancing, doing yoga, meditating, hiking, praying for the planet, singing and skipping through life.